Mercy's Embrace

Elizabeth Elliot's Story

A NOVEL IN THREE PARTS

Book 2
So Lively a Chase

Laura Hile

Publisher's Note: This is a work of fiction. Locales and public names are sometimes used for atmospheric purposes. Any resemblance to actual people, living or dead, or to businesses, companies, events, institutions, or locales is completely coincidental.

The characters Patrick McGillvary, Cleora, Claire, and Ronan McGillvary, and the butler, Longwell, are creations of Susan Kaye and are used with permission.

Book Layout ©2017 BookDesignTemplates.com

Cover Design by Damonza

Mercy's Embrace: So Lively a Chase: Elizabeth Elliot's Story Book 2/ Laura Hile. – 2nd ed.
ISBN-13: 978-1984015471

TABLE OF CHAPTERS

For my loving mother, Janet,
who has so eagerly anticipated this second volume

1 MAKING THE BEST OF IT

With a hammering heart, Elizabeth Elliot pulled open the door to Bailey's Tearoom and stepped inside. Surely he would be here! There—was he seated at the table in the corner? Or perhaps behind those ladies? That burst of laughter—certainly it was his voice she heard!

Or perhaps not.

The Abbey clock struck the hour—one, two. She became aware of the proprietor's stare and the knowing look he exchanged with the serving girl. Mortified, Elizabeth turned away. This was not the first time she had come looking for him, and these people obviously remembered. But where else was she to find him?

There was a tightening in her throat, and her chin began to quiver. Elizabeth pulled open the door. She would not cry! He was not worth that! Patrick Gill was nothing to her—nothing! She left the tearoom, banging the door behind her.

It was, she reasoned, her wretched situation that made her so vulnerable to Mr. Gill's charms. For what was he, really? A clerk in a counting house. To think that she, of all women, would condescend to meet him twice a week for tea. Why, it was laughable!

She had danced with him at that assembly as well. Well, and what did it matter? He had not returned to Bath. Or, more probably, he had decided to end their friendship. In either case Elizabeth was left to play the fool.

Oh, he had made promises. He said something about a pond and a bench and a note beneath the seat. At the time Elizabeth thought he meant the small lake at Belsom Park. But that could not be right—there was no bench at Belsom Park. And so, like a simpleton, she had visited every park in Bath. And didn't she look the idiot, sitting down on each bench and then feeling underneath for a note!

Elizabeth made her way to the hacking stand. That she must now spend precious pennies to hire a sedan chair was added to the list of Patrick Gill's offenses. What had possessed her to come today? She should have remained at home.

And here was another source of trouble. She ought to be living with her father in the fine house he had hired on Camden Place. But he had given it up to seek refuge in The Citadel, placing himself under that horrible physician's care. Elizabeth was now a guest of her newly-married sister, Anne. It was grossly unfair that she, the eldest sister, must become a dependent!

The journey to Anne's house on St. Peter Square was easily arranged, although the chairmen took their time ascending the hill. Presently the chair was lowered, and Elizabeth counted out the fare. It was then that she noticed a carriage waiting in front of Anne's house. She sighed. Mr. Rushworth was calling again.

James Rushworth had come every day since the assembly, though she did not always grant him an interview. Those conversations, conducted under Estella's watchful eyes, were an exercise in perseverance. Yesterday, for example, he laboured on about a French meal he had taken at The Clarendon. Elizabeth did not consider *filet de boeuf au jus* to be worthy of so much enthusiasm, but there it was.

One of the chairmen came to assist her. "I have changed my mind," she told him. "Take me to The Citadel—Mr. Savoy's establishment. Do you know it?"

Elizabeth found her father in his rooms, handsome as ever in a silk brocade dressing gown. Today he was occupied with the pages of a booklet. He rose to his feet when she entered and waved her to a chair.

"My dear," he said, "listen to this. It's the most extraordinary thing. Fortuitous, I call it."

Elizabeth smiled. Only one event would fit this bill. "Have we come in to a fortune, then?"

Over the top of his spectacles he gave her a look. "Mr. Savoy has recommended that I study this." He held up the booklet for her to see.

Elizabeth leaned in to better read the title. "An almanac? What do you want with an almanac?"

"It is a source of Information."

"For farmers," she said. "Or for gentlemen like Mr. Musgrove, who must oversee crops. But surely not for you."

"There is more here than tables of the moon and tides. There is, you see, the rotation of the stars to consider. The positions of the planets."

What nonsense was this? "You cannot be serious, Father."

"Mr. Savoy believes there are messages from the stars themselves."

"He would. I suppose he'll have you consulting a fortune teller next?"

"This is an ancient science and one worth attending to. Listen to this. It is the forecast for April." Sir Walter found the page and read:

> The mutual Aspects this month are but few
> and amicable.

Elizabeth wrinkled her nose. "That is a prediction?"

"If," he said severely, "you will kindly refrain from commenting until I have finished?" He cleared his throat and read:

> Fear not poor Soldier, I expect thy Condition
> to be good about these Times. Much civil Ac-
> tion, confident Hopes that we shall recover
> our Freedom, and enlarge our preceding Priv-
> ileges.

Elizabeth nearly laughed. "In what way is this help-ful?"

"You have not been attending," cried Sir Walter. "Consider our situation!"

"I am! Father, we are not soldiers."

"Prisoners, more like," he said. "Prisoners to debt and deprivation. But this tells me that, due to civil action, I shall recover my freedom. Freedom, Elizabeth! With priv-ileges."

"Enlarged privileges, according to your gypsy." She rose to her feet. "I meant to bring the post, but I came away too quickly and forgot to stop at Lady Russell's."

He waved her apology aside. "She will be by with it later, I am sure."

"Lady Russell now comes every day?"

"Why not? Now that I may have visitors, you ought to do the same."

"I haven't a carriage at my disposal as Lady Russell has. Now that I am here, is there anything I may do for you?"

But Sir Walter had returned to his almanac.

"Father?"

He waved her on. "Farewell, then. Give my regards to your new companion, Cousin Whatever-her-name-is."

"Estella Stevenson-Bragg. Surely you remember."

Sir Walter did not look up. "One of the Stevensons. Pity, that."

"Do not blame me. It was Captain Wentworth who asked her to come."

He looked up and twinkled. "I trust she is better at backgammon than poor Mrs. Clay?"

This comment stung. Penelope Clay, Elizabeth's former companion, had been her particular friend—and now she was gone. "I wouldn't know," Elizabeth said and went out.

Fortunately the sedan chair was waiting, and so within a short time Elizabeth arrived at St. Peter Square. Of Mr. Rushworth's carriage there was no sign.

Captain Wentworth had taken what Elizabeth suspected was a second-rate house for his new wife. It was both cluttered and undignified, being the residence of an admiral who was currently out of the country. Elizabeth had lately learned that Anne, scandalized by his artistic taste, had hidden several of his statues and paintings in the attic. This came as no surprise. Everyone knew that admirals were lascivious brutes.

Anne's butler opened the door with his usual silent precision. Elizabeth eyed him as she surrendered her gloves and hat. With Mr. Yee one never knew. He had, however, become an unlikely ally in her war against Estella.

Yee presented a silver salver on which calling cards were arranged. "Mr. Rushworth has called, Miss Elliot. A matter of some urgency. He plans to return. And,"—Yee's eyebrow lifted—"a gentleman by the name of Elliot left his card."

"Botheration," muttered Elizabeth. Mr. Elliot's presence in Bath was a nuisance. He also claimed to have urgent business to discuss, a thing she wished to avoid.

Yee made no move to withdraw the salver. "There is a notation on the reverse," he said softly.

William Elliot was her father's heir and, save for a brief period last winter, had been at odds with the family for years. That Mr. Elliot should be so attentive now, while her father's health was in question, did nothing to improve her opinion. Elizabeth turned the card to read:

Off to Brighton for a spell. I'll call when I return.

Elizabeth tossed the card onto Yee's tray. As if she cared for Mr. Elliot or his plans! Then she realized there were voices—Estella was speaking to someone. But wasn't the house empty? Elizabeth rounded on Yee. "She has a caller? In the dining room?"

The dining room was adjacent to the entrance hall, so Estella's voice carried perfectly. "I must say, this coffee is not at all fresh!"

Elizabeth pursed her lips. Trust Estella to serve coffee in the middle of the day—and in the dining room, of all places! "To whom is my cousin speaking?" she whispered.

Before Yee could answer, Estella spoke again. "Your Mrs. Yee is so inconsistent with her cooking! On some days the coffee is perfectly made, but on others—! Would you like me to ring for a fresh pot, dear Anne?"

Dear Anne? What was this?

"Anne is supposed to be in Shropshire," Elizabeth whispered to Yee.

"Mrs. Wentworth arrived just after you left," he murmured.

Anne's reply to Estella was indistinct, but Elizabeth heard the sound of a bell. Was Estella usurping Anne's role as hostess? What nerve! Elizabeth caught hold of Yee's sleeve. "Don't answer that," she ordered.

"I think the coffee is perfectly delightful," said another voice. "So refreshing after our journey."

But this was her sister Mary! What was Mary doing in Bath?

"Mrs. Charles Musgrove is also here," Yee remarked.

"Who else?" Elizabeth demanded.

Mary went on talking. "I happen to know that dear Captain Wentworth brought this coffee especially for Captain Benwick. He likes to sample different sorts; I heard him tell Charles so yesterday. This coffee," she added, "is from Abbey-sinia."

"Captain Wentworth *and* Captain Benwick are here?" whispered Elizabeth. "And Charles Musgrove as well?"

"He comes later in the week," Yee said. "Captain Benwick departs tomorrow. Will you join the ladies for coffee?"

Elizabeth gave Yee a look. "No," she said evenly. "I'll learn more this way."

Yee's brows went up. "As you wish."

"Do not look at me like that. All servants listen at doors—even you. How else does one learn anything?"

"I," said he, "have no need for such tactics."

Elizabeth returned her attention to the conversation. If Mary was referring to Captain Wentworth as *dear*, she and Estella had come to dagger drawing! Wasn't that delightful!

"My best hope," she confided to Yee, "is that Mrs. Stevenson-Bragg will be sent packing. Won't that make life easier for all of us?"

The bell sounded again. Apparently Estella was growing impatient.

Again Yee's eyebrow lifted. "And yet, 'Hope deferred maketh the heart sick, Miss Elliot,'" he quoted. He made a slight bow and went into the dining room. Straightway Estella began complaining. Yee came out with the coffee pot. He did not look at Elizabeth.

"I trust your time with Elizabeth has been pleasant, Cousin Estella." This was Anne's voice. Trust Anne to maintain peace.

"I must say, your sister is not at all the lady I expected."

"Of course she is a lady!" cried Mary. "What else would she be?"

"I never expected her to be a hermit," countered Estella. "Which is exactly what she is. And bookish too."

"Elizabeth, bookish?" Mary sounded incredulous.

"Indeed, yes," said Estella. "For she loaned me her 'favorite book,' a flaming nautical romance, and insisted that I read it."

"You must forgive our surprise," said Anne. "We have not found Elizabeth to be fond of reading."

"Except for the *Baronetage*," said Mary, "which is certainly her favourite book. For my part, I think it would be a complete waste of your time. Why should you wish to read about a set of people with whom you are so thinly connected?"

Elizabeth smiled. Mary and Estella were most definitely—what was the saying? Ah, yes—on the warpath!

"I understand from Yee," said Anne, "that Elizabeth has taken you to see the sights. Did you enjoy yourself? Bath is particularly pleasant in the spring."

Elizabeth's smile grew. Poor Anne was desperate if she was calling Bath pleasant. Anne hated Bath.

"The shifts I was put to, to convince your sister to take me anywhere!" Estella cried. "She is so beautiful and so well-connected. I expected her to attend parties and dinners every night of the week, but she did nothing of the sort."

"Even if she had," said Mary hotly, "she could hardly have taken you along! If you haven't noticed, Elizabeth is rather particular about those she is seen with."

"Mary—" Anne's voice held a warning tone.

"Don't come the innocent with me, Anne. You know very well how it is! Elizabeth remained at home because she could do nothing else. Not with Father ill, you gone, and a complete nobody as a guest. Honestly!"

"A nobody?" cried Estella. "I like that!"

Anne spoke more forcefully. "Did you enjoy the assembly, Cousin Estella? As Elizabeth is out, you must tell us all about it."

"She is either out, or she is sleeping the day away ... again," Estella put in.

"Which is exactly as a lady should do!" said Mary.

"The assembly?" prompted Anne.

There was a pause. "Well. It was very elegant and very crowded," Estella said at last. "Which came as a surprise, for are not many ladies and gentlemen—the most genteel—in London during April?"

"And," persisted Anne, "did you enjoy the dancing?"

"Oh, ever so! And you needn't think I was left to languish with the matrons." Estella spoke more easily now. "Your sister provided me with the most delightful partners."

"She did?" squeaked Mary. "Imagine that, Elizabeth being considerate! Who were they?"

"Let me see. There was Mr. Rushworth—he is such a funny one and so awkward, though I hear he is fearfully rich. I think he would have preferred to be your sister's for every dance. He has come to call nearly every day since; he stares and stares at her. And he consumes a great quantity of cake."

Elizabeth felt a flush rise to her cheeks. What an appalling conquest she'd made!

"Mr. James Rushworth?" Mary sounded puzzled. "Isn't he the fellow whose wife ran off with another—"

Anne interrupted. "And your other dance partners?"

"There were ever so many; I cannot recall. But how could I forget dear Colonel Wallis?"

"Colonel Wallis?" Anne's voice was sharp.

"Let me tell you, he is my idea of a gentleman! So courtly and distinguished! But then, I do adore regimentals, even on an older man. But I believe my favourite partner was your cousin. He is so witty and handsome. He dances divinely."

"My cousin?" Anne sounded dumbfounded. "Do you mean William Elliot?"

"I thought Mr. Elliot had disappeared," said Mary. "You must mean someone else."

"No, William Elliot is the man I mean," said Estella. "And what is more, I think he admires your sister very much. But she does not seem to return the sentiment."

"Elizabeth, not like Mr. Elliot?" cried Mary. "Nonsense. When I was here last winter, she was very fond of him. He called every evening just to see her. It was the talk of the town."

"No, I cannot agree," said Estella. "She is much fonder of that other fellow, the one she danced three sets with."

"Three?" There was wondering rebuke in Anne's voice. Elizabeth set her teeth. She had done no such thing! If only Estella would stop talking!

"That cannot be right," said Anne. "Elizabeth's public manners are flawless."

Elizabeth could not miss the implication. Anne would do well to keep her opinions to herself!

"Only think of it, Anne," cried Mary. "Mr. Elliot has returned to Bath. Do you suppose he'll call?" There was a pause. "I know! That officer's dinner that Captain Wentworth is putting together. Why not invite Mr. Elliot to come?"

Anne did not reply right away. "Our cousin is not an officer, Mary," she said at last. "I really do not think—"

"Rubbish! Neither is Charles, and he is certainly coming."

"So Estella," said Anne, "you say that Elizabeth is fond of Mr. Rushworth? She danced often with him?"

"Good gracious, no. Where did you get that idea? The man your sister admires is Mr. Gill."

Elizabeth's heart began to hammer. This was dreadful. Had she been so obvious? Had Estella guessed her secret?

"He is rather dashing," Estella went on, "for he rescued us when we were drifting in that boat."

"Boat?" demanded Mary. "What boat?"

"The one at Sydney Gardens, of course. After poor Mr. Elliot fell into the canal, Mr. Gill came out of nowhere and rescued us."

"What?" cried Mary.

"Not that Mr. Gill isn't a charming man," continued Estella. "He is. And he is rather nice looking too, in an athletic, animal way. Still, I find it delicious that your so-fine sister, who is obviously a stickler, has fallen for someone like him." Estella gave her trilling laugh.

Elizabeth's fingers curled into fists.

"What I think," said Anne, "is that you have been reading too many novels, Cousin Estella. That is not what you were invited here to do."

"But—what else was there? I could hardly accompany your sister to her love-trysts."

"Her *what?*" cried Anne.

Elizabeth's mouth dropped open. How dare Estella say such a thing?

Mary's ringing laughter was even worse. "Love-trysts?" she crowed. "Elizabeth? I don't believe it for a moment. Anne, she is jesting—she must be! What man in his right mind would have Elizabeth?"

"Think what you will, but it's true," said Estella primly. "Every Tuesday and Thursday afternoon she disappears. And I am never invited to accompany her. It's Tuesday today—and where is she?"

"A fine companion you've been!" cried Mary. "Even Mrs. Clay did better than that!"

"I expect Elizabeth was calling on Father at those times." Anne's tone was sharp, which did not bode well for Estella. "Shall we go into the drawing room?"

"But the coffee—?"

"Yee will know where to find us," said Anne. "He is quite resourceful in that way." There came the sound of chairs being pushed back.

Elizabeth wheeled and retraced her steps to the bottom of the staircase. She placed her hand on the bannister rail, turned round, and waited. One by one the ladies emerged.

"Why, good afternoon," she said, stepping down.

The stricken look on her sisters' faces was delightful to behold.

2 WELL YOU DESERVE

Estella Stevenson-Bragg did not remain in the drawing room for long. This suited Mary Musgrove perfectly. "Well!" she said, after the door closed. "She is prettier than I expected, although I daresay that golden hair is not genuine. And to dress in such a showy manner! Bless me, what a vibrant shade of green!"

Elizabeth, who was standing before the mantelpiece, turned. "You have not yet seen her tangerine get-up," she remarked.

It was all Mary could do not to gape. Since when did Elizabeth use slang expressions? The look on Anne's face spoke volumes. Elizabeth must have noticed this, for she pursed up her lips and moved over to the windows.

It was left for Mary to continue the conversation. "A married woman," she said, "ought to dress more modestly and in better taste." Here Mary paused to adjust her cap.

When one had attractive curls, it was important not to cover them.

"But then," she went on, "perhaps having a showy companion is not frowned upon in Bath. I recall that Mrs. Clay had several daring dresses."

Anne gave her a look but said nothing.

Mary's chin came up. If Anne was guarding her tongue, Elizabeth would do the same—and their afternoon together would be dull as ditchwater! And then Mary had to flinch, for here was one of her husband's cant expressions. Really, the man was impossible. No matter that he was the future squire, he must insist on talking like a stable hand. Charles was poisoning her speech!

As her sisters remained silent, Mary went on talking. "Surely you recall Mrs. Clay's grey evening gown, Anne. Scandalous, I thought it. Such a neckline! She might as well have carried her,"—Mary paused to giggle—"*feminine charms* on a platter! And did you not tell me, Anne, that Father was the one who purchased that gown? What was he thinking?"

"Might we speak of something else, please?" said Elizabeth. "Such as the weather? Or perhaps the state of the roads?"

Mary gave an unhappy huff. Elizabeth must always be domineering. But the look on her face promised trouble, so Mary complied. "Our journey was quite pleasant, thanks to Captain Wentworth. He hired a comfortable coach, and we changed horses often. We covered the fifty-odd miles in good time. The boys fared surprisingly well."

"The boys?" Elizabeth sounded shocked. "Never tell me you have brought your sons to Bath!"

Mary fired up. "And why shouldn't I?"

"Because, dear Mary, Cousin Estella has done the same, so the nursery is already full. Her son and daughter are quite wild. To have them here has been a trial for everyone."

"Oh dear," said Anne. "I don't suppose Frederick said anything about her children in his letter. So of course she felt at liberty to bring—" The drawing room door opened, and Anne left off speaking.

Anne's butler addressed Elizabeth. "Mr. James Rushworth has returned, Miss Elliot. Are you at home?"

A look passed between Elizabeth and Anne. Mary straightened up. "Of course we are at home," she hurried to say. "Well we are, Anne. As no one is going to say anything interesting, we might as well see Mr. Rushworth."

Anne just looked at her—as always, Anne must think everything out, which was such a nuisance! —and then she nodded to the butler. Moments later Mary heard laboured footsteps climbing the stairs to the drawing room.

"... seed cake?" she heard Elizabeth whisper. "He is so fond of it."

Mary understood this all too well. The gentleman would get his cake whereas she, who would very much like a second piece, would not be offered any. But why was she surprised? It was always so among her family. No one thought to enquire after her preferences.

And so James Rushworth came into Anne's drawing room. Although he had been pointed out to her—for he was the subject of much gossip—Mary had never been introduced. Today he was looking painfully shy, and it seemed to Mary that he was fatter than before. He hadn't much conversation, but it was obvious where his interest lay. As Estella had noted, he had eyes only for Elizabeth. He lowered himself onto the chair Anne indicated and sat there without saying anything, nervously rubbing his knees.

Elizabeth was surprisingly kind. "And what have you brought, Mr. Rushworth?" she said, indicating the parcel beside him. "I understand from Yee that it is a matter of some importance."

Mr. Rushworth flushed and produced a folded newspaper. "It's ... the article I told you about. The trial for *crim. con.* was printed up all over again in *The Times*. It's required for the petition for the ... divorce."

Mr. Rushworth removed his gloves—a slow process— to better turn the pages. His hands trembled a little as he did this. He spread the newspaper on a low table so that Elizabeth could see. "It's coming up in a bill before Parliament," he explained.

Anne looked shocked, but Mary edged nearer. To speak about such a trial was not in the best of taste, but it was so intriguing! Why, the criminal conversation article looked like an advertisement for the theatre! There was a drawing of a man and a woman embracing, with Mr. Henry Crawford's name featured prominently. Mr. Rushworth's wife was identified as his Mistress. Printed

in very large letters were the words *TRIAL* and *ADUL-
TERY*. Then came the amount that Mr. Rushworth was
asking in damages: five thousand pounds.

Mary's mouth came open. Why, one could become rich
through lawsuits!

"My solicitor says it won't be long now," she heard Mr.
Rushworth tell Elizabeth, "and so I must be off to London. I thought you might ... show this to your father. As
proof of my ... situation."

"Do you think that is wise?" This was from Anne, and
she did not look pleased. "Forgive my interference, Mr.
Rushworth, but perhaps you ought to show this to our
father yourself."

Mr. Rushworth gaped at Anne, his mouth opening and
closing like a fish's. A scarlet flush spread over his neck.
"D-Do you think so?"

"I do." Anne was about to say more when the door
came open again. Lady Russell was announced.

Mr. Rushworth jumped to his feet. "I-I'll go now," he
stammered. He attempted to fold the newspaper, but it
was large and he made sorry work of it. He bowed to each
lady and to Lady Russell.

"Good gracious," said Lady Russell, after he had scut-
tled away. "I hope I'm not as fearsome as that. Poor Mr.
Rushworth!"

And then Lady Russell had to hear all about their trip
from Uppercross, which was a great bore. It was all Mary
could do not to yawn! It seemed that she had come to
invite Elizabeth to join her for her afternoon calls, ending

with a visit to Sir Walter. When she learned that Elizabeth had already been, she decided that Mary must come in her place. This was the last thing Mary wished to do, but she knew better than to argue with her godmother.

Together they descended to the entrance hall. "How are you feeling today, Mary?" said Lady Russell. "Did you have a pleasant journey?"

Mary shrugged. "What can one expect, being shut up in a stuffy coach with so many others? We departed Uppercross at a frightful hour—before the sun was even up! Captain Wentworth *would* change horses as often as possible; it was so provoking! Just when I had the boys asleep, we'd arrive at another coaching inn. The driver would blow his wretched horn, and up they'd jump. I am worn to the bone, truly."

Mary paused, and then added, "I ought to be taking a nap." She searched her godmother's face for traces of sympathy.

"Well then," said Lady Russell crisply. "The sooner we depart, the sooner you'll return."

Mary gave a great sigh. As usual, she had wasted her breath. Lady Russell was as unfeeling as a stone!

"What a curious young man," Anne said, as soon as Mary and Lady Russell went out. "I am sorry for him, of course, and yet—" She paused, her brows perplexed in thought. "Elizabeth," she said at last, "do you think it is proper for Mr. Rushworth to be courting you so soon? For that is obviously what he is doing."

Elizabeth squirmed in her chair, uncomfortable under her sister's frank gaze. It was one thing to encourage Mr. Rushworth at Lady Eleanora's house party, but in the presence of her family it was more difficult. "La, what notions you have," she said lightly. "I think his admiration is sweet—like that of a devoted spaniel. I doubt he means anything by it."

"He certainly means something if he's wishing to speak with Father," said Anne. Again she furrowed her brows. "I feel for him, truly, for Father will not hear his suit kindly. If only Father were not so particular about personal appearance."

Elizabeth felt the sting of this. Anne had no such qualms; their father had once said that Captain Wentworth would look well in their drawing room, and he was right. He would never say the same about James Rushworth.

"How fortunate for you that Captain Wentworth is thought to be handsome," she said. "And his new-made fortune has certainly smoothed your path!"

"As Mr. Rushworth's fortune and estate will likewise smooth yours," flashed Anne. Her tone softened. "Elizabeth, what are you about? How can you give this young man so much encouragement? I cannot believe you like him."

Elizabeth rose to her feet. "Mr. Rushworth's charm lies in his good nature," she said sharply, "which must make him acceptable to any woman. I do not need you to throw his deficiencies in my face, Anne. I have Lady Russell for that." Elizabeth strode to the door and opened it.

"Elizabeth, it was not my intention to—"

Elizabeth banged the door shut. As always her sister must be prosing and moralizing—it was the height of impertinence! She descended to the entrance hall and rummaged in the cloakroom for her broad-brimmed hat. Now that the house was filled with people she despised, it was the perfect time for a stroll through the park.

But visiting the grounds of the Belsom estate was an awkward business, for Elizabeth was hardly an invited guest. Shortly after she came to live here she discovered the gate—Mr. Norman's gate, Yee called it—and as Yee did not issue a reprimand, she assumed that the neighbours were welcome to trespass. But she was never entirely comfortable there, for Belsom Park was owned by the loathsome Admiral McGillvary. The less she had to do with him, the better!

As Elizabeth trod the pathway behind the mews, Anne's words continued to plague her. Anne was right. James Rushworth was everything she had once scorned in a suitor, but he was a suitor. That, at least, was something.

The lure was Sotherton, the Rushworth estate, as well as the fine London residence he'd taken on Grosvenor Square. Elizabeth turned her mind toward happier thoughts, such as imagining what the Sotherton mansion might be like. Mr. Rushworth had described it in great detail. Images inspired by her beloved Kellynch Hall rose in her mind: a grand and lofty house, shining floors, solid mahogany, rich damask, gilding and carving—and James Rushworth's eager face as he demanded that kiss.

Elizabeth gasped, aghast. That wretched masquerade ball! That horrible kiss! Why must she continually remember it?

She stalked to the gate, determined to put James Rushworth out of her mind. But another set of memories came boiling up. *He* had opened this very gate. *He* had helped her evade Mr. Elliot, and then they had fled through the park together. Not Mr. Rushworth, but Patrick Gill.

Elizabeth sighed heavily. The very last person she wished to think about—besides James Rushworth—was Patrick Gill.

But it was no use. Again she was in the Assembly Rooms, dancing with him. Their time together had been so brief, and yet she could recall every precious moment: the feel of her hand in his, the words he had spoken, the way he had smiled, the tender light in his eyes ...

Tender?

Elizabeth brought a hand to her cheek. This was ridiculous. Patrick Gill was not a suitor—he was not even a gentleman. He had a profession, which meant he was a *person*, a man similar to her father's solicitor, Mr. Shepherd. He was not admissible in company.

But this line of reasoning did not hold, for she had allowed herself to be seen with him at the assembly. Not only that, she had consented to dance with him.

"No, I did not consent," she said aloud. "He forced me to dance with him, and then—"

And then he had said good-bye.

He'd rattled off some rigmarole about a bench in the park, when she knew very well there was no such thing. Elizabeth felt her throat grow tight. She wrenched open the gate and went through; it shut behind her with a clash. A sloped lawn was before her and she strode to the top. Below, flanked by willows, was a small lake—a pond, he'd called it. There was no bench. Patrick Gill had been hoaxing.

"Hoaxing." Elizabeth grumbled the word as she descended. Was she surprised? "Fine!" she flung at the sky. "Lovely! And now he has gone away, just like all the other men I've ever—"

Elizabeth's words died on her lips. For there, on the western side of the lake, were people. A woman and two children whom Elizabeth recognized as the Braggs. They were feeding birds. And the woman with them was sitting on a bench.

Mary complained all the way back to St. Peter Square. "To hear Father talk, that Citadel is the most delightful place on the face of the earth." She gave an unhappy huff. "Not once did he enquire about me—his own daughter! —or about Little Charles or Walter. What do I care if there are musical concerts in the salon? What do I want with his new set of friends?"

"I must admit, I had my doubts about his physician," said Lady Russell, "but under his care your father has made remarkable progress. It is gratifying to see his happy spirits."

Presently Lady Russell's carriage pulled up before Anne's house. Mary gathered her things together. "Will you be coming in?" she asked politely, hoping Lady Russell wouldn't.

"I believe I shall," was the answer. "It is such a pleasure to have Anne among us again. And you too, of course."

"If that horrid Estella were not here, it would be a pleasure." Mary continued to scowl as she clambered out of the carriage. Lady Russell gave her a look. "Well it would be," Mary insisted. "The woman is a perfect goose. She cares for nothing but herself."

"Do you think so?" Smiling, Lady Russell stepped up to the door and lifted the knocker.

"And her taste in clothing is beyond anything!"

The door came open, and Mary marched into the house ahead of her godmother. "Hello, Yee. Has anyone called? Has my husband arrived?"

She made at once for the staircase. "At Uppercross," she said over her shoulder to Lady Russell, "Charles spent all his time with Captain Wentworth and Captain Benwick. It was so provoking. After he arrives, it will be more of the same."

Lady Russell followed. "So I would expect when a house is filled with women. Be reasonable, dear. What else is there for him to do?"

"What else is there for *me* to do?" Mary came in to the drawing room and cast herself on one of the sofas. "I wonder where Anne has got to."

"Presumably she is resting."

"I must say, it is much more amusing to visit Bath with the Musgroves."

Lady Russell did not answer. She began wandering through Anne's drawing room, pausing to examine this or that. Mary sighed some more. It was wretchedly unfair that Anne should have such a spacious drawing room. Mary's home in Uppercross, which at one time had been a farmhouse, had only one formal parlor. Thanks to the antics of her young sons, the once-fine furniture was now hopelessly worn.

Lady Russell paused before the pianoforte, a gift to Anne from her husband. "What a pity you have not kept up with your playing."

Always her godmother must be critical! "As you may recall, we do not have an instrument," Mary pointed out. "The Musgroves did offer us their old spinet—so outdated! No one plays the harpsichord any more. I made Charles take it away."

"Mary!"

"What else was I to do? The boys would not leave it alone. I dearly love music as much as anyone, but you have no idea. My poor nerves!"

"What a pity." Lady Russell resumed her examination of the pianoforte. "This is a lovely instrument. Anne must be so pleased."

"I do not see why everyone must go into raptures over it. I declare, all the way to Bath I was having to hear about the pianoforte or the officers' dinner. You cannot imagine how dreary. And now that we are here, it is Father this, or Estella that. No one listens to any of my suggestions."

Lady Russell came to sit near Mary. "Such as?" she said encouragingly.

"Such as the guest list for the officers' dinner. I make one suggestion—and it was a very good one! —and I am told to mind my own business. Or words to that effect."

Yee came in with the tea tray; Lady Russell took charge and filled a cup for Mary. "What did you suggest, dear?"

"Only that our cousin be added to the guest list."

"William Elliot?" The silver teapot shook in Lady Russell's hand. "That is out of the question."

"What is wrong with Mr. Elliot? Why has everyone suddenly turned against him? He practically lived in the house on Camden Place, and Father was always pleased to welcome him."

"We will leave your father out of this discussion, if you please." Lady Russell passed the plate of biscuits. "If you must know, Mr. Elliot has behaved in an infamous manner."

Mary shrugged. "If he prefers the company of Mrs. Clay, what is that to us?"

Lady Russell put down the plate with a snap. "Their supposed cohabitation is merely gossip," she said sharply, "which you would do well to ignore. I suggest we change the subject. How are you finding Bath?"

"You asked me that before." Mary dug a spoon into the jam pot. "If you must know, I am having a horrid time. There is nothing worse than to be in a place like this, at the height of the fashionable season, and be strapped for cash."

"I imagine not, but must you use such language?"

It was all Mary could do not to grind her teeth. Conversing with Lady Russell was such a trial! "Anne and I did some shopping in Crewkherne the other day," she said. "I saw an adorable lilac parasol—the most precious thing imaginable. But could I buy it? No. But Anne did. She has money aplenty now that she is married, while I live the life of a pauper."

Mary took a bite of jam-covered biscuit and added, around a mouthful, "Charles is a beast."

Lady Russell lowered her teacup. "Lilac does not become you, dear," she said.

Mary made an impatient gesture. "Anne is no longer forced to wear provincial fashions as I am. It is most unfair. Indeed, I wonder why I ever accepted Charles Musgrove."

"Mary!"

"I was deceived, thoroughly deceived. And you and Father thought it was such a good match."

"I did, and it is." said Lady Russell. "In that district, the Musgroves are second only to your own family, Mary. Someday, when Charles is squire and the Great House is your own—"

"You mean when I am old and worn down," Mary cried. "What use will the Great House be to me then? In the meantime, I must be married to a farmer."

Lady Russell just looked at her.

"A farmer," Mary repeated. "Do you know what Charles is doing this very moment? Riding every rutted road in the district, dressed as a bumpkin, chatting with his father's tenants. He has hatched a scheme to breed horses, and he must hear every yokel's opinion on the subject. He says there is much to be learned from tenant farmers. I ask you!"

"I call that being an attentive landlord. His father does the same."

"Mine never did. It would be too humiliating!"

"We will leave your father out of this discussion, if you please." Lady Russell reached for the plate. "Have another biscuit, dear."

Elizabeth was so stunned by the bench that she did not realize that Miss Owen was waving. "Hello," she heard her call. "Isn't this a lovely afternoon?"

She lifted a reluctant hand and saw Miss Owen make room for her to sit. "Please join us," she called.

Stepping cautiously, for her knees had suddenly become wobbly, Elizabeth made her way down the grassy slope. The bench was here—it was real. Patrick Gill had spoken the truth. Did this mean there was a note? Elizabeth did not like to sit beside Miss Owen and converse, for what did one say to a plain woman with no taste or social connections? But if she did not, how would she check for a note?

The bench was made of carved stone, substantial and real. Elizabeth ran her fingers along the armrest. How could she have missed something so obvious? In her heart a curious feeling was welling up—a singing sort of happiness that had nothing to do with anything. She closed her eyes, savouring the deliciousness of it.

"I want more bread."

Elizabeth blinked her eyes open. Johnny Bragg stood there with the sun full on his face. What an unattractive, scowling child he was!

Miss Owen produced a marketing basket. "Here you are, Master Bragg," she said cheerfully. She filled his outstretched hands with bread crusts. "Have a care now. The geese are not shy."

Johnny eyed her with distaste. "I want more," he said. "Give me the basket."

Elizabeth's eyes narrowed. She knew exactly what she would give this stubby little weevil—a kick! And then she had to smile, for *weevil* was one of Patrick Gill's expressions. It described Johnny Bragg perfectly.

Miss Owen was patient. "We must share the crusts, Master Bragg."

As if on cue, Bella presented herself. "I need more," she said.

Miss Owen likewise filled her hands. Her brother made a face. Bella looked from her supply to his. "No fair," she cried. "You gave Johnny more!"

"As I told your brother, we must share."

Johnny stuck out his tongue, and Bella stomped off. With an Indian yell, he ran at the geese, causing a great flapping. Bella began to shriek.

Miss Owen was undaunted by this display. "The real trouble," she said, "is that geese can be quite aggressive.

In country places, geese are sometimes used as watchdogs. As you see, these are accustomed to being fed."

A duck waddled up and cocked its head, enquiring. Miss Owen smilingly shooed him off. "There is no teaching manners to ducks and geese," she said. "They will not learn."

"There is no teaching manners to these children either," said Elizabeth. "Not so much as a please or thank you. I like that! What is their mother think—"

The words died on Elizabeth's lips. What was she thinking? She was actually conversing with this woman!

"I expect that she isn't thinking," said Miss Owen. She hesitated and then said, "Your cousin's children are an inconvenience, but she bears them no ill will. With my father it was different. To him we were a source of income. When we could not pull our weight ..."

Elizabeth did not know how to reply. At last she said, "Now that my sister and her husband have come, the Braggs will probably return home."

"And I will miss them."

Elizabeth shook her head at this. There was such a thing as too much politeness.

"I see you do not believe me," Miss Owen said, smiling, "but it is quite true. The Braggs are healthy and, for the most part, they are happy." She hesitated. "You see, I sometimes assist my cousin in his work. By the time I am called into the sickroom, the children are usually in desperate straits, poor lambs. I can do so little, save to comfort them and pray."

"You nurse children in the sickroom? How ... brave!"

Miss Owen studied her clasped hands. "You are kind to say so, Miss Elliot, but you do not see how I tremble as I work! My sole qualification is that I am available. And I am uncommonly healthy."

"And compassionate." This slipped out before Elizabeth could stop it. She had done it again; she'd spoken without thinking.

"At those times Michael—Mr. Minthorne, I should say—needs me so desperately. The mother is in no condition to help, being unskilled and overcome with grief."

"But a hired nurse?" said Elizabeth. "Surely the family can bring in a hired nurse and spare you the risk."

"There is little risk, as I have had most childhood illnesses. And also—" Again Miss Owen hesitated. "Sickness is expensive, Miss Elliot."

"Don't I know it? Why, my own father has—" Elizabeth broke off speaking. What was there about this woman that she must confide in her?

Bella Bragg's shrieks were piercing. "You miserable little beast!" she cried. "How dare you!" She came running up. "Johnny is throwing mud!"

Miss Owen sighed and rose to her feet. "We are finished here." She dumped the remaining crusts on the grass and turned to Elizabeth. "Thank you for bearing me company. I see that you enjoy this new bench as much as I."

"New?" echoed Elizabeth. "But this bench has been here for years."

"Ah, but it has not—and therein lies the mystery. Look here." Miss Owen pointed with the toe of her shoe.

"The turf at the base is a different colour. This bench has been moved from somewhere else."

Elizabeth's heart gave a thump. "Recently?" she faltered.

"Quite recently. I know this because I come nearly every day. On Friday last it appeared, just as you see. I suppose the gardener must have brought it."

"The ... gardener?"

"Mr. Burns." Miss Owen adjusted her hat against the sun. "Come, children," she called. "Good day, Miss Elliot."

Elizabeth waited until they were out of sight before dropping to her knees. Sure enough, wedged into a seam and affixed with court plaster was a flat packet of oiled parchment. She pulled it loose and, after an anxious glance to the hilltop, sat to examine it. There was no name, and it was closed with many daubs of sealing wax. The design on the seal was one she did not recognize—some kind of harp with an anchor. Inside was a stiff white card.

Elizabeth, My Dear,

Circumstances do not permit me to meet you
for at least the next week ...

Elizabeth stopped reading to hunt for the date. A week ago Thursday! With a hammering heart, she read on.

... as I must remain in London for an unspec-
ified time. Dare I presume upon your forgiveness?

"My forgiveness?" she whispered. What was there to
forgive?

I regret using such unorthodox means of delivery. In such situations, one does what one
can. I will notify you here when I return to
Bath.

Yours, as ever,
Patrick

Elizabeth gazed at the signature for a very long time.
Patrick. He had used his Christian name.
Sleep would not come easily that night.

3 STRONG REASONS MAKE STRONG ACTIONS

Mary's complaint—that it was more amusing to visit Bath with the Musgroves—was repeated, and after several days in the company of her sisters, Elizabeth had to agree. Whenever Mary's in-laws came, they indulged in shopping and concerts and theatre parties. Anne and her husband did none of these things. Instead, they spent much time in the company of Captain Wentworth's sister and her husband. It was left to Elizabeth to amuse and entertain the others.

Their days often began with a promenade through the Pump Room—easier now that Mr. Rushworth was gone—and then with the making of calls. Although Elizabeth could claim a wide acquaintance in Bath, she was not eager to display her cousin and youngest sister. The three women often remained at home.

On Sunday there was a mishap concerning church, which Elizabeth used to her advantage. Lady Russell's carriage could not accommodate everyone, and so Elizabeth found herself left to make the trip in a job carriage with Mary, Estella, and the two Bragg children. Elizabeth told the driver to take them to Argyle Chapel. How Mary would object!

And she did. After the service, Mary and Estella sat in stony silence. "I do not know what more I can say," Elizabeth told Mary. "This has become our usual habit for Sunday service. How was I to know you wished to go to the parish church with Anne? Next week you may do as you please."

Estella spoke up. "I fully intend to!"

Elizabeth adopted a thoughtful attitude. "Unless," she said, smiling a little.

"Unless what?"

"Unless I decide that I prefer Mr. Jay's sermons to those at the parish church. I believe you were invited to Bath as my companion. Where I go, you must likewise go."

After this remark, there was no bearing with Estella. Once the hack arrived at Anne's house, she gathered her children and went flouncing into the house.

Mary remained in order to visit Sir Walter with Elizabeth. "I suppose Father will be peevish again," Mary said, as soon as the carriage began to move. "I cannot see how Lady Russell puts up with him."

"She is certainly to be pitied," Elizabeth agreed. "You must admit, she has been a faithful friend to Father."

"She has nothing else to do with her time, that is all. And listen to you—you're beginning to sound as prosy as that Winnie Owen."

Elizabeth met her sister's look evenly. "I would not rail against Miss Owen if I were you," she said, "considering how much time she spends with Little Charles and Walter. You really should exert yourself to find a new nursery maid." Shortly after arriving in Bath, Mary's Jemima had abruptly given notice.

"But I *am!*" cried Mary, bouncing up in her seat. "Yesterday I found a perfectly suitable woman, which is no easy task, let me tell you. But when she learned that we are to live entirely in Uppercross, quite shut away from the world, she lost all interest!"

Mary gave an unhappy sniff. "As for that service today, why, it was beyond anything!"

"Were you attending to any of it? I thought you talked with our cousin the entire time."

"Bless me, no. It was Estella who talked to me, which is a very different thing. Honestly, how could that dreadful Mr. Jay say so much about that dreary text? Who wants to hear a sermon about the owner of an hostelry?"

It was all Elizabeth could do not to roll her eyes. Did her sister have rocks for brains? "It was the story of the Pharisee and the publican," she said wearily. "A publican is a Roman tax collector, not the owner of a public house. I thought the sermon was rather good."

Mary gave a snort of derision. "You might think 'God be merciful to me, a sinner' is interesting, but I do not!"

"Actually," said Elizabeth, "it was the bit about the other man—the self-righteous one who boasted of his good deeds and prayed to himself. I have never thought about it that way."

Mary examined one of her gloves. "Tell me, Sister-dear, how do you like being called a sinner? Do you beat your breast when you pray, like that horrid publican did?"

"Perhaps I should."

"I have no intention of doing so, ever," said Mary. "And I do not like being called a sinner, for I am no such thing."

Elizabeth nearly laughed. "What a liar you are, Mary," she said, smiling.

Mary straightened her bonnet. "I do not steal, nor have I murdered," she said primly. "Neither do I take the Lord's name in vain, or—"

"Or lie or gossip or covet," Elizabeth finished. "You are a pattern-card of virtue, in fact. Please."

By this time they were pulling up at The Citadel. Mary drew her wrap more closely around her shoulders and announced, "I do not feel at all well."

"Is that so? Elise will be pleased. She'll make up one of her mustard plasters straightway."

"Laugh if you will, but I *have* caught a chill, I just know it. It would be most unwise for me to visit Father. You go ahead; I'll wait here."

"In this draughty carriage? Don't be ridiculous."

But Mary remained where she was.

Perhaps it was for the best, because Elizabeth's visit did not go at all well. Sir Walter kept a running list of petty complaints. Presently she noticed something on the mantelpiece. "I see Lady Russell has brought your post," she remarked, as soon as he paused to take a breath. "And look, here is another of those letters."

Sir Walter waved it aside.

Elizabeth got up to retrieve it. "This looks important. You ought to open it."

"I have neither the time nor the energy to deal with trivial matters. This ought to be sent to Shepherd. All of the tradesmen's bills go to Shepherd. Confound it, Elizabeth, how many times must I remind you?"

"This is not a tradesman's bill. I thought Mr. Shepherd told you to see to this particular payment yoursel—" Elizabeth broke off speaking. She had learned this information by snooping through her father's desk!

Fortunately he did not notice the slip. "This is the worst of the lot," he complained. "Am I never to escape demands for payment? Every week it is the same."

"Very well, I'll send it to Mr. Shepherd."

"Money!" he cried out. "Do people think I am made of money? It does not grow on trees, my dear." His voice was raspy now, and his fingers curled on the arm of his chair. "Do you know what shall become of me? I'll be cast into prison, that's what!"

Elizabeth sighed Must he always be dramatic? "Surely not," she said lightly. "As a gentleman, you are not bound by the—" She stopped. What did the law say? Was a baronet subject to the civil courts?

"After all I have done for you," he lamented, "is this to be my reward?"

An attendant came in with the tea trolley. Sir Walter dismissed Elizabeth and reached for the plate of sandwiches.

The journey back to St. Peter Square was equally unpleasant. Mary went stomping up the stairs to the drawing room, leaving Elizabeth to follow. Estella and Anne were there, seated before a bright fire. Mary went at once to join them. Elizabeth expressed surprise, as the weather was warm.

Mary took instant offense. "I am cold," she said, "and so is dear Estella. So you needn't give me one of your looks. It will be a wonder if I haven't caught my death, for that horrible chapel was so draughty. I daresay I have the beginning of a sore throat."

So it was now *dear Estella*, was it? It was odd how some women formed alliances; a mutual disgust of Argyle Chapel had done the trick. "Next week, bring a cloak," Elizabeth said.

"I have no intention of repeating the ordeal, thank you."

Elizabeth could not resist a smile. "So you will be returning to Uppercross?"

Anne passed Elizabeth a cup of tea. "How was Father?" she said, before Mary could reply. "I trust he is well?"

"This was one of his bad days."

"I wonder why?" said Mary. "When last I called he was in such spirits. So full of plans for his return to Kellynch. I could scarcely get a word in."

"And when was that?" flashed Elizabeth. "Last week?"

Anne looked from one to the other. "Elizabeth, please," she murmured.

"Your pardon, madam." Yee's low voice caught Elizabeth's attention. "Miss Owen has come to collect the children."

Elizabeth put down her cup and saucer. No matter that she was not dressed for walking, this was the perfect escape. "I believe I'll join her."

"Is Miss Owen still hanging about?" Estella's penetrating whisper could be heard by all.

Elizabeth shook a scornful head. Her pretty cousin might have the better breeding, but Miss Owen certainly had the better manners.

She met with Miss Owen in the entrance hall, and soon their little party was hurrying along the path. Miss Owen had hold of Little Charles and her basket, and Elizabeth, who knew nothing about children, had charge of young Walter. He was almost three.

"Truly, Miss Elliot," said Miss Owen, panting a little as Little Charles pulled her along, "you needn't go to all this trouble. I can manage them quite well by myself."

Walter held tightly to Elizabeth's bare hand; his fingers were sticky. "I don't mind," she said gamely.

"Surely you wish to remain with your sisters. What about Mrs. Stevenson-Bragg?"

Johnny and Bella, who were well ahead, had the gate open. Elizabeth could hear its hinges squealing as it was pulled open and shut, open and shut.

"Hurry it up!" yelled Johnny.

"Aunt 'Lizbet," Walter shouted up to her. "We're going to play Ducks and Drakes."

"What on earth is that? And why must we go into the park to play?" She addressed Miss Owen, but Little Charles answered. He was four and, like his father, was very fond of talking. "We need water for Ducks and Drakes."

"Water," Elizabeth repeated. "How ... nice."

"You throw a rock," Little Charles explained, "and then you say, 'Duck-Drake-Duck-Drake' until it stops." His smile slipped. "I'm not a very good thrower."

"That is the game? Throwing rocks?" Elizabeth had never thrown a rock in her life.

"He means skipping stones over the surface of the water," Miss Owen explained. "Don't worry, Little Charles, you are becoming better at throwing every day." She raised her voice. "Follow me, children! And if we happen to see Admiral McGillvary, mind your manners! And stay clear of his horse!"

Little Charles looked back. "Hurry up, Aunt 'Lizbeth," he bellowed. Walter pulled at her hand.

Elizabeth sighed and trudged ahead.

Once the children settled down, Elizabeth found herself in conversation. As before, Miss Owen began it. "And how is your father?"

Elizabeth knew this was mere politeness, but since she could think of nothing else to speak about—save Miss Owen's ugly hat—she took it up. "To be honest, he was ... crabby." She attempted to speak lightly, but she suspected her listener was not fooled.

"My father is often the same," said Miss Owen, "but he does not seem to be able to rise above it. His situation is far different from your father's, I am sure." She gave a sharp sigh. "Papa's health is poor, but he brought that on himself by drinking far more than is good for him. And—" She hesitated. "And he has money troubles."

"Don't we all," said Elizabeth.

"However," she continued more cheerfully, "he is free now, thanks to my brothers. I hope and pray things will be better for him."

Elizabeth looked hard at Miss Owen. "Free," she repeated. "How do you mean, free?"

Miss Owen flushed; she began to study her clasped hands. "He could not pay his debts, you see. And so—" She made a vague gesture. "For a time Father was confined."

Elizabeth was shocked. "Do you mean he was imprisoned?"

Miss Owen sighed. "When a man is unable to pay his creditors, then ..."

Elizabeth did not know what to say. She had heard of such things, but to meet the daughter of a bankrupt man made the threat terribly real. Would she face a similar fate? If so, what could be done? She shot a look at Miss Owen and spoke her thought. "How was your father to raise the money if he was—" Elizabeth hesitated. She did not like to say the word *imprisoned.*

"That was left for my brothers to do."

The tight feeling in Elizabeth's chest, which had been growing steadily worse, now threatened to overwhelm her. If her father were in similar straits, what would happen? For she had no brothers.

It was not until later that night that the answer came. Elizabeth might not have brothers, but she did have *brothers-in-law.*

And so one fine afternoon, when Captain Wentworth was at home and looked to be in a receptive mood, Elizabeth presented herself at the door of his ground floor office. He rose when she entered.

"Good afternoon," he said, with unbecoming surprise. When he realized that she had something to discuss, he indicated the chair in front of his desk. "Won't you sit down?"

Elizabeth drew a long breath. She expected to be uncomfortable, but she had no idea how much she would feel it now that they were face to face. "I have come to speak to you on a matter of some importance."

"So I see."

Apparently this was his invitation to continue. What shabby manners Captain Wentworth had! "It is a matter of business," Elizabeth said, "in which you will be acting on behalf on another."

Captain Wentworth's stern expression relaxed. "Is this about Mrs. Smith?" he said, smiling. "Anne has already informed me of the particulars. You may rest easy. I am prepared to act on her behalf."

Elizabeth frowned at him; she knew no one named Smith. "I have lately learned that our father is facing severe financial troubles, Captain Wentworth."

His smile froze. "This is hardly a new situation." He leaned back in his chair. "But please, continue."

"He is truly worried. In fact, I fear his anxiety is affecting his health." She waited for a response, but there was none. "He is despondent, Captain Wentworth," she added.

"So I would imagine."

He gave her no encouragement! How despicable it was to be reduced to begging!

"What I would like to ask," she managed, "is whether you would consider assisting him to pay his debts. It would certainly give peace of mind to Anne."

Captain Wentworth did not answer right away. "I take it you refer to paying his shot at The Citadel," he said.

"His shot? Do you mean his bill? Is he behind in his payments there as well?"

"Is this a surprise to you?" Captain Wentworth's smile became unpleasant. "Mr. Savoy is most insistent about being paid on time. At the moment he is not happy with your father."

Captain Wentworth's eyes studied her face. "So," he said, "I must assume that you are speaking of his other obligations. How much does he owe?"

Elizabeth moistened her lips. "I do not know," she said truthfully. "Several thousand pounds, perhaps?" She came to the edge of her chair. "You see, I've been think-ing. Anne told me the story of how you paid for the pian-oforte—with that unexpected money—and I was wondering if you could do the same for poor Father."

Captain Wentworth said nothing, so Elizabeth plunged ahead. "Surely there must be some way you can assist him. Anne would be extremely grateful. And," Eliz-abeth continued, warming to her subject, "Father would be able to return to Kellynch Hall and not be a bother to you—or to her— any longer!"

"A tempting inducement."

"You see?" she cried. "Everyone benefits."

"Everyone benefits," he agreed, "except my estate. It's a nice bit of wishful thinking, but fundamentally unsound. What you are suggesting is that I rob Anne and our chil-dren of 'several thousand pounds.' Oh," he added, raising a hand, "you are not the first to suggest this. Mary also thinks it a praiseworthy notion."

Elizabeth froze to haughtiness. "Isn't it?"

He lifted a quill and began to toy with it. "I find it ironic," he said, "that those who do not earn a living are always quick to tell those who *do* how to spend their money."

"I am not asking you to *spend* anything," Elizabeth flashed. "I am merely suggesting that you help Father!"

"Allow me to give you perspective. At my current rank, my yearly pay is in the neighbourhood of five hun-dred pounds." He tapped the quill lightly on the desktop. "A year's worth of work, Miss Elliot, during which time I must support myself while at sea, as well as my wife and children here in England."

Embarrassed, Elizabeth cried, "I am not asking you to hand over your slave's wages to Father! But surely you can relieve some of his distress!"

"I am in no way obliged to shoulder the load of his financial obligations." He raised an eyebrow. "Have you consulted with Charles Musgrove on the subject? You will find him even less sympathetic. How many acres of his family's land, I wonder, would he be obliged to sell to raise your 'several thousand pounds'?"

Elizabeth eyed him with growing resentment. Unfortunately there was more. "The simple fact is this," he went on. "When a man fails to provide for his family and shows not a particle of remorse, he is little more than grain for the grist mill of life's consequences. To put it bluntly, if a man refuses to swim, the sharks will eat him."

Elizabeth was too shocked to say anything. Did Captain Wentworth hate her father so entirely? Did he likewise hate her?

He smiled slightly. "Let us say, for the sake of argument, that I do discharge your father's debts. What then?"

Elizabeth found her voice. "Father will return to Kellynch Hall."

"Where he will retire quietly? And meekly live within his means?"

This was unanswerable.

"You know very well that he would not." Wentworth tossed the quill aside. "Within two or three years he would be back where he is now, just as much in the hole as ever."

Elizabeth said, in a rough whisper, "People change, Captain Wentworth. Perhaps he will reform. Turn over a new leaf, so to speak."

"Perhaps." The sarcasm in Captain Wentworth's tone was palpable. "It occurs to me that your father has had sufficient motive to make such a reformation before this—and has refused. He does not scruple, for instance, to deny his daughters of their rightful settlement income."

Elizabeth could no longer look Captain Wentworth in the eye.

He broke the silence. "If ever I do agree to discharge your father's debts, understand this: It will be after he is dead. Never before."

"Think of Anne!" Elizabeth cried. "Think of her peace of mind!"

"I am thinking of Anne," he replied. "While he lives, your father must find his own way." The finality in Captain Wentworth's declaration was unmistakable. The interview was over.

Elizabeth rose to her feet with as much dignity as she could muster and said through clenched teeth, "Is this your final answer, sir?"

Captain Wentworth likewise pushed back his chair. "It is."

"Then," she cried, "may God help poor Father."

"What an excellent idea." Captain Wentworth's cold smile reappeared. "I suggest you apply to Him for the money."

4 Pribbles and Prabbles

In the days following, Mary Musgrove did indeed develop a full-blown cold. She complained so much that eventually Yee was sent to summon the physician.

Winnie Owen met him at the service door. "I am afraid Mr. Minthorne won't have time until this evening," she told him. "Is she very bad? Is there anything I might do for her?"

"She is anxious because her husband has not come," said Yee. "He sent a letter, but she has, I believe, a nervous disposition."

Winnie considered. "She has been alone for all this time?"

"Today her breakfast tray was untouched."

"Mr. Minthorne won't like that. She must eat."

Yee's brows went up. "We shall prepare another tray if you wish, but it is well to remember: 'The spirit of a man will sustain his infirmity; but a wounded spirit, who can bear?'"

"A wounded spirit," Winnie echoed. "Do you suppose she will see me? Sometimes it helps to speak about one's troubles. While we talk, you can bring in a plate of sandwiches."

"I shall enquire."

Some minutes later Winnie followed Yee up to Mary Musgrove's bedchamber. Although she had never conversed with Mrs. Musgrove, Winnie was too well acquainted with the rigors of the sickroom to be shy. She went directly to the bed.

"Good morning," she said pleasantly. "I am Miss Owen, Mr. Minthorne's cousin, come to visit you. Mr. Yee will bring us tea and sandwiches, and while he does, you must tell me exactly how you are feeling."

Although Mary Musgrove made no move to return the greeting, Winnie knew herself to be on solid ground. She drew a chair forward. "Mr. Yee tells me your husband did not arrive as expected. You must feel it deeply."

Mrs. Musgrove turned her head. "My husband," she repeated. "My husband is the greatest beast in nature!" Her face crumpled. "He was supposed to arrive with money and my trunks, but it seems he has more important things to do."

"Oh dear," said Winnie. She located a fresh handkerchief. "Suppose you tell me about it."

"He is cruel and selfish and horrible," Mrs. Musgrove said, dabbing at her eyes. "I ought never to have married him. Truly, you have no idea how I am treated. As if I am nothing!"

Winnie sighed; it was always the same story. She was almost glad to be unmarried! "Has he a temper?" she asked a little fearfully. Her father had a vicious temper, especially when he had been drinking. It was well that he lived in Wales!

"The worst." Mrs. Musgrove hitched herself higher on the pillow. "You should hear the things he says to me."

Winnie closed her eyes, remembering. "Does he fly into a rage and curse?"

Mrs. Musgrove looked startled. "Not exactly," she said. "But he is terribly unkind."

"I'm sorry," said Winnie. "You know how men's tongues will run away with them, especially when they've been drinking."

Mrs. Musgrove sniffed. "Charles," she said "is altogether too fond of drinking! You would be shocked to learn the lowly sort of drink he prefers."

Winnie was all sympathy. "Rum," she said wrathfully, "and demon gin. Horrible stuff. Altogether wicked."

Mrs. Musgrove's eyes went wide, and Winnie realized that she must be unaccustomed to plain speaking. "I am sorry to offend," she said gently, "but there is nothing like facing the truth of a matter. Tell me more."

"Well," said Mrs. Musgrove, warming to her subject, "Charles cares nothing for my feelings—my own sincerest feelings! Indeed, no one knows what I suffer at his hands."

Winnie caught her breath. "Does he *beat* you?"

"Er—no," Mrs. Musgrove said. "But I daresay he would like to!" She twisted the handkerchief. "He has no regard for the state of my health, Miss Owen, which is quite delicate. Indeed, Charles is forever comparing me to ... to other women! It is horrible, I tell you, horrible!"

Winnie laid a gentle hand on her shoulder. "Mrs. Musgrove you cannot mean he keeps a mis—a—" Winnie blushed; she could not bring herself to say the word! "Does he—keep another woman?"

There was a pause. "Well, no," said Mrs. Musgrove. "But his brother! His brother, Richard, certainly did. Or he would have if he had lived long enough. You know how habits run in a family."

As two of her brothers were now following in their father's footsteps, Winnie knew exactly.

"He complains how I manage the boys. And how I handle money. You have never met a more tightfisted, stingy man in all your life. The things other women receive as a matter of course he denies me." Mrs. Musgrove's tears began to flow again. "The basic necessities of life! It is too, too hard."

Winnie poured out a glass of water and offered the plate of sandwiches. Mrs. Musgrove helped herself. Soon color returned to her cheeks. Mr. Minthorne would be pleased, although it had cost Winnie to hear the sad tale. The woman's husband was obviously a monster.

Still, it would be some time before her cousin would arrive. She might as well hear it all. "What else is troubling you, Mrs. Musgrove?" she said gently.

Lady Russell stood uncertainly outside Sir Walter's door. She had been searching without success for an attendant to announce her arrival, for she wished to visit him. The sound of voices within his room caught her attention, and she came nearer to listen. Was the phrase *good day* among the babble?

The handle of the door turned. Apparently someone was coming out.

Lady Russell stepped back a pace. A moment later a gentleman emerged, and he carefully closed the door. He was a wide fellow. Lady Russell coughed, and he turned round.

"Why, Mr. Rushworth," she said. "How do you do?"

Mr. Rushworth pulled the hat from his head. "Very well, ma'am," he said and made a little bow. "Very well indeed. In fact—" His polite smile dissolved into a boyish grin. "In fact, I was never better in my life."

"How thoughtful of you to call on Sir Walter. Charity toward the sick is a becoming virtue."

Mr. Rushworth was now twisting the brim of his hat. "I came all the way from London, ma'am," he confessed, "on an errand for Mama. So I thought I would—you know—pop by."

"I trust you enjoyed your visit?"

"Very much, ma'am. He was most agreeable about— about everything. I didn't think he would be." And then Mr. Rushworth's supply of words deserted him. He mumbled a brief farewell and moved off.

Puzzled, Lady Russell watched him go. Such an odd young man! She looked again for an attendant but eventually gave it up. "Good morning, Sir Walter," she called and opened the door a crack. "May I come in?"

Sir Walter's greeting was clear and strong, an excellent sign. He sat in a chair by one of the windows; sunshine streamed through the panes to light his head and shoulders. At his side was a small table upon which were spread writing materials. Apparently he was working on a letter.

"This is perfect," he said and returned his attention to one of the pages. He bent and signed his name with a flourish. "There we are—finished. Your timing is superb."

She brought out a bundle of his most recent letters. "Where would you like me to put these?"

"Oh, anywhere. On the chair, on the bed, on the floor—it matters not." He read through what he had written and nodded. "Yes, quite perfect."

Lady Russell smiled; she would never put his letters on the floor. "I'll just set these on the mantelpiece," she suggested, "where they won't be misplaced. Several look to be rather important."

Sir Walter turned his head. "Invitations?"

"I believe these are letters of business."

"Oh," he said. "Business." He became occupied with the sealing wax. When he finished, he glanced up. "Good gracious, forgive my appalling manners. Please, do sit down." He waved a hand toward a chair adjacent to his. "I have had such a morning."

"Indeed?"

"I have had a caller, you see. With news."

It must have been some news, for Sir Walter's eyes were shining.

"And so, as you see," he continued, "I have written to Shepherd." He held out the newly-sealed letter. "Would you be so kind as to have this sent by express? He must come to Bath straightway, for I have need of his counsel."

Lady Russell took the letter with raised brows. "By express," she repeated.

"I must see Shepherd about several things. The settlements, for one. He needs to be on hand to record the settlements."

"The—settlements?" Was someone contemplating matrimony?

"There is another little problem," he said, "regarding the loan payment. But no matter, Shepherd will handle it admirably, I am sure." Sir Walter sat back in his chair. His fingers drummed on his knee. He hummed a tune and tapped his foot. "I say," he complained. "Aren't you going to ask about my caller?"

The late afternoon was golden, so uncharacteristic for that time of year. The sunshine, brilliant clouds, and caressing breeze made being out-of-doors a delight. Even Elizabeth, who had been under a cloud since her interview with Captain Wentworth, was drawn out to enjoy the park. The added benefit was that she would not find Captain Wentworth there. The sooner she was married and out of his house, the better!

When she reached the top of the slope, she heard the sound of children laughing. Sure enough, Miss Owen and the Musgrove boys were beside the lake. She turned to go, but then she remembered Captain Wentworth and thought better of it. It was far nicer to be here.

Little Charles came running up. "Aunt 'Lizbeth," he shouted. "There's frogs in the mud! By the rushes! I caught one! Want to see?" He held out cupped hands, the prison for the unfortunate frog.

Elizabeth brought a gloved hand to her breast. "Er— no, thank you, Little Charles," she said, as kindly as she could. She had noticed that Miss Owen was gentle with children and received much better responses from them.

Together she and Little Charles made their way to the bench. "Have you found any birds' nests?" Elizabeth enquired politely. The boys were wild to find one, she knew.

Little Charles's face lit up. "Oh lots!" he bellowed. "Miss Ow'n found a dandy one in that bush over there." His face fell a bit. "But it's old. Miss Ow'n says it's not time for nests."

"Little Charles," Miss Owen broke in. "Have a care for the frog! Do be gentle."

Little Charles glanced down at his hands. "Oh," he said. "Sorry." He parted his fingers to peer at his captive. "He's trying to get out."

"Perhaps you should return him to his friends in the mud?" Elizabeth had to smile at her advice—what did she know about frogs? Little Charles's stockings and breeches were covered with mud; what harm could more do? He went galloping away.

"What an excellent suggestion," said Miss Owen merrily. "What is it about getting dirty that is so attractive to a boy?"

Elizabeth sat down. "I have no idea." She allowed herself to relax against the back of the stone bench. Since it was only Miss Owen, it did not matter if she indulged in the luxury of lounging. "I know nothing about boys," she admitted, closing her eyes against the bright sun.

"I do," said Miss Owen, "and young or old, when it comes to adventures they are all the same. The dirtier, the better."

Elizabeth opened an eye. "They are the same, aren't they?" she said, caught by a sudden memory. "Climbing through hedges and jumping into canals and—"

How had Patrick Gill put it? Ah yes. "And messing about in boats." Elizabeth's smile faded. It was better not to think about Patrick Gill.

"Aunt 'Lizbet?" Walter stood at her knee. "I looked," he said solemnly, "but there's nothing hiding under there." He pointed to the bench.

His question brought a pang. When they were here last, she had asked him to check for a note. But this was before her interview with Captain Wentworth. Had Mr. Gill placed one? Given the severity of her situation, it was better not to know. Patrick Gill had been a charming diversion, nothing more.

"I thank you, Walter," she said and gave his curly head a pat. "You needn't look under the bench anymore."

"Are you brave now?"

"Yes," she said. "I think I am brave now."

He scampered off to join his brother.

"He is a fine little fellow," said Miss Owen. "Always checking for creatures beneath the bench."

"He is," said Elizabeth softly. "And I am a simpleton."

"There's nothing to be ashamed of. Mice give me a terrible fright. Although ..." Miss Owen paused. "To say truth, I am most afraid of people. My Great Aunt Minthorne in particular. I shouldn't be, but there it is." She glanced shyly at Elizabeth.

"I know exactly what you mean."

"Mr. Yee says I must overcome it. He says 'The fear of man bringeth a snare,' and I daresay he is right. You know how fond Mr. Yee is of quoting texts." Miss Owen paused to smile. "It's odd, isn't it? I cannot imagine him being afraid of anyone. Yet to hear his story, he and his wife have had very difficult lives.

Had Yee a story? Elizabeth eyed Miss Owen wonderingly. She had never thought about servants as having lives. They were just—servants.

Miss Owen gave a sharp sigh. "How the time does run away," she said. "I'd best get these fellows home. They want a good washing and clean clothes. We're having a bit of a treat later this afternoon."

Elizabeth chose to remain behind. She adjusted the brim of her hat against the glare of the sun. Now that it was quiet she ought to enjoy the beauties here. The willows were covered with the new green of spring—a pretty sight—and the water sparkled merrily.

Elizabeth could only frown and kick a toe against the turf. Birds flitted in and out of trees, singing and trilling.

Each blade of new grass shone golden. But Elizabeth was too occupied with her thoughts to care.

If only she could stop thinking! Was this why Anne was so fond of reading? To avoid thinking of Captain Wentworth after their father sent him away? Perhaps next time she should bring a book.

A slight sound caught her attention, and she glanced up. A lone horseman was cantering along the top of the hill. She quickly looked the other way, feigning unconcern. Perhaps he would not notice her and go away? To her distress, she heard the hoof beats draw nearer.

Hating herself, Elizabeth finally looked up. The rider, who was now very near indeed, was dismounting. He removed his hat, exposing unruly brown hair. And then he smiled.

Elizabeth caught her breath in surprise.

"Miss Elliot," he called. "Good afternoon." It seemed as if he would say more, but no words came.

Elizabeth's heart was pounding alarmingly. "You've returned," she cried and rose from the bench. She could feel a smile spreading across her face—a foolish smile, she knew. She had forgotten how handsome he was.

Patrick Gill held up a sealed letter. "I have no need to place this, have I?" There was a pause. "You've found the bench, I see. Do you like it?"

Elizabeth discovered that she'd been staring instead of listening. His face held an expectant look; had he asked a question? She must say something. "Is this not a lovely day?" she managed.

He came nearer. Left to itself, his horse began to tear at the grass. "Yes," he said, "it is a very lovely day."

"I—was beginning to wonder whether you would return." She was finding it difficult to breathe properly.

"But I had given my word." He flashed another delightful smile. "Did you doubt me?"

"It has been my experience that gentlemen often change their minds."

His eyes glittered, or so it seemed to her. "Ah, but I am not a gentleman. Or so I have been told."

"You certainly look like a gentleman today," she countered. "Are you helping Burns to exercise the horses?"

Mr. Gill seemed pleased by this. "Have you met Burns?"

"Miss Owen has." Elizabeth stopped. "He—Burns—told her that it was permissible to be down here. I doubt this is true. If our gardener at Kellynch told trespassers such a thing, I would be angry."

Mr. Gill's smile turned into a grin. Why was he so pleased by this?

Elizabeth swallowed. She had to say something—she couldn't just stare! "The horse you are riding is beautiful." And it was. Large and handsome, it was as black as jet.

"Would you like an introduction?" Mr. Gill patted its neck and shoulders. "This," he said, "is Aoife."

"Ee-fa." Elizabeth repeated the unfamiliar name. "That's Irish, isn't it?" She reached out a tentative hand. "I have always longed to ride."

Mr. Gill had become occupied with untwisting Aoife's bridle, but at this he looked up. "How do you mean?"

"My father never kept saddle horses. He does not ride—and neither do his daughters."

He gave her a sidelong look. "You cannot expect me to believe that. Come, confess your cowardice and be done with it."

"I am no coward," she retorted. "My father thinks horses are dirty animals and would never let us near them. I would gladly ride if given the chance."

Mr. Gill straightened. His eyes were very blue. "Very well," he said, looking her over. "Is that a good dress you are wearing?"

"Not particularly."

"Excellent. Come here." He bent down and cupped his hands together. "Put your foot here, and I'll throw you up."

"You'll do what?"

"Hold on tightly—use your knees to grasp Aoife's sides—until I'm up behind you."

Elizabeth caught his arm. "What do you mean?"

"I mean," he said, grinning, "to teach you to ride— now. Are you game?"

"*Am I?*" she cried.

Before Elizabeth had time to settle herself, McGillvary swung up behind. He threw his free arm round her waist and reminded her to use her knees.

"My knees," she repeated, a little out of breath. "But surely this is not the way I ought to sit. As a lady, I mean."

McGillvary did not answer; he had all he could do to keep Aoife from plunging sideways. Obviously she was not happy at having two riders to bear.

"I do apologize," he said, making his seat secure. "This is how I taught my daughter. Now that I think on it, she must have been four or five."

He turned his head one way and then another, wondering how to deal with Elizabeth's wide-brimmed hat. "If you sit just here," he said, using his free hand to place her shoulder, "I shall be able to see—"

Instead of complying, she twisted round. "Is my hat in your way?"

"Think nothing of it," he said courteously, applying a firm hand to the reins. Aoife had taken to prancing. She was fresher than he thought.

To his surprise, Elizabeth's response was to pull roughly at the hat's ribbons. "There," she said, removing it. "Since I am riding like a hoyden, I might as well look the part." She made a move to toss her hat to the ground.

McGillvary intercepted. "Gently, my dear, gently," he said. He brought the horse forward until she was alongside the bench. "There you are, milady," he said, smiling. Elizabeth dropped her hat neatly on the seat.

"And now," he said, "shall we ride?"

"You *will* keep away from the house, won't you?" This was said with some anxiety. "I don't mind riding like a gypsy," Elizabeth confessed, "but I'd hate to be caught looking like one."

"Your wish is my command. In fact,"—McGillvary pulled off his own hat—"there!" He tossed it onto the bench beside hers. "Now we both look like ... what was the charming word you used?"

"Gypsies," she said, laughing with him. "Trespassers, in fact."

"We are definitely not trespassers." He urged Aoife into a walk, and slowly they made a circuit around the far side of the lake. "Am I taking it too fast?"

"Oh, no! Not at all!" She turned her head. "May we not ride faster?"

"Not yet." If he allowed Aoife a bit of liberty, she would break into a trot, which would be uncomfortable for both of them. "First," he said, bringing his lips near to Elizabeth's ear, "I'd like you to become accustomed to the feel and movement of the horse. Fair enough?"

This was only part of the story. McGillvary was very much enjoying becoming accustomed to Elizabeth, as they were pressed so close together. His left arm encircled her waist, drawing her to rest against his chest. Best of all, she did nothing to resist. Strands of her hair brushed his cheek; her scent—a hint of jasmine—was intoxicating.

A series of sharp barks broke the silence. McGillvary turned to see two dogs racing toward them. "Hugo!" he cried hoarsely, "Tough! No!"

As Hugo and Tough rounded the lake they startled the geese, setting into motion a flapping cacophony. Aoife reared suddenly, causing Elizabeth to gasp. Ignoring

McGillvary's attempts to rein her in, Aoife charged up the hill in the direction of the mansion.

McGillvary and Elizabeth disappeared at a hand gallop, heading toward the avenue of chestnuts with the two dogs in joyous pursuit.

5 Is She Not Passing Fair?

When Yee brought down the two Musgrove boys, now wearing clean clothes, Winnie Owen was ready for them. She took a small hand in each of her own. "You are spending the afternoon with me at my cousin's house," she announced. "We'll play games and have an early supper. What do you say to that?"

Little Charles and Walter cheered, and Winnie smiled with them. Cook would not be happy—she hated impromptu entertaining—but she knew her cousin Michael would not mind. Yee opened the main door.

"Mr. Yee," she said, "if they are needed, you may come at any time. Please remember to knock hard at the service door, as Cook is so deaf."

"You should be calling me Yee," he said softly.

She flushed. "I forgot. I'm sorry, it's just that—"

"Why, Miss Owen," called a voice.

Winnie looked up to see Mrs. Musgrove standing on the landing above. She clung to the bannister rail as she made her way down the stairs. She was, Winnie noticed, wearing a lovely dressing gown of pink satin. "I cannot thank you enough," she said, "for taking charge of my sweet boys." She turned aside to cough.

"It's best for everyone. The older children have been twitting them so. And I very much enjoy the company."

Mrs. Musgrove came to pat Little Walter on the head. "The Braggs are perfect beasts," she complained. "And there is something else ..."

She lowered her voice. "It's their father," she said, behind her hand. "He's been due anytime this past week. As you might expect, the boys are wild to see him. And of course, nothing."

Mrs. Musgrove rolled her eyes heavenward. "Another delay. You know what *that* means."

Winnie did indeed. "I am very sorry," she said. "Let us hope he will arrive soon."

"In one piece and with my trunks." Mrs. Musgrove waved her handkerchief. "Farewell, boys. Mind your manners."

Little Charles and Walter jumped and skipped along the pavement, talking all the way.

"First," said Winnie, "I'll show you the house and arrange for our supper. And then we'll play games in the back parlour. What do you say to that?"

"Hide-And-Seek?" chirped Walter, tugging at her hand.

"And several more besides."

"Then Papa will come," said Little Charles, "and dance with Mama and she won't be cross anymore."

"What a very good thing that would be."

As they approached the door of the Minthorne house, Little Charles squeezed her hand. "Know what I want for supper?" he confided. "Scrumpy! Heated up!"

"Me too," bellowed Walter.

Winnie was struck speechless. Scrumpy was hard cider! A drink not fitting for a child! "I'll—see what Cook can do for us," she said faintly.

"Papa *loves* Scrumpy," Little Charles announced.

"I am sure he does," said Winnie. When—or if—Mr. Musgrove arrived in Bath was nothing to her, but she found herself hoping that he would come today—so that she could give him a piece of her mind. Scrumpy, indeed!

An hour or so later, a two-wheeled vehicle pulled up before the Wentworth house. Both horse and gig had obviously been on the road for most of the day. A solitary figure climbed down, removed several bulky parcels, and signalled his companion to drive on.

Hearing the commotion of his arrival, Mary Musgrove came out of the drawing room. "Bless me," she cried, peering down at him. "Have you come at last? And in such dirt, too."

Charles Musgrove shrugged off his overcoat and passed it to the butler. "It was a bit dusty," he admitted. "What we need is a spot of rain. Not easy in the gig, rain. Glad it was clear."

Mary became red in the face. "Never tell me that you have come to Bath in the gig!"

"Of course I did," he replied cheerfully. He removed his hat and used his fingers to comb his hair.

"How dreadful."

"It wasn't so bad. I could hardly ask my father for the coach and horses, not at this time of year. You've always complained about not having transportation in Bath, so I thought why not bring the gig?"

"But it's so shabby and provincial."

Charles began to mount the stairs. "The gig's in fine shape. Coney painted it not too long ago and—"

"Painted in black," she flung at him. 'Such a dreary colour."

He halted. "What's wrong with black? Would you rather it be yellow?"

"At least yellow is vibrant and alive. And sporting."

"A gig is not a sporting vehicle." Charles regarded his wife in silence. "You'll think differently when you need to go out. I'll tell you what: I'll take you out tomorrow morning—whenever you like."

"A handsome offer, to be sure, but as you see I am ill. I have no intention of being seen in a countrified gig. I'd as soon drive out in a dog cart."

Charles began to draw off his driving gloves. "I thought you'd be pleased," he said. "Bye the bye, where are the boys? Have you hired a new nursery maid?"

"I have not," she said. "They are with Miss Owen next door."

"At Minthorne's house?" He turned and descended the stairs.

"Are you leaving, Charles? But you've only just arrived!"

"I am going to fetch my sons home—if I can find where Yee put my hat," he said. "Burn it, where is the man?"

"Perhaps he took it below stairs for cleaning. I daresay it needs it." Mary shrugged. "You may as well go without it. The neighbours here are such *canaille* they likely won't notice."

Charles jerked the door open. "If that is the case," he said, "I wonder that you allow the boys to spend so much time with them." He went out, slamming the door.

Walter Musgrove dissolved into giggling, and Winnie smiled. An afternoon like this was exactly what these boys needed. "Very well, gentlemen," she announced, "in precisely three seconds I shall begin the count. Are you prepared to hide?"

Little Charles poked his head from behind the ancient wingchair. "Ready," he hollered.

"Me too," chirped Walter.

"Very well, I shall begin counting ... now!" Winnie faced the wall. "One, two, three ..."

She could hear more giggling and admonitions to hurry up.

"Four, five, six ..."

What could be better than Hide-And-Go Seek? Unless it was Blindman's Bluff. Winnie had played both with her brothers in their father's barn. Wally had a particular way of playing this game ...

"Twenty-eight, twenty-nine ..." She paused for emphasis. "Thirty! Ready or not, here I come!"

She turned round. The room was silent, save for the ticking of the longcase clock and the muffled giggles of the boys. Why not try Wally's trick? Winnie hunted up her cousin's fringed lap blanket and arranged it over her head, as Wally used to do. Now to imitate his voice ...

"When I find ye," she growled in a heavy brogue, "ye'll be sorry! For I'm the ..." Winnie thought fast; these were very small boys after all. "... for I'm the Kissing Monster! When I find ye, I'll be giving ye a kiss! So beware!"

Winnie slouched through the parlour in fine monster fashion, her face hidden behind the blanket's fringe. The boys were not adept at hiding—or remaining quiet—but she did her best not to find them. She had Little Charles cornered once, but she became tangled in the blanket and gamely let him go. After all, there was no hurry.

So diverting was the game that Winnie did not hear the opening of the door or Ruth's muffled announcement. She did hear the boys squeal more loudly, but that was not unusual.

"And when I find ye," she repeated, taking a new direction, "there'll be no escaping yar doom!" She bent over and took several monster-like lunges, growling in her best monster voice.

"The Kissing Monster! The Kissing Monster!" the boys shrieked gleefully. "Papa, Papa, save us!"

Papa? Winnie pulled up short. There, several paces away, was a pair of brown boots—a man's boots. They were travel-stained. Winnie pulled the blanket from her head.

The man bent and held out a hand to her—a broad hand that looked to have some strength in it. "Miss Owen?" His was a distinctly friendly voice.

Winnie took in his pleasant, round face, his wide smile, and his curling light-brown hair. But it was his eyes that held her attention: they were hazel with a twinkling cheerfulness. Surely this was not the brute Mrs. Musgrove had ranted about! He must be an uncle. But the boys called him *Papa* ...

Walter clung to his legs and Little Charles climbed onto his back, talking nonstop. Everything was poured into his ears: the games they'd played and the lake and the frogs and the birds' nests. The man was not at all put off by their noise. He ruffled Walter's hair affectionately and turned to her.

"Charles Musgrove, at your service," he said laughingly. "Please, allow me."

Reluctantly Winnie placed her hand in his. Her legs had become cramped from kneeling, so she needed his help to rise.

"I'm sorry to spoil your game," he went on. "For a minute there, I thought I'd be the one to get the kiss!"

Poor Winnie blushed all the way to the roots of her hair—which was falling down around her shoulders because of the blanket. "H-how do you do, Mr. Musgrove?" she stammered.

McGillvary cursed under his breath as, one-handed, he fought to rein in Aoife. It took all his strength to keep from being unseated. At last she came to a standstill, shivering as the two dogs pranced round her feet. Keeping a firm hand on the reins, McGillvary turned his attention to Elizabeth. Her head was down; he could feel her breath come in sharp gasps.

"Elizabeth, my dear, I am so sorry! I would not have had this happen for the world."

With a shaking hand she pushed back a fallen lock of hair. McGillvary braced himself for the worst. She tipped her head; her eyes met his.

"Is that all?" she said, in a voice as hoarse as his.

"An accident," he said, cursing Aoife's perverseness. "The fault is entirely mine. You cannot know how sorry I—"

"No, no," cried Elizabeth, taking hold of his arm. "I mean, is that *all?*" She was smiling.

"Is that ... all?" he repeated blankly.

"Must we stop riding so soon? Oh," she cried, "it was like flying. Flying with the wind. Speaking of flying, when are we to do that?"

McGillvary blinked. "I beg pardon?"

Elizabeth laughed. "Like they do in the Hunt. You know, sailing over the hedgerows and into the fields beyond. I don't know the word for it." Her smile dimmed somewhat. "I've always felt a little sorry for the fox," she confessed, "but oh! How glorious for the rider! To—how do they say?"

She smiled in sudden triumph. "Ah yes. *To give chase!*"

"You like to ride this way?"

"Oh yes," she said earnestly. "Hell-bent-for-leather! Er—as my brother Charles would say." She blushed adorably.

He felt his lips twist into a smile. "You do not lack for courage, Miss Elliot, I give you that. Allow me to get my bearings and we'll be off." He urged Aoife forward at a walk.

"Did you think I was afraid? Riding is not a feat requiring courage."

McGillvary guided the horse from the gravel drive to the turf of the lawn. "I quite agree. Boarding an enemy ship in the dead of night, now that requires courage."

"Not as much as hearing one's name announced at— oh, any of the London balls," she countered, "for the fifth or sixth season in a row. With no husband to show for it."

"It is in nowise the same," he retorted laughingly. "I faced death, Elizabeth, certain death. On every hand!"

A dimple appeared in her cheek. "And so did I," she said. "At least when you were boarding ships you did not have to worry about appearing unconcerned and keeping poise."

"I had enough to do to keep my wits," he pointed out, "as well as direct the men under my command."

"Ah, but could you do all that and look beautiful into the bargain?" She gave a gurgle of laughter. "I think not."

McGillvary could not help himself; this was too much. He reined in Aoife. His heart, his senses—his very being— were awash with desire. And there was something else: admiration. Desire and admiration, together. It was a heady combination.

Aoife bent to take a mouthful of grass; McGillvary let go the reins and brought his other arm to encircle Elizabeth. His feeling for her could no longer be denied. Tossing aside his fine resolutions, he moistened his lips. But as he bent to kiss her, he felt her body stiffen.

Elizabeth had not guessed his intention; she was gazing at something beyond. "What is that place, Mr. Gill?" she said quietly.

McGillvary's head came up; he was struck by the odd note in her voice. She repeated the question, this time more insistently.

He turned to look. "The Belsom mansion. Quite a beautiful house, actually. Have you seen it?" He studied her profile. All traces of her smile were gone.

"It is his house, isn't it?" She gave a perfectly genuine shudder.

His house. Meaning my house.

Sobered, he spoke his thought. "Have you considered that you might have misjudged the man?"

"Oh no," she said easily. "I have not misjudged him."

McGillvary sat silent, frowning.

"I know my opinion is not a popular one," Elizabeth went on, "at least not among the ladies. They chase after him in the most shameless way."

"They do, yes," he murmured.

"It is certainly on account of his fortune. And there is the dashing uniform. I don't suppose he objects." She continued to study the house. "What do you think, Mr. Gill?"

"To be completely honest, I am afraid he—"

Before McGillvary could say more, Elizabeth shifted in her seat. He found he was now looking her full in the eyes. The expression in them took his breath away. And then she smiled—an enchanting smile that trembled at the corners. "But why should we spoil our afternoon talking about him?"

"Because I ..." McGillvary fought to make the words come. Surely this was the moment to confess the truth! But all he could do was smile like an idiot.

She loves me. Without rank or fortune she loves me.

Elizabeth gave his arm a squeeze. "You promised to teach me to ride," she reminded gently. "So, *en avant!*"

McGillvary swallowed. The moment for confession was gone, but there would be another. Yes, there would surely be another. He could not kiss her now, but there would be time for that, too.

He gathered the reins. "As you brother Charles would say?"

"Certainly not," she answered, laughing. "Charles does not speak French. He has enough trouble speaking plain English."

McGillvary grimaced a little. "He is not the only one."

With shaking hands Elizabeth fumbled with the latch. She paused long enough to pull the gate shut, then gathered her skirts and took the path at a run. How could she have let the entire afternoon slip away?

She did not want to think about what would happen if anyone saw her. Her heart was pounding as she slipped into the house. Treading with agonizing care, she made for the servants' stairway. The ascent was a challenge, for her legs were sore from riding.

At length she reached the safety of her bedchamber. She tossed her hat on the bed and went hunting for her brush. Her hair was a sight! After pulling out the combs that remained, she bent over and began to work. Her arms ached, but she ignored this.

It was then that she got a good look at her skirt. The light blue muslin was covered with hairs from the horse! Elizabeth was so surprised that she dropped the hairbrush.

She brushed savagely at her skirts. She would wear *this* dress, and that horse would be black! At last she gave it up. There was no way to remove them all. What would Elise think?

Elizabeth resumed working with her hair, none too gently. She did not care what Elise thought—or what Anne thought—did she? She was a grown woman; she could do as she liked! All the same, if she hurried, perhaps her sister would not notice the time.

6 CAUSE AND EFFECT

On the following morning, Colonel Wallis came into his parlor, humming a tune. "Here you are, m'boy." He held a letter aloft. "While you were away in Brighton, nothing. And on the very morning you return, this. What luck, eh?"

William Elliot took the letter, broke the seal, and examined the signature. So she had found him. Penelope Clay was not stupid. She would guess that sooner or later he'd visit the Wallises—his friendship with them was no secret. He read it through twice and put it down.

His sour expression did not escape Colonel Wallis. "Bad news, what?"

Elliot threw him a look and returned to the letter. Like the lady herself, it was littered with cloying expressions of love and devotion. Its ending was predictable, a heartfelt plea for his return. Like a mother hen, she was scolding and then begging.

He put the letter aside. His late wife had begged continually. Everything about her was loathsome, save for
her fortune.

Nevertheless, Penelope's tone was troubling. There
was something she was hinting at, something between the
lines. Elliot sat back, sucking his teeth and thinking.
"Women," he muttered.

Colonel Wallis turned. "How's that? Trouble with a
woman?"

Elliot swallowed an oath. He'd forgotten that Wallis
was in the room. The man's bluff banter grew more irksome every day.

Colonel Wallis gave a wheezy chuckle and sauntered
over to Elliot's chair, a wineglass in each hand. "Miss
Elizabeth Elliot's a rare handful," he said, passing a glass.
"That Rushworth fellow now—best to keep an eye on
him. He's moving in for the kill, so my Annette says."

William Elliot cast his gaze to the ceiling. "Rushworth
is an idiot. He's always moving in for the kill, or so he
thinks. I know my cousin. Elizabeth is toying with him.
She'd sooner die than be his wife."

"I hear his divorce is about wound up. Not something
I'd like my daughter mixed up in—blot on the family
name and all. Plenty of women are willing when the stakes
are high."

"Rushworth's money will make a way for him," Elliot
agreed. "But not with Elizabeth." He thought of something else. "What of Sir Walter, by the bye? He lives, I
take it."

Colonel Wallis puffed out his cheeks. "That he does." He rotated the stem of his wineglass. "As much in debt as ever and falling behind every day, or so Traub tells me. Losing his tenant for that manor house of yours, too."

Mr. Elliot smiled. "Shall I offer to take the place myself? As a sweet surprise for my darling bride?"

"Oho! So the wind's in that quarter, is it?"

"Perhaps," was all William Elliot would say. Any day he might become Sir William, possessor of a landed estate. He meant to enjoy his new position, but there were also social obligations. He'd once had a simpleton for a wife. He had no intention of repeating that mistake.

"Thought you'd changed your mind about her."

Wallis was right, he had. And then he'd changed it right back. Elizabeth's open scorn that day on the canal still made his blood boil. And yet ...

"I want a woman who will be a credit to me," he confessed. "A beautiful, accomplished woman. Not—" His gaze travelled to Penelope Clay's letter.

"Miss Elliot will do you proud. Grows prettier each time I see her." Wallis drained the contents of his glass. "Spirited too," he added, smacking his lips.

Yes, Elizabeth was spirited. If he decided to make her his wife, that would need to change. Mr. Elliot was betrayed into a smile. "You should see her when she's in a rage."

"Time to have a little talk with Papa?" Colonel Wallis heaved out of his chair and took hold of Elliot's near-empty glass. "I'll drink to that. But first, we must reprovision, eh?"

Elliot returned to Penelope's letter. There was something here, he knew it. She held more cards in her hand than she was showing. Why?

"Wallis," he said suddenly, "is there any significance in a woman being ill?"

Colonel Wallis finished refilling the glasses. "Infectious illness? Or something else?"

"It must be something else, though I cannot imagine what."

"How long has she been under the weather?"

Elliot shrugged. "I have no idea. A month. Maybe more."

A look of smiling comprehension crossed Colonel Wallis's face. "Is this a particularly close friend of yours?"

Elliot's eyes narrowed. "What does that have to do with it?"

"My dear boy," said Colonel Wallis, smiling broadly, "it has everything to do with it. But it's early days yet. Time will tell. Yes, time will tell."

Elizabeth lowered herself into the chair, grasping the edge of the dining table for support. There was not one part of her that did not ache. She was paying dearly for yesterday's riding lesson.

As she unfolded her napkin, Yee placed a steaming cup of tea. Elizabeth touched the sides of the cup with her fingers, delighting in the warmth. What she longed to do was immerse her body in a steaming bath—again. But now that Anne was home, she did not dare to ask for another. Yee had been watching her since yesterday. Did he guess where she had been?

In silence he brought her breakfast. This was the best thing about Yee. Of anyone in the house, he alone had the good sense to leave her undisturbed at the breakfast table. The newspaper was placed at her elbow, along with several letters. The first was from James Rushworth—nothing surprising there. The second letter was more perplexing.

> My Dear E,
>
> I am delivering this by Mrs. S-B's hand, as I do not wish to impose upon your sister's hospitality by calling myself. However, it has become imperative that I speak with you privately. By this time your father knows the particulars of the situation, and he, I am certain, would approve of this somewhat unconventional request.
>
> Would you do me the honour of calling? At your earliest convenience, of course.
>
> Wm. E

There followed the address of the Wallis residence.

Well! Elizabeth recognized a command when she saw one; she had no intention of dancing to her cousin's tune. It did not suit her to call today, for today she had an engagement at Bailey's tearoom. Elizabeth put the letter aside, humming a little as she spread jam on a piece of toast.

There was also a note from Anne, informing her that Mary was asking to see her. According to Yee, Mary had spent a troubled night and this morning was feverish.

"Feverish, my foot," Elizabeth murmured. Mary would lie in bed, drinking tea by the pot-full, and then complain that she was ill and over-heated! However, Elizabeth could not very well ignore Anne's request. Later that morning she presented herself at the door to Mary's bed-chamber. Anne came in answer to her knock and brought her into the room.

"Good morning, Mary," Elizabeth said, coming up to the bed. "How do you do? Yee tells me you are feverish, although how he would know such a thing is beyond me." She paused to study her sister. "You don't look ill at all. That is quite a pretty cap."

Mary's expression changed. "It is nice, is it not?" she said. "I thought so when I saw it in that shop window. I think one should always look one's best, even when one is ill. And I so often *am*."

"There is no invalid in all of Bath as pretty as you," Elizabeth agreed. She watched Mary pluck at the ruffle on her nightdress. "I hear you wished to see me."

Mary blinked. "Oh yes," she said. "You must visit Father today. I would gladly go myself, but as you can see, I am indisposed."

Elizabeth eyed her sister with growing irritation. "How convenient," she said.

"I am sorry if it spoils your precious plans," Mary cried. "Do you think I wish to be confined to my bed in this odious way? I daresay you give no thought for your poor, ill sister who is forced to remain at home!"

Elizabeth was about to reply in kind when she encountered a burning look from Anne. She agreed to call on her father and then swiftly left the room.

"I shall call on him all right," she muttered as she descended the stairs, "but he'd better be quick about it, for I won't be late for tea!" Then she remembered something else. If there was time, she would ask him about the business with William Elliot. As for Mary, perhaps Mr. Minthorne would give her a whopping jug of that syrup she liked so much—if only to keep her quiet!

Patrick McGillvary was having an equally frustrating morning. He was now seated at Mr. Lonk's desk at Madderly Kinclaven going over accounts. On the whole, he was pleased by the way the quarter had finished out. Now Lonk was blustering his way through more awkward business: the list of delinquent accounts. McGillvary frowned; the list was longer than expected.

Mr. Lonk puffed out his cheeks. "These gents," he said defensively, "all of them, have been contacted personally about the payment policy, sir. Save for those at the bottom of the list, who could not be reached."

McGillvary took the paper from Lonk and directed a speaking look. "And what do you propose to do about them?"

Mr. Lonk was looking harassed; he passed his tongue over his lips. "We'll hire some fellows to keep watch. Sooner or later they'll go out—every gentleman goes out, you know—and then we'll have 'em before the magistrate straightway."

"Simple, but effective," muttered McGillvary. He tossed the page onto the desk. "Very well. And Lonk. Do make certain that your watchers are sober."

Elizabeth came out of the house just as Charles Musgrove pulled up, and he very kindly offered to take her to The Citadel in his gig. Since he was saving her money, she felt obliged to converse. But she needn't have worried, for Charles Musgrove needed little encouragement to talk. Indeed, within a very short time she learned more than Anne had ever shared—about the trip to Shropshire, the details of the coming officers' dinner, and even Captain Wentworth's plans to purchase a carriage. She also learned about an invitation Wentworth and Anne had received from Lady Angela Thorne. This stunner was a bit hard to swallow, as Lady Angela had never shown any interest in Elizabeth or her father.

"Mary is mad as fire," Charles said. "That's nothing new, is it?"

Elizabeth smiled. "Did Anne never tell you how it was? When Mary was a girl she used to throw herself on the floor, bang her forehead against it, and then hold her breath."

"You don't say! Did it work?"

"Certainly it worked. But when Mary came out of the nursery, she learned the difference between a wooden floor and a marble one."

Charles threw back his head and laughed.

Elizabeth laughed with him, until she remembered who she was with. It was all Patrick Gill's fault. She had learned these free and easy manners from him.

Charles talked on. Tonight's assembly was his topic now, and he was spouting cheerful complaints about having to attend. He was hosting a dinner beforehand at the White Hart. "You don't suppose Mary will be too ill to come?" he said, as he guided the gig through a maze of wagons on Queen's Way. "After all, she's sent for Minthorne." Charles sounded hopeful.

"There's nothing Mary loves more than dancing. She must always be—" Elizabeth broke off speaking. Almost she had added, "making a spectacle of herself" but somehow it did not seem right—or kind—to say so.

They arrived at The Citadel soon enough, and Elizabeth was handed out of the gig. She was surprised to see Charles resume his seat and bring out a newspaper. "You are planning to wait?"

"Aw, sure. You won't be more than half an hour."

"I won't be even that long." And she wouldn't, or else she would be late for tea. However, this presented another problem. She could hardly have Charles Musgrove drop her at Bailey's! Elizabeth became so intent on sorting out this dilemma that she paid no attention to her surroundings—and walked smash into Mr. Savoy. The physician received her apology coldly.

"Miss Elliot," said he, "if you would be so kind as to stop by our office, I have an important document for your father's solicitor."

Elizabeth drew herself up. "Do you mean Mr. Shepherd? What have I to do with Mr. Shepherd?"

"You may give him my letter," said Mr. Savoy.

"But his office is in Crewkherne."

Mr. Savoy looked annoyed. "Then you will be pleased to inform your father that it is in his best interest to summon him."

He stalked off, leaving Elizabeth staring. She found her father in his rooms. He was restless and fidgety, and he muttered to himself things that Elizabeth could not understand. When she told him of Mr. Savoy's message, he raised himself from his chair and began to pace about.

"Time, time," he fretted. "What is it about time? These lowborn persons always fret about the time. Shepherd will come—I have summoned him by express—and Mr. Savoy will be satisfied, along with the others."

He stopped to glare at Elizabeth. "I must tell you, daughter, that I have been sadly deceived in Mr. Savoy. Money! Money is his god—and his reason for living." Sir Walter heaved a great sigh. "Never did I think that such a fine-looking man with such noble ideals could have such a greedy heart."

But Sir Walter's irritation was short-lived. Soon his thoughts began to take a different direction. "So," he said. "Have you any news to tell me, daughter? Have you seen him? Have you laid out your plans?"

Elizabeth was in no mood for riddles. "If you mean Frederick Wentworth, no, I have not seen him. If you mean Charles Musgrove, yes. I came with him in his, er ... vehicle."

"Wentworth? Musgrove? No, no! Rushworth, Elizabeth. James Rushworth is the man I mean." His expression became coy. "As if you did not know."

"No, I do not know," she sputtered. "Mr. Rushworth said something about coming to see you, but that was days ago."

Sir Walter smiled broadly. "Ah, then he has spoken after all. I knew he would. Now you know why Mr. Shepherd has been sent for." He gestured eagerly. "Have you brought him with you? Do not leave poor Mr. Rushworth standing in the hall! Invite him in, Elizabeth, invite him in."

"I told you. I came with Charles Musgrove," Elizabeth said. "In his gig."

"Upon my word. Rushworth won't like that."

"He won't know anything about it," she retorted. "Mr. Rushworth is in London."

Sir Walter gave a shriek, and dropped into a nearby chair. "But he cannot go to London! Not now! He must be on hand to sign the settlement papers. Time is of the essence—every day we delay is crucial."

Sir Walter cradled his head in his hands and rocked back and forth. "How can this have happened?" he lamented. "You don't understand! No one can understand! My sanctuary, my place of refuge! My hard-won peace of mind—violated! Yes, violated. By money-grubbing tradesmen with outrageous demands. Even here there is no escape. Oh!"

Elizabeth stood by as her father carried on. At last she said: "Speaking of Mr. Shepherd, Mr. Savoy has a document he wishes him to have. Shall I fetch it?"

Sir Walter raised his head. "Do not mention that man's name in my presence! Oh, that Rushworth were yet in Bath!"

Elizabeth stole a look at the clock. "Mr. Rushworth did mention seeing to various matters of business. Something to do with Parliament."

An eager light came into Sir Walter's eyes "Parliament. Yes, that would be the divorce." Claw-like, his fingers grasped the arms of his chair. "And then, Elizabeth, you must be married. As soon as may be, do you understand? By special license."

Elizabeth felt hot and cold at the same time. "To say truth," she confessed, "I am no longer certain that I wish to marry Mr. Rushworth, Father. Divorce carries such stigma, you know."

She attempted an arch smile. "After all, I am an Elliot."

Sir Walter brushed her objections aside. "Yes-yes-yes," he said. "Rushworth is well aware of that, and he is prepared to pay—I mean, settle. Handsomely."

He turned aside to cough. "Generosity in a husband is an admirable trait, my dear. Especially generosity to one's father-in-law."

"Do I have this right?" Elizabeth said, finding her voice. "Mr. Rushworth is to give over money in order to marry me? Like a barbarian, he is going to *purchase* me? And you see nothing wrong with this?"

Sir Walter fidgeted in his chair. "Such arrangements are made every day," he bleated. "In fact, dear Mr. Rushworth's generous gift will come at a most opportune time." Sir Walter lowered his voice to a whisper. "You might not have noticed, but I am a bit behind in my payments to Mr. Savoy. But no matter. Soon all shall be resolved, for you shall be married."

"But I do not wish to marry Mr. Rushworth!" cried Elizabeth. "I have changed my mind!"

Sir Walter's eyes narrowed. "You mean to break your engagement?"

"What engagement? We have no engagement!" Elizabeth nearly screamed. "Only an idiotic understanding! Which we kept secret for fear of his mother! No one knows of it!"

"Indeed." Sir Walter's voice was cold.

"Father—Papa—I need more time! Please."

Sir Walter raised an eyebrow. "My dear, time is the one thing you cannot have. You should have voiced your doubts sooner. I'm afraid the announcement is about to be sent to the papers. You cannot turn back now."

"Sent to the— ! Father, how could you!" Elizabeth's breath came in angry gasps. "If you think for one minute that I am going to marry that—that booberkin, you are mistaken!"

She whirled about, intending to run from the room, and stopped dead in her tracks. Sir Walter's door was ajar—and her cousin's smiling face showed through the opening.

William Elliot rapped gently on the door. "Knock, knock!" he called. "It is I, the truant one, come to pay a visit to my family." He smiled charmingly at Sir Walter and then at Elizabeth.

"How do you do, sir? It took ingenuity to discover your new abode, but I persevered." He made his bow. "I trust I do not interrupt anything?"

"Of course not," cried Elizabeth. "I was just taking my leave. Good day to you."

William Elliot gallantly stepped aside. "As always, you are the most beautiful when you are angry," he said as she passed. "Dearest, loveliest Elizabeth."

"You have arrived at a most opportune time, my dear William!" she heard her father say. "It so happens that I need you to execute an errand—"

The door swung shut; Elizabeth heard no more. Her heels beat a sharp staccato on the floor of the passageway.

Dearest, loveliest Elizabeth? James Rushworth had used those words once—and now William Elliot! If any man dared to say that to her again, she would *strike* him!

There was simply no understanding Elizabeth. Not twenty minutes ago she was fine, talkative even, but now! She came out of the gate like a shot, mad as fire. Scorning assistance she climbed into the gig.

And wouldn't it figure; now it was beginning to rain. Charles felt on the floor for one of the umbrellas and opened it for her, but not before noticing how dirty it was. Fortunately, she took it without saying anything cutting.

As soon as they were underway, Charles stole another look. Elizabeth was staring straight ahead. The sound of Belle's hooves, the creak and rattle of the wheels on the cobbles, and the patter of rain on the umbrella were the only sounds to be heard. Charles turned up the collar of his driving coat. Rain never bothered him, but this silence did.

At last he could stand no more. "So," he said, very off-hand, "I take it Sir Walter was in his usual good spirits?" He figured this had to be the problem. If the man were ill, Elizabeth would have looked stricken instead of angry—and she was looking extremely angry. Very well did Charles understand this. Sir Walter often made him feel that way.

It began to rain harder. "I say," he said at last. "I'm sorry about the weather." He wiped water from the leather seat with his gloved hand, but to no avail. "Here," he said, reaching beneath the seat, "perhaps you can dry it with this." He held out a folded newspaper.

"Thank you," Elizabeth began stiffly, "but the umbrella is all I—" She broke off speaking and snatched at the newspaper. "How old is this?" she demanded.

"What difference does it make? It's dry, isn't it?"

Elizabeth did not answer. She was turning the pages, which was an awkward business because of the umbrella. "Confound it," she muttered, "where is the society section?"

"Estella removed it." The boulevard was crowded and he must negotiate the turn. Then he thought of something. "You're headed home, right?" A gust of wind caught at the newspaper.

"No," she said. "I have an appoi—" She stopped. "I have an errand."

"In all this wet? Can't it wait?"

"No! It ... is a matter of some urgency."

"Well, all right. No need to bite my head off. Where shall I set you down?"

She thought for a minute. "At the Abbey."

"How's that again?"

"Please set me down at the Abbey." She coughed a little. "I wish to pray. There's nothing wrong with praying, is there?"

"Well no, but ..." Charles caught the expression in her eyes. Wisely, he decided to keep silent for the remainder of the trip.

"I tell you, I am perfectly recovered!" Sir Walter's face was beaming.

Lady Russell looked at him for a long moment. "But Sir Walter," she said, removing her gloves one by one, "is this not a matter for the physician to decide? You are, after all, under his care."

"What does he know?" he said. "My health is completely restored, I tell you, and I intend to quit this place just as soon as Elizabeth is married. In fact, sooner!"

He rubbed his hands together. "Mr. Rushworth is a man of his word. I need not delay another day. It is quite safe for me to leave."

Lady Russell became even more puzzled. "Safe? Of course, it is safe."

He leaned forward and placed his hand over hers. "My dear," he said in a low voice, "do you suppose you could bring Anne to visit me tomorrow? I must see her as soon as may be—to make the arrangements."

Lady Russell stared at his hand. "Whatever you like," she faltered. "Shall I bring Elizabeth as well?"

"There is no need to see Elizabeth. Although—" Sir Walter grew thoughtful. "There is the matter of her bridal things. Doubtless she will wish to choose a gown and such. But there is so little time! May I count on your assistance, my dear? To find a suitable gown for Elizabeth?"

"Since when has Elizabeth needed help in choosing apparel?"

Sir Walter's voice sank. "Yes, but you see," he confided, "Elizabeth does not understand." He gave Lady Russell's hand a squeeze. "Mr. Rushworth is so very anxious to be married. Elizabeth has no notion of the eagerness, the understandable eagerness, of a young man."

"But would it not be better to wait? His divorce has only just been granted!"

"All the more reason for them to be married, my dear." Sir Walter gave a great sigh. "Think of Elizabeth's happiness."

Elizabeth said a brief word of thanks and scrambled out of Charles's gig as soon as he pulled up before the Abbey. The pain in her limbs was unbearable, but she made herself turn and wave to Charles. In her haste she forgot to return his umbrella, but she did not notice this until after he had driven off.

Dodging puddles, Elizabeth made for the entrance to the Abbey. Once inside she closed the umbrella carefully and left it with the others. It was a shabby thing and dirty, too. She was glad to be rid of it.

Coming inside the Abbey was only pretense, in case Charles happened to see her. She would only stay for a minute or two—just until the rain tapered off. As her eyes adjusted to the light, she could see that she was not the only one who had this idea. There was a sizable group gathered along the rear wall, with more coming in the door. These people were every bit as shabby and careworn as Charles's umbrella. Elizabeth edged away.

As the rain increased, the street filled with carriages. Charles slowed Belle to a walk and bit back an oath. A gust of wind blew rain into his face. With his free hand, he tipped the brim of his hat. How bothersome life in the city could be! It was not the rain, he was accustomed to that, but to be snarled in traffic was miserable.

He was not the only one who was caught. Small knots of people hiding from the rain peered from doorways. A few continued walking, though at an increased pace. There was the woman just ahead on the left, for instance. Charles felt for her, for she was bedraggled; and yet she toiled on. There was something familiar about her. With-out thinking, Charles called out a name: "Miss Owen!"

The woman turned, and then she smiled.

Charles motioned wildly. "Get in!" he cried. Miss Owen hesitated, but only for a moment. She gathered her sodden skirts and ran toward the gig.

"I've an umbrella, somewhere." Charles now remem-bered that Mary insisted on keeping two umbrellas in the gig. But he didn't like to think about Mary just now; he was too busy helping Miss Owen. Grinning, he jumped down and held out a hand to her.

He helped her into the gig and then climbed up after. He fished out the other umbrella and opened it for her. "I'm afraid it's old and shabby," he explained, "but it's the best I can offer."

Miss Owen took hold of it willingly. "It's perfect," she said, smiling at him. "I too am rather shabby. We match."

Charles couldn't help himself; he continued to apolo-gize. He wiped at the seat with the newspaper Elizabeth had discarded, which caused Miss Owen to laugh.

"Please," she said, "don't trouble on my account! I'm so very grateful for the ride. You have no idea how weary I am."

Charles knew all about feeling weary—but he didn't feel weary any longer. He grinned at her and gave the reins a shake. "Walk on, Belle," he called.

Elizabeth did not know how it happened, but she found herself moving down the aisle toward the front of the sanctuary. Every pew was empty, save for the occasional old woman. Elizabeth eyed them warily. They looked so worn and dismal, these women. She decided they must have nothing better to do, so they came to pray. As she slid into a pew, Elizabeth tugged at the brim of her hat. Her hat today was very smart and its brim was small, but she wished to conceal as much of her face as possible.

As she sat, a gasp of pain escaped and the pew creaked. These small sounds were alarmingly large in the vast building. Elizabeth held her breath and willed herself to remain absolutely still. Several minutes passed before she dared to look up. Everything within the Abbey seemed shrouded—even the windows looked dark. Odd little sounds came from everywhere, unnaturally magnified: a cough, a door closing, the rasp of turning pages, the echo of footsteps, and the sound of rain drumming on the windows.

The rain was coming down in earnest now. If she tried to dash across the street to Bailey's tearoom, she would be drenched. There was nothing to do but wait it out. Fortunately, she was early for her appointment with Mr. Gill. Since she was there, she might as well say a prayer. She had not brought her prayer book, but surely she could remember one.

Elizabeth bowed her head and searched for the proper words. But instead of words, images came hurtling forward—hateful, wretched images: her father, frowning and scolding; Mr. Rushworth's eager face; the page from today's newspaper.

This would never do. Elizabeth composed herself, took a deep breath, and made another attempt. This time, Estella and Mary leered at her. Elizabeth covered her face with her hands, but the awful images continued to come: Anne's tired face and Miss Owen's trusting one, Captain Wentworth's sneer as he cruelly refused to assist her father, and Yee's calm visage, always watchful.

And there was more. Lady Russell came forward with a reproachful look and Lady Eleanora, too. A lump rose in Elizabeth's throat; she had abused Lady Eleanora's hospitality shamefully. And Elise—she was quite harsh with Elise this morning. Why had she been so unkind?

Elizabeth's head came up. She was not on trial here! She had done nothing wrong! She had merely come to say a prayer!

Through sheer force of will, Elizabeth dredged up a prayer, one she had recited every day as a child. She was determined to say it, come what may. Somehow she had to drive the horrible faces from her mind. She set her teeth and once again bowed her head.

"Our Father, Who art in heaven, hallowed be Thy name," was what she meant to say; every fiber of her will was focused on it. But instead, Elizabeth found her lips whispering these words: "Lord, be merciful to me, the sinner."

Sometime later, Charles Musgrove was settled in Wentworth's library. He accepted the glass of sherry with a grateful sigh and propped his stocking feet before the fire. What could be better? The chair adjacent to his gave a leathery whisper as Frederick Wentworth lowered his form into it. A gust of wind lashed rain against the library windows.

"Beastly weather," Wentworth remarked, lifting his glass to his lips.

"Not a day for the gig," agreed Charles. "You should have seen Elizabeth's face when it came on to rain. As she was already in a rare tweak thanks to His Highness, we had a pleasant trip together." He took a sip of sherry.

"Pleasant," echoed Wentworth. "I see."

Charles lowered his glass. "Do you know," he said, "I used to think Mary's tirades were bad. But Elizabeth's silences—gad! I thought she was going to bite my head off, but she just sat there and glared. And when I came to a stop she went bounding off. Strange."

"M'm," said Wentworth.

"I hope you didn't want today's paper, Frederick," Charles continued, "for she's ruined that. Something was the matter with it, but I never found out what. Whatever it was, she seemed to think it was your fault."

Wentworth cocked an eyebrow. "At the moment the old girl is probably drowning her troubles in a hot bath. So, we are safe until dinner."

Charles looked up. "Oh, Elizabeth's not here. She had me drop her at the Abbey, of all things."

"The Abbey?"

"Said she had to pray." Charles grinned. "Don't that beat all?"

Wentworth glanced at the clock. "Just past two," he said slowly. "And—what day is this, Charles?"

"Tuesday." Wentworth rotated the stem of his glass between his fingers.

"What's the matter with Tuesday?"

"Elizabeth has been leaving the house on Tuesday and Thursday afternoons."

Charles thought for a moment. "Mary mentioned that. Estella told her Elizabeth is having secret meetings with some fell—say!" He leaned forward. "You don't think Elizabeth's sneaking around with a curate, do you?"

Wentworth did not return the smile. "I don't know what to think," he said. "Estella is not a reliable source of information."

"But you do suspect something."

"Yee does," Wentworth said. "And that's enough for me."

Charles set his glass on the table. "I say! How about we pop over there? Catch her in the act, eh?"

"Charles."

"Never mind the weather! I *like* driving in the rain!"

"Charles."

But Charles was on his feet. "What do you say, Frederick?" He looked around. "Where'd Yee put my boots, anyway?"

"Not yet. We wait, and we watch. When the time is right, we act."

Charles scuffed the carpet with a sock-clad toe. "Burn it, we won't get anywhere that way."

"What we won't do is set Elizabeth on her guard," Wentworth said. "We will certainly do that if we barge in today, unprepared."

Charles threw himself into a chair. "I suppose."

"I suspect the Abbey is only a meeting place. Elizabeth could easily get into a carriage and no one would be the wiser."

Charles's smile slipped. "Get into a carriage, you say?"

"With a gentleman. You know."

"I see what you mean, but ..." Charles gave a tug to his collar. "Perhaps she's simply going for a little drive with a friend. Around the town, seeing the sights. Is that so wrong?"

"Seeing the sights with a friend." Wentworth raised both brows. "In the rain, Charles?"

How long she sat in the pew Elizabeth could not say. She had begun badly, and from such a start there could be no recovery. Every worry and hurt in her overburdened heart came pouring out. Like a child, she buried her head in her hands and wept, though silently. Long ago Elizabeth had learned this skill.

At last there were no more tears left. Elizabeth remained huddled in the pew, not wishing to move. The accusing faces were gone now, and in their place had come peace—and something else. Dare she name it ... forgiveness?

And there was music. Elizabeth listened for some time before she realized that the organist was playing the introit; the afternoon service was about to begin. She wiped her cheeks with the back of her hand. She knew that her eyes were red and puffy, but that did not matter, not any longer. The service was set to begin at three o'clock. She had missed her appointment with Mr. Gill.

Elizabeth drew an uncertain breath. It was probably still raining, and she had no way home. She did not want to think about Mr. Gill or of what he thought of her. But as she was straightening her hat, she noticed something— and stiffened. She was not alone. Someone was sitting beside her in the pew.

"Elizabeth," he whispered. "Dearest, loveliest Elizabeth, what is wrong?"

7 HARD DOWN THE HELM!

The Abbey was not so dark that McGillvary could mistake the stricken expression on Elizabeth's face. She had been weeping, but why?

She gave him a fleeting look, then turned away to wipe her tears with bare fingers. "I'm s-sorry I missed our appointment," she whispered brokenly. "I did not intend to, but my father ..."

Immediately he had his own handkerchief out and slid nearer to offer it. The pew creaked. Elizabeth gave a start. "Your father," he repeated gently. "He is worse?" This must be the reason for her grief; he could imagine no other. Indeed, he had been watching her carefully; she flinched when he said it. Was this not confirmation? Sir Walter Elliot must be at death's door.

"Yes," whispered Elizabeth. "Oh yes. My father is very much worse."

"In what way may I serve you? You have only to say, you know. I am yours to command at any time."

Elizabeth's chin came up. "Thank you, Mr. Gill," she said, "but I do not believe there is anything you, or anyone, can do." She paused and then added, "You are very kind, but this is something I must face myself."

"Alone?" said McGillvary.

"Not alone." She smiled a little; her eyes traveled to the altar. "I am never truly alone, am I? Then too, I have my family to—good gracious, my family!"

Abruptly Elizabeth stood and began gathering her things. "I must go. I have been away too long." She attempted to put on her gloves, but they were too wet.

McGillvary was on his feet too. "Not before you've had some tea." He took a firm hold of her elbow. "Come."

"But—there is no time for tea, Mr. Gill."

"Please don't call me that," he said. He led her into the aisle and offered his arm.

Elizabeth looked at him in frowning surprise. "Very well ... Patrick," she said. She placed her hand on his arm. "But not for long. Mary and her husband are taking us to dinner, and then we attend the assembly. I must prepare."

"You must be joking."

"It's for Estella, you see," Elizabeth explained in an undervoice. "I'd rather not go at all, but Estella sets great store by such things. I should go to entertain her. For Anne."

McGillvary struggled to digest this. "For Anne," he repeated. "But what about your father?"

"He will be all right."

When they reached the door, she took her hand from his arm and pulled an umbrella from among a pile of others. McGillvary stepped forward to open the door. "I take it Anne will be staying with your father?"

Elizabeth crossed the threshold and paused to open the umbrella. "No," she said. "I expect Anne will attend the assembly with us. But she'll wish to dance with her husband or others and not be plagued by Estella."

McGillvary took the umbrella from her. "Do you mean to leave your father alone tonight? Shouldn't you be keeping vigil?"

"Vigil! Why would I do that?"

He turned his head in surprise. "Isn't your father dying?"

"Certainly not!"

"But I thought you said he was worse!"

"He is!"

He blinked and made another attempt. "You mean his illness is worse."

"No," said Elizabeth crisply, "I mean my father is a worse liar than ever!"

McGillvary gave a shout of laughter. "Great heaven!" he cried. "What will you say next?"

"Well, he is," she muttered. "It's the honest truth. I'll not make excuses for him any longer."

"Oh, I believe you," he said gaily, offering his arm. "My father told lies too, God rest his soul. What has the man done this time?"

Elizabeth fell into step beside him. "He treats me as if I were chattel! As if my life, my future, my—" She gave a huff of frustration. "As if my only reason for living was to further his purposes!"

McGillvary grinned. "I believe that is the way of fathers—to be overbearing."

"You would never treat your own daughter in such an infamous way, I am sure."

"My daughter." McGillvary sighed. "So far as my daughter is concerned, I am every bit the tyrant."

"Not you," Elizabeth said warmly. "You would never run roughshod over her future plans, with a total disregard for her happiness, or—"

"That's just exactly what I have done," he interrupted. "If I had an ivory tower handy, I'd lock her in!" He had to smile at the dismay on Elizabeth's face. "My sweet daughter," he explained, "has had the misfortune to fall violently in love with her music teacher. He has been dismissed, but I caught her writing to him."

Elizabeth thought for a moment. "I remember," she said slowly. "You told me that she had fallen in love with someone ineligible."

"I did?"

"Yes, at our first tea together. You asked for my advice."

McGillvary frowned. He might have said such an outrageous thing, by way of conversation, although it was not true at the time.

Elizabeth's father is not the only liar, his conscience whispered.

"I suppose I did," he said, and guided her across the street. "And yes, I would like your advice. When you are feeling up to giving it."

He opened the door to Bailey's, and she gave him a wry smile. "I am always up to giving advice, unfortunately. It is a habit I learned from my father—that of being pleased with my own opinions."

"Along with being a liar," he joked, following her to their table.

Her voice grew wistful. "I am very good at lying, too."

"You have never lied to me." McGillvary held the chair for her. "I, on the other hand—"

She interrupted. "On the other hand, everything my father says is a lie, or very nearly! I am thoroughly sick of lies! I shall never tell another!"

He regarded her solemnly over the top of his menu. "Never?"

"Not if I can help it," she said seriously. "And let come what may! Lying is ... cowardly!"

Her words made him wince. "Not everyone tells lies out of perverseness, Elizabeth," he said quietly. "Sometimes a lie begins as a simple jest, which then gets out of hand and grows."

"There was nothing funny in what my father said to me today."

"He has been ill," McGillvary reasoned. "You must forgive his overbearing ways and short temper."

He hesitated, suddenly suspicious. He did not like the look of open doubt in her eyes. "Your father *is* ill?"

"In all honesty, I do not know," she said. "At one time he was. Now I wonder whether that was part of the ruse."

"His sickness was a ruse?"

She sighed heavily. "I think it has something to do with his debts."

McGillvary's eyes narrowed. "How do you mean?"

"My father owes money," she said slowly, "and I think it suits him to feign illness."

"Hiding from his creditors, eh? An old trick."

"Is it?" She looked wonderingly at him. "I expect he thought he was being clever. At any rate, he is bored with being an invalid now. I think he's planning something."

"Your father owes a great deal of money to Madderly Kinclaven. I trust his plans include paying off his creditors."

"I think not," Elizabeth said. "He ignores the letters they send."

"A handy notion."

"To say truth, he burns them unopened," Elizabeth confided. "Father believes that handling business matters is beneath him. He leaves it to our solicitor and other inferior persons."

The girl came with the tea just then, so McGillvary was kept from answering. This was just as well, as the words he swallowed were not fit for her ears. Elizabeth's comments today served to strengthen his resolve. Sir Walter might as well learn now that his future son-in-law was nobody's fool.

"So," he said, as soon as the girl departed, "is your father planning to flee England on a moonless night?" He spoke lightly. "Because barring that, he is out of options. He'll have to sell something."

"There isn't much to sell."

"I expect he'll find something he can bear to part with: a piece of property, an art collection, jewelry ..."

"... or his firstborn," Elizabeth put in. "That would be me."

McGillvary reached across the table and covered her hand. "You leave him to solve this. It's surprising how resourceful a man can become when he's pressed."

"That's exactly what I'm afraid of."

"Elizabeth," he said firmly. "Leave your father to fight his battles. This is not your affair."

Her shoulders sagged. "I think I ought to go home now. I'm sorry; I've barely touched my tea. How I am going to find strength for that assembly I do not know. Every inch of me aches." She smiled ruefully. "I fear I'm not a very good horsewoman."

"Nonsense," he said bracingly. "You've courage enough for anything."

She shook her head. "Not this afternoon."

"I know, my dear. But remember this: tomorrow is another day."

He smiled. "You know what sailors say: Don't give up the ship." He gave her hand a squeeze. "Bear up, my dear. Where there's life, there's hope."

"Where there's life, there's hope." Elizabeth repeated it, but not very convincingly.

"In a city like this, having a trustworthy nursery maid is everything." Estella paused long enough to take the cup and saucer Anne offered. "After all, she walks out a good deal, does she not? And with no companion but the children? Any sort of person might accost her—which generally does happen, especially when soldiers are about."

Estella paused only to click her tongue in disapproval. "My dear Mary," she went on, "one can never be too careful. You are right to be discriminating."

Anne studied her sister. Mary looked pale and worn, and yet it was a good thing that she had come down for tea. If only Estella would not talk so much! She would speak to Frederick tonight about sending Estella home. It was more than time.

"I must say, it is rather nice not to have Miss Owen here," Estella continued. "The woman can be such a nuisance."

"I do not find her so." Anne offered a plate of sandwiches. "She has been very helpful, and I enjoy her company."

"You are not the only one to enjoy her company." Estella primmed up her lips. "Do you know what I saw this afternoon? Your Miss Owen returning from a drive. With a man."

"What does that have to do with anything?" said Mary.

Estella turned. "Ah, but they were alone!"

"Perhaps it was her cousin," Anne suggested. "There is nothing improper in that."

"I could not see his face, but he was *not* Mr. Minthorne. What is more," she leaned in, "Miss Owen was soaked to the skin—it was raining dreadfully! But she did not look at all bothered by it, nor did he. Laughing and carrying on, they were! He even held her hand while she climbed out. Scandalous, I call it."

"How could anyone get so wet riding in a carriage?" scoffed Mary. "Only a simpleton would leave the top down."

Estella lowered her teacup. "Ah, but Miss Owen did not come in a carriage. It was one of those two-wheeled affairs, the kind without a top. I forget what they are called. Like a pony cart, only larger."

"A gig." Mary adjusted her position on the sofa. "Charles was talking about taking the gig out today, but I'm sure he changed his mind. No one would be that stupid."

"But he did," Anne said, before she could stop herself. "That is, he took Elizabeth to see Father."

"In all this rain? Oh, famous! Is she pouting in her bedchamber?"

"I don't believe Elizabeth has returned." Anne looked up to see the drawing room door open.

"Hallo!" called a cheerful voice. "Wentworth and I are going out, as the rain has let up. We'll be back in a bit."

Mary looked her husband over. "Charles, what have you done with your shoes?"

"Huh?" Charles looked down at his stocking clad feet and grinned. "Aw, they're in the library. I was drying my feet by the fire a while back. Sorry."

"Your shoes are ... wet?"

"Sure," he said. "From the rain."

Mary glared at him, and Charles spread his hands. "What?" he said. "What did I do now?"

"You should not have done this, Patrick," Elizabeth said softly. "I know how dear it is to hire a carriage."

McGillvary tore his gaze from her face. "I can afford it," he grumbled. "I was not about to let you walk. Don't worry."

"But I do worry," she said. "You will have to do without something in order to pay for this. I don't like that."

"Elizabeth," he said, "believe me, it is no sacrifice."

"You have given me something you can ill afford. I thank you from the bottom of my heart." The tender expression in her eyes only made him more annoyed with himself. The fare was nothing, yet she saw it as sacrificial gallantry! The lowly Gill grew nobler every day—and there was nothing he could do to stop it!

Unfortunately, his irritation must have showed on his face. "Ah, you see?" she cried. "My friend, you cannot hide it! I have put you out!"

The wisest course, McGillvary knew, was to remain silent. With difficulty, he averted his eyes. He could not stop her from gazing at him, though. He felt her eyes studying him.

"Shall I see you at the assembly tonight?" she asked.

"No," he snapped. "I—" McGillvary could feel his jaw tense. He would have given up his right arm to be able to skip this evening's obligation, but he was trapped. "I am hosting a dinner," he heard himself say. "A small affair; nothing grand. For some of my colleagues."

This was quite true—Admiral Mather and Commodore Ashby were colleagues, of a sort. They were also very fond of after-dinner conversation—and burgundy. There would be no slipping off to the assembly tonight.

William Elliot counted as he paced the length of his borrowed bedchamber. Eight steps forward, turn, eight steps back. The boards of the floor creaked beneath his weight, but he did not care. To go down to the front parlor meant encountering Annette Wallis, and Elliot had had quite enough of her.

It was the same old story. Wallis had married her for her looks and her fortune, but what had it brought him? All flash and very little substance. The public rooms of this narrow little house were fitted up in the first style, but the rest of the house was definitely shabby. The walnut paneling added to the oppressive feeling of the room. The worst of it was, until dinner he had nothing to do. After that was the assembly, and then there would be excitement enough—if he could find Elizabeth.

Elliot's eyes followed the frayed border of the carpet. Her behavior had become so odd, so unaccountable. Then too, so had Penelope's. He gave a snort of derision.

A soft knock sounded at the bedchamber door. It opened to admit the Wallis's footman. "If you please, sir," he said, "you have a caller. In the back salon." Mr. Elliot did not bother to conceal his irritation. "Who is it?"

The man consulted the card he held. "Mr. John Shepherd. A solicitor, sir."

"Tell him I am not at home." The footman shifted from one foot to another. "Begging your pardon, sir," he said, "but he said to say that he has come on business. About his daughter."

"His daughter? What have I to do with his daughter?"

"Name of Clay, sir." The footman swallowed. "That's the name he said, sir. Clay."

William Elliot's brows descended, and the footman took a step back. "The devil it is!" he snapped. "Very well," he said, through clenched teeth. "Kindly inform Mr. Shepherd that I will be down directly."

Elizabeth had fallen silent. The interior of the job carriage was not so dark that her face was hidden. She kept her eyes averted; her mouth trembled slightly.

McGillvary cursed silently. Like a fool he had thoughtlessly allowed his irritation to show in his voice. Now he had hurt her, the very last thing he intended to do.

"Elizabeth," he said quietly, "forgive me, please. My schedule of late has been impossible. I did not mean to be harsh with you."

"I understand," she said in a small voice.

He moved nearer. "It's just that I don't like leaving you to fend for yourself tonight."

Elizabeth's head came up. "I am not a child. I have been 'fending for myself' for a good many years now."

"I know that," he said. "And I can see that this has been a trying day. The last thing you need is to be cornered by Farley ... or your cousin."

Elizabeth sighed heavily.

"And whatever you do," McGillvary went on, "don't kiss Rushworth!"

"Oh for heaven's sake!" cried Elizabeth, "I have no intention of kissing him! Besides," she added, "Mr. Rushworth is in London."

"Good. I hope he stays there. Indefinitely."

"And I'll have you know," she continued, "that I do not make it a practice to kiss people at an assembly! I mean—" Elizabeth broke off in confusion.

"I do not mean you shouldn't kiss anyone," he interposed. "Just not anyone tonight. Not Rushworth. Or your cousin. Or Sir Henry Farley."

"Sir Henry?" She gave a perfectly natural shudder, which pleased him. "You needn't worry," she said. "I expect I'll have a dreadful time." She glanced out of the window; they were not far from St Peter Square. "Let me out at the corner, please."

McGillvary reached for the check string. "When shall I see you again?"

"Tuesday, I suppose."

"No." The word came out before he could stop it.

Elizabeth looked at him in sudden surprise. McGillvary kept his chin up. He had spoken his thought; there was nothing to be done but continue. "I need to see you sooner. Tomorrow. Can you manage to meet me tomorrow?" The carriage drew to a halt.

"I don't know."

"Tomorrow at eleven." This was not a question.

"I'll be asleep at eleven."

McGillvary smiled. "Bailey's, at two o'clock. Fair enough?"

She looked doubtful. He took hold of her hand. "Elizabeth," he said, "it's important." He looked directly into her eyes. "Do not fail me ... please?"

"Patrick, I ..." Elizabeth's hand trembled in his. "Very well," she relented.

McGillvary caught hold of her other hand. "And tonight," he said firmly, "remember: No kissing."

She gave an exasperated sigh. "Yes, Papa."

Papa? Was this how she saw him? His hold on her hands tightened. Before she could take avoiding action of any kind, he bend and pressed a warm and possessive kiss on her lips. At length he drew back, smiling a little at her confusion.

"No kissing," he repeated, but gently. "I'll see you tomorrow." McGillvary released her and gave the door handle a twist. The door swung open.

Elizabeth's eyes were wide. "No ... kissing," she repeated softly.

8 BAG AND BAGGAGE

Exactly how she extricated herself from the job carriage
Elizabeth could not say. Fortunately, it was no longer
raining. She found herself standing on the damp pavement, gazing stupidly at the houses across the square. She
heard the box creak as the driver resumed his seat; he
clucked to the horse. Elizabeth whirled round—she
couldn't help it! Through the window glass she could see
Patrick. He was watching her; his face was very near to
the glass.

And then he smiled. Elizabeth felt her knees turn to
jelly. "Patrick," she whispered, and realized that he saw
her speak his name.

She felt vulnerable and exposed and foolish, but did it
matter? His expression changed; the smile faded. He
reached for something above his head—the check string?
Immediately the driver pulled up.

Elizabeth stood rooted to the pavement. The handle of the door slowly turned, and his hand—Patrick's own hand—pushed it open. Elizabeth's heart was beating fast. Was Patrick coming out? Or would he invite her to rejoin him inside?

And then Elizabeth heard her name, faintly at first—and it was not Patrick Gill who said it. Involuntarily she turned. "Heigh-ho! Elizabeth!" the voice repeated. "I see you found your way home!"

It was Charles Musgrove coming around the corner, rather unsteadily. Behind him was Captain Wentworth.

This was worse than anything! In a pathetic attempt to appear calm she turned to face them, and behind her back she made a warning gesture to Patrick.

"Hello!" she called out, in a strangled sort of voice. She did not dare look behind at the carriage. She heard the door shut with a click, and then the carriage rolled away.

"So," called Charles, "how was the Abbey?" He grinned over his shoulder at Captain Wentworth. "Hob-nobbing with the old ladies to her heart's content," he said. "Flirted with the curate, too. Wouldn't take a ride from me, no-oh. Had to brave the rain."

Elizabeth gave a start and glanced down—she'd left Charles's umbrella at Bailey's! What if he asked after it?

Captain Wentworth caught her eye. "I beg your pardon," he said quietly. "I fear he's a bit on the go. Had a pint on an empty stomach." He linked his arm through Charles's. "This way, Musgrove," he said. "How about something to eat?"

Charles considered this. "Keep me out of Mary's way, it will," he said. "Always sick, my wife." Elizabeth fell into step behind the two men. "Believe I'll return the favor," Charles announced, as Wentworth opened the door. "Feeling a bit under the weather myself!" He giggled as he passed his hat to Yee. "What's it to her if my boots got wet? It was raining, wasn't it?"

Elizabeth kept well back. She heard Captain Wentworth give instructions to the butler and then moved off. She felt weak with relief. For instead of peppering her with questions, Captain Wentworth was taking Charles Musgrove to the library!

Slowly Elizabeth mounted the stairs, grateful for the support of the banister rail. Had there ever been such a day? And tonight was the dinner and then the assembly—where she was to kiss no one. Elizabeth almost giggled aloud, very much like Charles Musgrove had.

Smilingly, she pictured Patrick's face. How could she have thought him scruffy? His eyes held such sparkling directness! His demeanor was so decisive! And his looks? Oh, he was handsome, definitely!

And the kiss! Elizabeth's cheeks became warmer still. It was nothing like the kiss from James Rushworth—or anyone! Patrick's lips were so warm, molding to the shape of her mouth with such intensity. She hadn't wanted it to end!

As one in a dream, Elizabeth drifted into her bedchamber and tossed her reticule onto the bureau. She would have cast herself headlong onto her bed when she noticed, too late, that someone was already there! Elizabeth could not stop her fall and landed on top of a pair of feet.

Mary gave a start and sat up. "Good gracious!" she shrieked. "Have a care, Elizabeth!"

Elizabeth scrambled to her feet. "Mary!" she said, keeping a rein on her rising temper. "What are you doing in my bed?"

"I have the headache," Mary cried. "Well, I do! Can I help it if this house is so noisy? Estella will carry on, and her children shriek and run about and ask for this and for that! The maids run up and down the stairs all day! I must have peace and quiet."

Elizabeth pulled open the draperies one by one, ignoring Mary's protests. "Yes, I know the light hurts your eyes," she said. "You must get up now if you wish to be ready on time."

She glanced at Mary's face. "You haven't had your hair washed. You'll need to do it now so that it will have time to dry. Otherwise, Anne's new maid will use the curling irons."

"Heaven preserve us," Mary exclaimed weakly. "My poor hair, frizzled beyond recognition! That dreadful girl!"

"It served you right, if you ask me," Elizabeth said. "You were too harsh with her the other day. She was scared out of her wits. Now get up."

Elizabeth pulled at the coverlet, but Mary resisted. "I'm not going," she said, clutching it with both hands.

Elizabeth's brows rose. "You and Charles are hosting the dinner tonight. Of course you must go."

Mary raised her chin defiantly. "Charles is a perfect beast! He will not invite the Wallises! He refused, bold as you please, even when I asked him nicely! Which was perfectly Byzantine of him! So, I am not going."

"Then you are a bigger simpleton than I took you for," Elizabeth said. "One of these days, Mary, your pride is going to choke you."

"You're a fine one to talk," Mary retorted. "Where have you been all afternoon?"

"If you must know, I visited Father. And then went to church to pray. And then ..."

Elizabeth hesitated. She had vowed to tell no more lies, and she meant to keep her promise. "I met up with a handsome, dashing man who invited me to take tea with him, and then he saw me home in a carriage—and made violent love to me!"

Mary plucked at the coverlet. "What a stupid, hoaxing story," she complained. "You must think me a sapskull. You went to see Father; Charles told us that." Her lips twisted into a smirk. "And then, as you had nothing better to do, you had tea. Alone. And came home in a chair."

"As you wish," said Elizabeth.

"By the bye," Mary continued, "Lady Russell sent a note for you. It's there on your bureau. You and she have received an invitation."

Elizabeth's lips hardened into a line; Mary was such a snoop! As expected, the note was unsealed. "Mrs. Buxford-Heighton's ball," she read aloud. Lady Russell had enclosed a note of explanation, written by the hostess, explaining the lateness of the invitation.

"It is quite a feather in your cap, dear," Mary mocked. "For my part, I think it's awfully rude of Mrs. Buxford-Heighton not to invite the rest of your family. Poor Anne—think of her lacerated feelings!"

"Yes, well ..." Elizabeth knew very well that Anne would be glad to escape such an overblown affair. As for herself, she had no desire to attend a ball, no matter how prestigious, accompanied only by Lady Russell!

Besides, of what use to her was a ball without Patrick?

William Elliot's brows went up. "With whom am I supposedly cohabiting?" he said. "Who the devil is Mrs. Penelope Clay?"

He frowned, as if making an effort to remember. "Ah yes," he said at last. "Sir Walter's daughter's companion." He laughed softly.

"You are correct." Mr. Shepherd's tone was cold.

Mr. Elliot spread his hands. "Surely you jest, sir. Your daughter flatters herself."

"I speak truth, Mr. Elliot," Mr. Shepherd said. "I have seen Penelope quite recently. She told me the sorry story of your escapade together."

"I take it you have evidence? My name on the lease of the house, for example? Or an incriminating piece of correspondence, perhaps?" William Elliot's brows rose in hauteur. "If the lady is residing under my protection, surely you have proof?"

"I have my daughter's word of honour," Mr. Shepherd said hotly. "Can you deny what has transpired between you?"

"I can and I do," Elliot said evenly. "Your accusations insult me, sir. A man of my status and position, involved with such *canaille*? It is unthinkable."

He gave the bell cord a series of tugs. "We have no more to say to one another on this subject. I bid you good day." Elliot pulled open the parlour door to admit the Wallis's butler. "Mr. Shepherd," he said sharply, "is leaving."

Mr. Shepherd was taken into the hall. "You have not heard the last from me," he shouted. "Do you hear me, Elliot? You have not heard the last from me!"

William Elliot stood motionless in the centre of the room. So this was Penelope's little game. Having lost her bid to ensnare Sir Walter into matrimony, she had set her sights on himself! He was all too familiar with the allure of the future title. How his late wife's family had fairly salivated over the prospect! Mr. Shepherd might spout righteous indignation, but he was no different. The man had some nerve, bringing along the legal paperwork.

He began to pace, calling down curses on both father and daughter. He had no desire to marry Penelope Clay or any other strumpet of low birth. As for Wallis and his little joke about marrying his cousin Elizabeth ...

Elizabeth.

The thought burst upon William Elliot like an explosion. It was so bold that it made him shiver. The idea grew in strength. He began to laugh softly. "A man who is already married," Elliot said aloud, savouring the words, "cannot be forced to the altar, now can he?"

He drew out a cigar and lit it. His hostess wouldn't like him smoking here, but what of it? He blew out a stream of smoke. If he played his cards right, it would be perfect. He could even allow Elizabeth to think that she had entrapped him!

When Charles had first presented his plan for that evening, Elizabeth assumed that she would enjoy the assembly far more than the dinner. As it turned out, she was wrong. The dinner was quite nice, even if the company left something—or rather, someone —to be desired. Elizabeth found herself looking for Patrick Gill's face everywhere. His presence at the assembly was impossible—he was hosting a dinner himself—and yet she knew he was a man of considerable talents. Would he find a way to put in an appearance by evening's end?

Elizabeth chose not to dance, but kept occupied by picturing how he would look in evening dress. Would he wear the beautiful faux-diamond stickpin?

A voice recalled her to her surroundings. Apparently she had dropped her fan. Sir Henry held it out to her.

"Thank you, sir," she said politely. Her fingers closed on the fan, but Sir Henry did not let go.

"I am so very sorry to hear about your father." Sir Henry brought his other hand to rest upon hers in a warm clasp of friendship.

As luck would have it, a set was forming for the next dance. Elizabeth knew what would follow. To dance would be a good thing, for then Sir Henry would have to release her hand.

And it was not so very bad. Sir Henry Farley was an accomplished dancer, even at his age. As they moved through the figure of the dance, Elizabeth's gaze strayed now and then to the crowd—it seemed she could not help herself.

"Your father?" Sir Henry was saying. "How is he, truly?"

"I believe he is pining for visitors, sir," she said. "His health does seem to be improving." They were parted in the dance just then. She tried to ignore the squeeze Sir Henry had given her hand.

"I did hear," he continued, as soon as the dance brought them together, "that your father's troubles are considerable. You are so brave, Miss Elliot. Unbowed by gossips and tattlers. I salute you."

Elizabeth murmured assent and made her turn. She could not help but notice how intensely he gazed at her. "A lesser woman," he said, "would have been undone by such events. But not you."

"You are too kind, Sir Henry." Common politeness was now uncomfortable. She kept out of reach as much as possible.

But the figure of the dance worked against her. As soon as he was able, Sir Henry took hold of her hand and gave it another squeeze. "I only hope, my dear, that what transpires next will not be too distressing for you."

Elizabeth kept her head high. The closing bars of the dance could not sound soon enough!

At last it was over; Sir Henry led her from the dance floor. "Do bear in mind, dear Miss Elliot," he said softly, "that I am your friend. Troubling times reveal true friendship, *n'est ce pas?*" Again his disturbing smile appeared. "It would be my pleasure to assist you in any way I can."

"T-thank you, Sir Henry," she stammered.

Patrick Gill had warned her about this man, and like a fool she had brushed his concern aside. Sir Henry's eyes were shining with open admiration—as if she were a common trollop! Had her father been present, Sir Henry would never display such obvious regard!

Smiling, he raised her hand to his lips. Thank heaven she was wearing gloves!

Elizabeth looked up to see William Elliot come into the ballroom. Never was she more relieved to see him. She carefully pulled her hand from Sir Henry's grasp and excused herself.

Having endured Sir Henry's compliments, Elizabeth was unimpressed with what her cousin had to say. Mr. Elliot talked on, while she kept an eye on Sir Henry. Once he was out of sight she opened her fan. "This room is so close," she complained. "If you will excuse me, I would like to speak to my sister." She moved away.

William Elliot followed. "What is this I hear about you and Rushworth?" he said.

"Nothing," she replied, over her shoulder.

"An engagement, perhaps?"

Elizabeth stopped. So he had overheard her conversation with her father. "Perhaps," she said. "But it is none of your business, Mr. Elliot." Again she attempted to slip into the crowd.

He caught her elbow. "As acting head of the family, it is my business," he said. "I cannot countenance an engagement that will bring dishonouor to us all."

If her cousin felt disgraced by James Rushworth, what would he say when he learned about Patrick Gill? "Head of the family, indeed," she scoffed. "My father lives—or hadn't you noticed?"

"He lives." There was bitterness in Mr. Elliot's tone. "He told me of your secret engagement. Really, Elizabeth!"

"Then he betrayed a confidence. I do not wish to discuss it. Good night."

Again he pulled her back. "Hang it all, this is too much! I understand your desperation, truly I do. But I cannot stand by while you make a disastrous misstep. He is unworthy of you!"

Elizabeth bristled, thinking of Patrick Gill. "Is he indeed?"

"You deserve a better man."

"Pray keep your voice down, Mr. Elliot. You will cause a scene."

"You worry about causing a scene, yet you think nothing of shaming your family?"

"You are a fine one to talk! You, lecturing me about marriage! You can have nothing to say. Your own behaviour was appalling."

Mr. Elliot's hold on her arm tightened. "Ah, but I believe I do have a right—speaking from experience!" His gaze never left her face. "Be sensible, I beg you," he said more quietly. "The ink on the divorce decree is scarcely dry. You have not considered." He moistened his lips and added, "There is another alternative."

"Pray enlighten me!"

"Very well, if you must know, there is ... myself."

"*What?*"

He bowed modestly. "I adore you. Surely you must know that."

"Indeed I do not." She twisted from his grasp. "Is this the way you court a lady? With bruises?"

William Elliot colored slightly. "I have not spoken until now out of respect for my late wife," he said stiffly.

Elizabeth laughed. "How can you say that," she mocked, "when you so obviously preferred Anne?"

"She was a distraction, but only for a time. It is you I love."

"Oh please. I, who am disgracing your name by allowing a lowborn man to court me?"

"Rushworth isn't lowborn, Elizabeth," he pointed out. "And I am a forgiving man." He spread his hands. "There is much I am prepared to forgive in the woman I choose to love."

Elizabeth felt her lip curl. Was he insulting her, even as he proposed?

"This time," he said, "I am determined to follow my heart."

"How very nice. Mrs. Clay will be delighted to hear that."

He was rendered speechless, and Elizabeth concealed her smile of triumph. "Pray excuse me, Mr. Elliot," she said frostily. "I have the headache and wish to go home."

Again his hand closed on her arm. This time his voice was harsh. "Your father has given me a commission, the consequences of which you will not like. Cross me, and I will be forced to follow through with his request."

"Who am I to stand in your way?" she flashed. "As the self-styled head of the family, you must do as you see fit."

"Very well," he said roughly, "I will. But bear this in mind: You have not heard the last from me!"

9 A DAY OF RECKONING

On Wednesday morning John Shepherd presented himself at The Citadel. He glanced at the clock. Sir Walter might not yet be dressed for the day, but Mr. Shepherd's business could not wait.

As he walked along the passageway, Mr. Shepherd reviewed yesterday's painful interview with William Elliot. He had made a tactical error—he knew that now. It was naïve to think that Penelope's seducer would succumb without resistance.

Jonas Clay had not put up a fight when confronted all those years ago. For a monetary settlement, the man had been quite willing to marry Penelope and remove her disgrace. William Elliot, who rated himself higher, would not be run to earth so easily. But he would yield eventually, of this Mr. Shepherd was certain. If Elliot thought to fob Penelope off like so much baggage, he had another thing coming.

Mr. Shepherd would now enlist the aid of Sir Walter Elliot. Not for nothing had he cultivated a business relationship with the baronet—although God knew it had not been easy or profitable. As a gentleman, Sir Walter knew what was due a lady in Penelope's condition. If anyone could bring pressure to bear, it would be Sir Walter.

Sir Walter's rooms were located at the corner of the building and overlooked a charming garden—not bad for a man who was hiding from his creditors. A pretty comfortable life the baronet led, and that without working a day! Among the landed gentry there were few who took their responsibilities less seriously than Sir Walter Elliot. Without shame he wrung every last groat from his tenants, and as landlord did as little as possible. Sir Walter would do more than whine today.

An attendant came to the door. Mr. Shepherd gave his name and stepped back to wait. Sir Walter must have overheard the exchange, for he called "Shepherd!" with genuine pleasure.

"Just the man I wish to see. When did you receive my express?"

Heartened, Mr. Shepherd checked his timepiece. Yes, he would have time to finish here, return to the Wallis residence for the necessary signatures from William Elliot, and post back to London tonight. Things were definitely looking up.

Charles came into the drawing room, asked after Captain Wentworth and, after receiving a vague answer from

Anne, dropped into one of the large chairs. He took up the newspaper.

Mary was silent for a minute and then began to talk. "Of all the insensitive, unfeeling creatures, Elizabeth is surely the worst."

He did not look up from his paper. "What has she done this time?"

"She thinks I should visit Father today—she told me so at breakfast. Me, in my miserable, weakened condition!"

Charles turned a page. "You seemed well enough last night."

"That," she said, "was a demonstration of silent suffering. No one gives me credit for the agonies I endure."

Mary fell silent, and then said, "Charles, I am running low on my medicine. Won't you tell Anne to speak to that physician about it? He has a special sort he makes up himself."

"Do you mean Minthorne? Ask him yourself. The walk will do you good."

"You know how my feet always ache after a ball." Mary wound her handkerchief around her fingers. "That sleeping draught is most effective," she added. "I never sleep well when I am in Bath."

"Then perhaps we ought to go home."

"But if I have my medicine there is no need. As you know, I am never as well at home as I am in Bath."

Mary coughed a little, and he looked up. She eyed him expectantly. "Would you mind, Charles?"

He sighed and crossed his legs. "What is the name of the stuff?"

"Bless me, I don't know. Syrup of poppies or some such thing." She began to hunt through her pockets. "I have the name written somewhere. Ah." She brought out a scrap of paper. "Here it is. This tells what I need."

Charles threw down the newspaper and heaved out of the chair. Mary's paper was twisted into a screw, which he carefully unfolded. Then he exploded.

"Burn it, Mary, this is not a prescription! This is a bill. Why was it not given to me?"

Mary was taken aback. "Why, I don't know."

"Did you pay Minthorne yourself?"

"Good gracious, of course I did not." Mary's voice rose higher. "So I haven't paid him. I shall. Eventually."

"Yes, eventually," Charles said, growing red in the face. "The question is, when? Next year? In the meantime, here I am having to face Minthorne and Miss Owen any day of the week. A fine fellow I am, to be ignoring my debts."

"There is no need to fly into the boughs with me, Charles Musgrove," Mary cried. "I don't know why you make an issue of such a trifling thing. It really is most shabby of you."

"Shabby?"

"Yes, shabby! Uncouth and ungentlemanlike as well!"

"We Musgroves pay our debts. Unlike certain people I could name." He flung over to the door.

"Charles," cried Mary. "Where do you think you are going?"

"To pay this debt. Tell Wentworth I'll meet him later."

John Shepherd paused only to slam the door behind him. After years with the baronet—slaving for him, negotiating for him, shouldering the burden of his financial catastrophe, laughing at his inane jokes—and this was the answer he received? Such things Sir Walter had said about Penelope! Unbelievable!

Not only had he disbelieved the information about William Elliot, he flatly refused to speak about the matter. Nor would he agree to interview his heir in order to ascertain the truth. He had the audacity to say that William Elliot was hoaxing him—as if Penelope's condition was a joke! And then he had smiled and changed the topic of conversation.

Shepherd ground his teeth. "If you think you have heard the last of this," he muttered, "you are sadly mistaken." So intent was he on his thoughts that as he rounded the corner he ran smash into someone.

He stammered an apology, but the gentleman waved it aside. "You are Sir Walter Elliot's man of business, are you not?"

John Shepherd stiffened; the fellow was looking him over as if he were some sort of vermin!

"My secretary tells me," the man continued, "that Sir Walter's account is seriously in arrears. If you would kindly step into my office?"

Mr. Shepherd's chin came up. "As of this morning, I am no longer handling the baronet's affairs." Habit made

him put out his hand. "John Shepherd, of Crewkherne,"
he said. "And you must be Mr. Savoy."

Savoy shook his hand. "This is most peculiar," he said,
"most peculiar indeed. Has Sir Walter engaged the services of another?"

"I am afraid I cannot say." Spite made him add, "He
may shift for himself, for all I care."

Mr. Savoy's brows rose. "Is that so?" He spoke behind
his hand. "Rumor has it that the man is bankrupt," he
said softly. "Can this be true?"

"Again, I cannot say. Nor can I prevent you from
drawing your own conclusions. The man owes money everywhere and has not the resources to pay."

Savoy spoke sharply. "If I am not to be paid, the least
I can do is vacate the baronet's rooms."

"You must do as seems best to you," said Mr. Shepherd. "And now, if you will excuse—"

Savoy gripped Shepherd's arm. "You did notice the
men," he said meaningfully.

"I beg your pardon?"

Savoy glanced this way and that. "Come with me," he
murmured, and led Shepherd down the hall to an office.
He unlocked the door and pushed Shepherd inside. "Those
men hanging about on the street," he said, speaking low.
"Surely you saw them—just outside the gate? They are
watching Sir Walter on behalf of the bailiff. Their wagon
is concealed around the corner."

Mr. Shepherd's brows rose. "A most interesting coincidence."

"A most *useful* coincidence," agreed Savoy. He indicated a chair before the desk. "Do sit down, Shepherd. I believe we can resolve this situation to our mutual benefit." He reached for the bell. "Would you care for some refreshment?"

Without hat or gloves, Charles Musgrove trod up the walk to Mr. Minthorne's residence. How could Mary be so thoughtless? He reached for the knocker—and grimaced. Yesterday he'd burned his hand and had forgotten about it—until now. Lifting the brass knocker with his good hand, he gave it a series of raps. To his dismay, Miss Owen opened the door.

"Why, Mr. Musgrove," she said, smiling. "Hello."

Charles felt his lips curve into an answering smile, but no words came. He did not know why this was so; he only knew that his irritation was gone. He did not seem to be able to keep from smiling. Miss Owen was looking almost pretty in a gown of blue gingham. Curling tendrils of her hair had escaped and framed her face. Miss Owen had a pleasing face.

Charles pulled himself together. He had come to transact business, not to smile at a pretty woman! "I have come to pay for my wife's medication." He held out the scrap of paper. "Is this the correct amount?"

Miss Owen took it from him. Charles felt his face grow warm. He dug in a pocket for his wallet.

"It is, Mr. Musgrove, but please don't trouble yourself about repaym—"

Charles interrupted. "We Musgroves pay our debts," he said, more harshly than he intended. "I mean," he amended, "I don't like to have these trifling bills pile up." He counted out the coins, but awkwardly because of his hand.

"Why Mr. Musgrove! You have an injury."

Such ready sympathy made Charles uncomfortable. "This?" he said, shrugging. "It's nothing. Just a flesh wound."

Miss Owen was frowning. "Is it a cut? A burn?"

Charles raised his eyes to hers. "A burn," he said, feeling like a schoolboy. "Came up against the chimney of the lamp last night. Didn't realize it was so hot."

"You bandaged this yourself?" Her tone was severe, but her green eyes were twinkling. "Is it a clean bandage, Mr. Musgrove?"

Charles grinned in spite of himself. "Oh you know," he said. "More or less."

Miss Owen bit her lips. "Yes, I do know," she said. "Which means you must come into the surgery at once. At the very least it ought to be cleaned and properly bandaged."

This was not what Charles wanted to hear. "Please," he objected. "I don't wish to disturb Mr. Minthorne. I'm sure he has more important things to do."

"He does, and you shan't disturb him at all." Miss Owen drew him into the entrance hall. "It happens that my cousin is not here. I can do it myself."

Charles's brow cleared. This was different! "I'm not putting you out?"

"Not in the least," she said. "Come."

Rather sheepishly, Charles allowed her to lead him to Mr. Minthorne's surgery. She had him sit at a square table by the window while she assembled supplies on a tray.

Removing the handkerchief was an awkward business. She was gentle, but he could tell it pained her to hurt him. That she should be so compassionate was oddly touching.

At last Charles could stand no more. "Here now, Miss Owen," he said. "That's not the way! Let me do it for you." He jerked at the handkerchief, which tore the newly-formed scab. It broke out bleeding.

"Oh, Mr. Musgrove!" Miss Owen rushed to blot it with a towel. "You are too rough." She held his bleeding hand in both of hers.

Charles bit his lip, but not for long. A merry laugh bubbled up inside; he could not contain it. "Ow!" he cried.

With effort, Savoy curbed his rising impatience. This John Shepherd was such a fellow for caution! He had explained the situation more than once. And then what must the man do but take a turn about the garden. He said he had to think, as if there was more to think about! Shepherd had examined the gate and the street—did he doubt the watchers' existence? Just as Savoy gave up hope of seeing him again, Shepherd came through the office door.

"I apologize for my reticence," he said. "I have been puzzling over what should be done. I believe I have come up with an acceptable plan."

"So long as your plan includes summoning the constable, I am content," replied Savoy.

"It is not quite so simple, I'm afraid. While Sir Walter is an inmate here he is, in a manner of speaking, safe. In other words, he cannot be seized."

"But this is my property, not his," cried Savoy. "Is there nothing I can do to evict him?"

"There are several options available. Of these we must consider which would be wisest to pursue. Unless you would like to figure as the man who delivers his patients over to the law ..."

This was an unexpected jolt. "I most certainly do not!" cried Savoy.

Could it be that Mr. Shepherd's eyes were twinkling? "The fact remains that you *do* wish to hand him over. We must come up with a way to accomplish this without appearing to do so." Mr. Shepherd sat down.

Mr. Savoy did likewise. "You have a plan." It was all Savoy could do not to rub his hands together.

"Sir Walter cannot be taken into custody unless he is on a public street. Obviously he is aware of this fact. I believe this is one of the reasons he chose to come to your establishment."

"He will not be the last," observed Savoy dryly.

"Somehow we must get him out of his rooms and off the grounds," continued Mr. Shepherd. "Unfortunately, he no longer trusts me. Which means ..." He raised an eyebrow.

Savoy was not slow to take the hint. "My dear Shepherd," he said, "it would give me great pleasure. I shall accompany him on a stroll across the lawn, taking pains to stray near to the gate ..."

"If I might make a suggestion? You could perhaps encounter an acquaintance of Sir Walter's? Say, in a barouche on the street? He has spoken of a Mrs. Leighton."

"Better yet," crowed Savoy, "Sir Henry Farley. The man sent in his card the other day; Sir Walter was beside himself with excitement." He passed his tongue over his lips. "I will see Sir Henry waving, just beyond the baronet's line of vision. We will move beyond the gate in order to greet him ..."

"... and the bailiff's men," said Mr. Shepherd, "will take it from there."

Mr. Savoy lost no time in putting the plan into action. Unfortunately, the street was remarkably clear that afternoon. No elegant barouche presented itself during the time he and Sir Walter walked the front lawn. Mr. Savoy was about to give it up when two vehicles rounded the corner.

"Sir Walter," he cried, with real excitement in his voice. "I recognize that gentleman. It cannot be—but it is! Sir Henry Farley!"

Sir Walter slewed round. As his arm remained linked with Savoy's, this was an awkward maneuver.

"I say! I do believe the man is waving!"

"What? Where?" said Sir Walter. "I do not see him!"

"Come closer." Savoy deftly unfastened the gate-latch. Shepherd had thought to have someone oil the hinges; the gate swung open without a sound.

"I do believe his carriage is pulling up," agreed Sir Walter.

This was perfectly true. One of the carriages had drawn aside. Sir Walter smoothed the folds of his brocade dressing gown. "I am not precisely attired for callers, am I?"

"My dear Sir Walter," said Savoy, leading him into the street, "of all my patients, you are the most elegant." He stood back and watched the men jump into action.

And so it was that when Lady Russell arrived at The Citadel for her daily visit, she encountered a most unusual sight. Here was her old friend, wearing a sumptuous dressing gown, being helped into a shabby black coach without windows. Sir Walter looked about with obvious dismay. Before Lady Russell's horrified eyes, the door was pulled to. The windowless coach rumbled away.

Lady Russell could not believe it. Was Sir Walter being *kidnapped?* Forgetting the check string, she pounded on the ceiling. The door was pulled open, and Hullin's worried face appeared.

"Follow that coach!" Lady Russell shrieked. "Something *dreadful* is happening to Sir Walter!"

Winnie Owen finished the bandage with a flat knot. She studied her handiwork with critical eyes; would it hold? She glanced at Mr. Musgrove. He did not seem as careless as Wally or Gareth, but with men there was no telling.

He was a talkative man and so very pleasant—just like her youngest brother.

"Now what are you thinking, Miss Owen?" he teased. "I've been rattling on like a chucklehead. You must think me a dead bore."

Winnie shook her head. "You remind me of one of my brothers," she said. "Wally, who has the happiest nature. He would like your horse-raising scheme, I think."

"Wally, eh? A youngish fellow?"

"Cadwallen, I should say. A grown man does not like to be called by his nursery name."

"I'll attest to that," Mr. Musgrove said, grinning. "Cadwallen has a ring to it."

"It means battle-scatterer. My brothers and I have Welsh names."

Mr. Musgrove tilted his head to one side. "I didn't know Winifred was Welsh," he said.

Winnie pushed back her chair and stood. "But my name is not Winifred. It's—"

"Yes?" His eyes had an expectant look—just like his son's!

"No, no," she said, laughing. "You'll not get that out of me. I never use my proper name." She gathered a stack of clean bandages.

"Family name, eh? You have my sympathies. My family's littered with fellows named Charles. It's my father's name as well, so I have been called Master Charles or Mr. Charles since I can remember. And what must my sister do but marry a chap named Charles?"

"And your son?" The words slipped out before she could stop them, but Mr. Musgrove did not look offended. He merely shrugged.

"You have me there. But the name's been passed from father to son for generations. I wouldn't want him to feel slighted."

"That is why he is Little Charles."

"Now then," he said, "you still have not told me your name. Shall I guess? Is it ... Wilhelmina?"

"No," she said, smiling. It was a good deal worse, but she did not intend to tell him that.

Somehow he guessed her thought, for he gave her a twinkling look. "Gwendolyn?"

"No, no. That is a pretty name." Winnie returned to the table and took up the basin of water. "You'll never guess."

"I don't know about that," he replied cheerfully. "Let me see." He thought for a minute. "I know," he crowed. "Winola."

"No."

Worse?" he said. "Very well. Wilma? Waluga?"

Winnie almost spilt the water for laughing. "What mother would name her sweet baby Waluga?" Something about his expression made her suspicious. "I don't believe there is such a name, Mr. Musgrove."

"You're right," he confessed. "I made it up." With his good hand he took the pitcher and brought it to her. "Tell me, won't you? I won't tell a soul."

Winnie hesitated. Her lips parted.

"Aha," he said. "Go on."

"It's a Welsh name," she said, feeling foolish.

"So it has a meaning. Perhaps I can guess. Is it stubborn goat?"

She gave a gurgle of laughter. "Of course not. If you must know," she said, unable to resist the teasing look in his eyes, "it means flower."

"Now we're getting somewhere," he said. "I've only to ask Wentworth. I bet he can come up with a book about Welsh words."

This never occurred to her. Mr. Musgrove and Captain Wentworth would talk about it and joke—and would they discuss it with others? Perhaps it was better to trust Mr. Musgrove? "If I tell you," she said slowly, "you must promise not to use it."

"Not even to you?" he teased.

"Especially not to me!"

"Very well," he said, more seriously now. "I promise."

Winnie took a deep breath. She lowered her voice. "My name," she said, "is Blodwyn.'

Oaths were shouted (by passers-by, not Hullin—or so Lady Russell hoped!) as her carriage swung round another corner at breakneck speed. She clung to the armrest. How Hullin managed to follow that windowless coach through the crowded streets Lady Russell did not know. She glanced out. They were passing into the lower section of Bath. Surely Sir Walter knew no one here!

Lady Russell could hardly bear to think of him. The expression on his face, and the brusque way in which the men had forced him into that coach—it was horrible! For they did force him, this she knew. Without a doubt, Sir Walter had been taken from The Citadel against his will.

If only Anne or Elizabeth had called on him this morning, as they ought to have done, this might never have happened! Anne, she knew, was fighting fatigue, but surely Elizabeth could have bestirred herself. Once she got to the bottom of this, things would certainly change! Sir Walter's daughters—particularly Elizabeth—would no longer be allowed to neglect him!

The carriage came to a stop. Lady Russell peered out. Her driver's boy was in the street engaged in earnest conversation with a group of labourers. His father gave a shout, and the boy came running back. Lady Russell hurried to let down her window.

The boy obediently came up. "Don't you worry none, milady," he panted. They can't have got far."

Lady Russell's heart skipped a beat. Had Hullin indeed lost track of Sir Walter's coach? She struggled to speak. "Every street," she called out hoarsely. "Do you hear? Tell your father that you are to search every street, every alley and mews, until we find that coach!"

"Yes, ma'am." The boy pulled at his forelock and went clambering onto the box.

The coach lurched forward and Lady Russell shut the window. She pressed her hands to her temples, willing down panic. "Dear Father in heaven," she whispered, "please, please let us find him."

10 The Indignity of It All

Lady Russell's carriage came to a halt before a tall house of stained brick. This was a very modest quarter of Bath. Hullin went to enquire, and for Lady Russell every moment was agony. Fortunately he did not keep her waiting long.

Again Lady Russell let down the window. "Well?" she demanded. "What is this place? Is Sir Walter here?"

Hullin took a moment to answer. "It's the bailiff's house, milady," he said. "The man you're asking about is here."

"Thank God for that. Kindly inform him that I have come and will take him home."

Hullin hesitated. "He won't be going nowhere just yet, ma'am. He has business with the bailiff."

Lady Russell peered over Hullin's shoulder. "What *is* this place?"

Hullin coughed and said, "It's a sponging house, milady. But not to worry," he added quickly. "There's
plenty worse than this." He jerked a thumb over his shoulder. "Few streets over are some real hellholes. Places a
man oughtn't to be after dark. Right proper, this is."

Lady Russell would not have described it in those
terms, but she swallowed her comment. Again the building came under scrutiny. A sponging house, she knew, was
the prelude to debtor's prison—and bankruptcy. Sir Walter's future would be littered with writs, law expenses,
and ruinous sacrifices. But surely this was all a mistake!

She addressed Hullin. "Is this sponging house a fit
place for me to visit? I would like to call upon Sir Walter."

"He'll be right pleased to see a friendly face, ma'am,
and no mistake. Perhaps you'd best wait a bit? I imagine
he'll be settling in, so to speak."

"Very well." Lady Russell closed the window and sat
back. Yes, there was much to sort out. The merchants of
Bath were fiends! A man of Sir Walter's standing ought
to be treated with dignity and consideration! But now he
was cast to the wolves, as it were, over what was obviously a simple misunderstanding.

Well. She would see him soon enough. God only knew
what she would say to him.

Presently she remembered the Bible. She'd brought it
along today because Sir Walter's thoughts could use a
nudge in the proper direction. Now that he was taken by
the bailiff, it appeared he needed more than a nudge!

Lady Russell spent some minutes leafing through the pages. The psalms, she knew, were often used to bring comfort. One particular text caught her eye.

> Many are the afflictions of the righteous,
> But the Lord delivereth him out of them all.

Lady Russell hesitated. Sir Walter Elliot was not precisely a righteous man. She flipped several pages back.

> He trusted on the Lord that He would deliver
> him;
> Let Him deliver him, seeing as he delighted
> in Him.

Well. As much as she valued her old friend, he was hardly one who delighted in the Lord! At last she found something that might do. Sir Walter was not a perfect man, but he was a good man—or so he tried to be.

> The steps of a good man are ordered by the
> Lord,
> And He delighteth in his way.
> Though he fall, he shall not be utterly cast
> down,
> For the Lord upholdeth him with His hand.

Unfortunately, Lady Russell had reservations about this one as well. Although the text was suitable, the word *good* was a bit troubling. When referring to Sir Walter

Elliot, the most honest use of the word *good* was in the term *good-looking*! Lady Russell did not think the steps of a good-looking man were necessarily ordered by the Lord. In fact, it was so often just the reverse!

Wherever Elizabeth went that morning she took dancing steps—to the dressing table to peek at the looking glass, or to the bed (where she sat and dreamed of an impossible future), or to the wardrobe to sort through her gowns. Humming a tune, she removed her favorite day dresses for inspection. Soon her bed was awash with colour.

Yellow would be perfect, she decided. Pale yellow muslin—layers of it, drifting about her as she walked—and a straw hat trimmed with a wide ribbon. Unfortunately Elizabeth owned no yellow dresses. Instead, she selected the green walking dress and gave it to Elise to press. Green was an even better choice, for was Patrick not an Irishman?

All that morning his name floated through her mind like music, wrapping her thoughts with a tender whisper of romance. She took up pencil and paper to write a note to Anne, but she wrote *Elizabeth Gill* instead. And then she had to laugh, for this was a perfectly dreadful name! Why did she not care?

Now that she thought on it, every aspect of her future would be dreadful! She would be married to a man of no distinction like Anne and would grow coarse like Mary. And have a nursery filled with children.

The thought of becoming a mother, once so repulsive, now brought only smiles. She had become rather fond of her young nephews. What would it be like to have a nursery filled with Patrick's children? Elizabeth discovered that she was blushing.

She did not know what Patrick's income was, but did it matter? Was it so expensive to marry and raise a family? People did it every day! Then too, had she not become wise in the ways of money? They would take one of those narrow houses, she decided, with lace curtains in the front windows and flowers in a bed out front. She could adjust to living in smaller quarters—had she not done so when her father took the house on Camden Place? A little house could be quite charming. And she would be sharing it with Patrick—Elizabeth paused to sigh—which would be absolutely wonderful.

Suddenly she laughed. Such thoughts were lunacy, for he had not yet asked for her hand. Would he do so today? Would he again bring her home in a job carriage and demand another kiss? She rather hoped so.

Elise came in to dress her hair, and this put an end to romantic speculations—almost. Soon Elizabeth was busy with her thoughts. Patrick Gill was intelligent and industrious. Surely he would succeed in his business endeavours, and then everything would be better. She had nothing to blush for in his manners. He was both handsome and distinguished, unlike certain pedigreed gentlemen she could name. And she wouldn't be a *cit* or a mushroom, for she was an Elliot. Perhaps, she thought recklessly, she had enough breeding for the both of them?

The parlor in which Lady Russell was left to wait was littered with old newspapers and smelled strongly of smoke and sweat. She used a clean handkerchief to cover the seat of a rather grimy chair. Presently Sir Walter was brought in. The elegant dressing gown was gone. Instead, he wore an ill-fitting jumper of coarse brown cloth over striped pantaloons. On his feet were woolen stockings, well-darned. Lady Russell's compassionate heart was wrung. "Oh, Sir Walter," she whispered.

Once they were alone, he gave a mournful sigh. "These clothes," he said, making a futile gesture. "Have you ever seen anything so disgraceful?" His eyes brimmed. "It is bad enough to be in this place, Amanda, but to be so attired is ..." His chin quivered.

Lady Russell did not know whether to laugh or cry. Who but Walter Elliot would think of clothing at a time like this? And what was he about, to be using her Christian name? "My friend," she said, "I am so sorry."

Again he sighed. "This is all a dreadful mistake."

"Of course it is. And as soon as you feel able, we shall discuss what must be done." She indicated the chair opposite hers. "Do sit down."

He looked so glum that Lady Russell decided to bring out her Bible. "Even in the face of shocking injustice," she said, turning the pages, "we must not abandon hope.

Sir Walter lapsed into silence; then his countenance brightened. "A brief confinement in the sponging house," he said hopefully, "is not unknown among the more reckless members of the nobility. Due to gaming debts and such."

She looked up. "Thank God you are not a gamester."

"Or," he went on, "after a bit of a drinking spree."

Lady Russell pursed up her lips. "Crapulous behaviour," she said, "is unbecoming in any man, regardless of his station." She hesitated, wondering how to phrase a delicate question. "You ... have not encountered anyone we know here, have you?"

He shook his head. "Alas, I have not a friend in the world. Besides yourself, that is." His voice rose higher. "Oh the horror of it all!"

Lady Russell made sympathetic sounds.

"The most pressing matter," he went on, "is that I am obliged to provide tonight's dinner."

Her brow wrinkled. "You must procure your own food? Nonsense! You are confined!"

"Well—" Sir Walter paused to sniff. "I suppose I could arrange for one of the inns to deliver it. The meal is not only for myself, you understand. I am to provide dinner for everyone."

Lady Russell was shocked. "But—what about the expense?"

"Bother the expense! The question is, how can I host a dinner while wearing these clothes?"

"Clothes be hanged," cried Lady Russell. "You are in the sponging house!"

"My dear, we are speaking of Tradition. Since when is Tradition affordable? I am to give the poor fellows a treat, as befits my station as the New Man." He puffed out his cheeks. "It is rather like a Public Day, is it not?"

Lady Russell thought it was nothing of the sort. "This is outrageous!"

He lowered his voice. "I needn't provide a *splendid* dinner," he said. "Think of the savings!"

Lady Russell could only stare.

"The meal will be below the mark, but my attire needn't be." Sir Walter rubbed his hands together. "Now then, I recall that you have several of my trunks at your house."

"But you must leave this place," she protested. "I cannot bring your trunks *here*."

"No, no, dear friend. That would be too much. However, perhaps you could bring a change of raiment?" He grew thoughtful. "There is a very fine waistcoat in one of those trunks. White satin, embroidered with leaves and pomegranates."

"You wish me to bring *evening clothes?*"

"For the dinner, Amanda." His eyes were pleading. "I'll need morning wear as well, but we can discuss that later." He paused. "The clothes in those trunks are sadly out of fashion."

"How can you think of fashion at a time like this?"

Sir Walter gave a heavy sigh. "I suppose it cannot be helped. I do so dislike being behind the times! Ah well, anything will be an improvement over these … togs." He attempted a wan smile.

Lady Russell's heart was touched. "Do not fret," she soothed. "I shall bring the clothes straightway—and some soap and a towel. Longwell will arrange for the dinner."

She paused. Did inmates of a sponging house keep town or country hours? "Is seven o'clock convenient?"

"It is, and I am most grateful." Sir Walter lifted his chin manfully. "I might be quartered among the ranks of the Great Unwashed," he said. "But I am not required to be wholly given over to barbarianism."

Elizabeth descended at half-past the hour, pulling on her gloves as she came. She took a brief look into the drawing room and found Mary on one of the sofas.

"Hello," she said pleasantly. "I see you are better." Elizabeth knew her sister's illness was a hoax, but she was not of a mind to twit Mary today. "I am going out. Is there anything you need?"

"There are a great many things I need." Mary's mouth puckered into a pout. "No one thinks of me at all; it is all rush-rush-rush! Everyone runs away, and I am left alone."

"I am sorry," said Elizabeth. "It is a lovely day. The garden should be pleasant."

"I do not like the garden. It reminds me of the country." Mary began to hunt in her pockets. "I have another clean handkerchief somewhere."

Elizabeth gave her one of her own. "You really ought to visit Father," she said. "He has been grouchy lately. The two of you should get on very well."

With a final look at the clock, Elizabeth nodded to her sister and left the drawing room.

"And now," said Lady Russell, "we must attend to business." This, she knew, would be difficult. How delicate was a gentleman's sense of dignity! How dearly she wished to avoid giving offense! He looked at her with expectation, which leant her courage. "Sir Walter," she said, "exactly how much are you in arrears?"

"Are you referring to ... money?" His voice quavered as he said the word.

"Yes, dear," she said gently. "How much money do you owe the bailiff?"

Sir Walter's face fell. "I do not know," he said slowly. "Shepherd has handled everything for me."

"Then we must contact Mr. Shepherd."

Sir Walter plucked a thread from his sleeve. "You cannot imagine my distress, to be so brutally treated. I haven't even had my morning bath."

"Yes, lamb, I know. I shall send for Mr. Shepherd, and he will see to everything. My express should reach him this very day. As soon as you are free of this place, you may have a lovely soak in the tub."

Sir Walter looked up. "You needn't send for Shepherd. He is here in Bath."

Lady Russell brightened. "Why, that is wonderful."

He sighed again. "Not at all. The man is no longer in my employ. I dismissed him."

"But—who is to handle your business if Mr. Shepherd does not?"

Sir Walter hung his head. "I am sure I do not know."

"Well then," said Lady Russell bracingly, "let us see for ourselves what must be done. Would you be so kind as to summon the bailiff?"

Sometime later, after the warrant had been produced, Lady Russell and Sir Walter sat together at the parlour table. She spent some time examining the charges against him which, as it turned out, had been brought by that evil physician, Mr. Savoy.

"Two hundred fifty pounds," she read aloud. "That is not so much." She looked up. "My dear, do you have this amount at hand?"

He cast up his hands. "How should I know? This is all a mistake."

"Very probably, but it is in your best interest to pay the bailiff."

"Thieves and robbers! That is what the lot of them are."

"I quite agree," said Lady Russell, thinking of Mr. Savoy's heartless tactics. "And yet you cannot go free until that amount is paid. Therefore you will give me a draft on your bank, and I shall get the money."

Sir Walter did not answer right away. "I ... do not know if I have that much," he confessed. "I did, but there have been expenses." His voice rose to a wail. "The excessive fee charged by Elizabeth's *modiste*, for one. Unbelievable."

"Elizabeth!" Lady Russell made a clucking noise. "Vanity, vanity! And what has been the result?"

Sir Walter was not attending. "Elizabeth!" he shouted joyfully. "By Jove, why did I not think of this before?

Elizabeth must contact Rushworth, do you hear? She'll have to send an express, but he won't mind the expense. Men who are in love never do. Tell her to say this: I need that settlement money right away."

"Settlement money?"

"Yes, yes. For the engagement. Elizabeth knows nothing about it, but Rushworth *does*."

"Sir Walter, of what are you speaking? Money paid out at an engagement? I have never heard of such a thing. That is not a settlement!"

His voice took on a pleading tone. "A little honey to sweeten the deal, that is all. Think of it as a gift."

Lady Russell's brows knit. "Do you mean a *bride price?* Surely you did not ask it of him!"

"He offered! Which was most generous, considering the sensitive nature of his proposal." Sir Walter lowered his voice. "He is, after all, divorced. Think of the disgrace."

"Would it be any worse, having a father-in-law in the—" Lady Russell broke off, horrified at what she'd been about to say. It was unwise to remain here. She needed time to think and so, it appeared, did he.

She pushed back her chair. "Leave everything to me," she said, refolding the warrant. "I shall see to your clothes and have Longwell arrange for the dinner."

Sir Walter's face was eager. "And the express to Rushworth? He is in London, you know. At his house in Grosvenor Square."

"You may leave everything to me."

Sir Walter came round the table to assist her with her chair. "You know best, my dear," he said meekly. "You always do."

As she reached the door, she heard him call her name. She turned. He held out her handkerchief. "Did you drop this?" he said. His smile, she noticed, was singularly charming.

The drive back to Rivers Street gave Lady Russell time to think, and yet her thoughts did not follow a proper direction. For some reason, she could not stop thinking of the handkerchief. There it was on the seat beside her, soiled with the dust—an ugly thing, really—and yet to see it made her smile. How long had it been since a gentleman was so gallant? A very long time indeed.

At last she pushed the handkerchief aside. There were things to be decided; so many things to be done. For as she was leaving, the bailiff had mentioned a most interesting development. Apparently there was a second warrant ready to be issued against Sir Walter, but because of a technicality—a missing seal or some such thing—it had not been brought forward. If Sir Walter were able to pay the amount he now owed, before the defective warrant was reissued, he would go free. The question was, how long would that freedom last?

Lady Russell smoothed her gloves, tracing the ridges of the seams. Such a tangle Walter Elliot had made for himself, and all so unnecessary! If Lady Elliot were yet alive, this catastrophe would never have occurred. Mr. Shepherd made attempt after attempt, but the sorry truth was this: Sir Walter Elliot could not be made to mind a manager's instructions. It was not in him to submit to a lesser man.

Well. She had come up with a solution, though he would not like it very well—and neither would her solicitor. Fortunately, Mr. Hinks had his office here in Bath. Lady Russell squared her shoulders and reached for the check string. It would be best to see Mr. Hinks at once, before she changed her mind.

11 BEAT TO QUARTERS!

The window of his bedchamber was open, allowing the breeze to tug playfully at the draperies. McGillvary finished buttoning his waistcoat. That flapping reminded him of canvas, stout and seaworthy. Oh to be at sea on such a day as this—in command of his own ship and pacing the quarterdeck!

His mind came alive with memories. From the lookout in the crosstrees came the shout: "Sail ho! Sail ho to the wind'ard!" And his bellowing answer: "What do you make of her?"

"Full-rigged ship, sir! French, by the cut of her tops'ls—"

French indeed. As if he could forget the day he'd intercepted the *Durance*. Glass in hand, he'd swung into the ratlines, bringing the enemy ship into focus, his mind racing to meet the challenge—

"Mr. Jones, you may beat to quarters."

"Beat to quarters it is, sir." Jones raised his trumpet. "All hands to clear ship!"

Everywhere around him, the ship came alive. Bulkheads were knocked down, gunports hauled up, the guns run out and loaded with double shot—

"Beg pardon, sir."

McGillvary gave a start. His man Pym stood at his elbow.

"Your carriage is ready, Admiral, sir," he said.

Reluctantly, McGillvary pulled himself from the imaginary quarterdeck. He would now be heading into battle of a different sort, this time alone at the helm. Pym helped ease him into a dark blue coat of exquisite cut. As Pym adjusted the set of it across the shoulders, McGillvary surveyed his unsmiling reflection.

Why the devil had he kissed her? He had worked so blasted hard to keep Elizabeth at arm's length. And it was for nothing. He had slipped—but for a moment—and the damage had been done. The woman he loved, his darling Elizabeth, had kissed not him but another!

What would happen today, when he confessed the truth to her? McGillvary sighed heavily. If there was a way to extricate himself from this tangle, he did not know it.

His secretary met him in the hall. "Mr. Lonk's report," he said, handing a sealed packet. "And the afternoon's *Bath Gazette*, sir, just arrived."

McGillvary accepted both with a word of thanks. There was more. "Mr. Lonk was wishful to know, sir, if you plan to call this afternoon to discuss the problem accounts."

McGillvary had forgotten; he gave a noncommittal answer. As he went out to the carriage, the breeze pulled at the lapels of his frock coat. McGillvary removed his hat and allowed the breeze free rein with his hair. He would no longer dress like Gill, but he ought to wear his hair in the man's unruly style.

The door was closed smartly behind him, and the carriage lurched into motion. On the seat was the newspaper Starkweather had given him. On a whim, or perhaps because his thoughts were filled with Elizabeth, he turned past the more tempting front pages to those featuring society news. He scanned the latest *on-dits* and announcement—always the same, these were. He felt his eyes begin to glaze.

Suddenly McGillvary sat up. Frowning, he scanned the text. "Oh hell!" he spat at the page. "What the devil does she mean by *this?*"

It took every bit of willpower to hold back what Elizabeth knew was a foolish smile. What else could she do? Just to see him sitting at their table made her feel giddy. But as soon as her eyes adjusted to the dimness of the tearoom, Elizabeth suffered a shock. Patrick Gill was not smiling, and his jaw was tensed. His eyes did not sparkle. Instead, they were watchful, as if he was weighing what to say to her.

With customary grace, he assisted her with the chair but said nothing while she drew off her gloves. A little fearfully, Elizabeth raised her eyes to meet his.

As soon as the serving girl left them, he spoke. "I thought I told you not to kiss anyone." There was no smile in his tone.

"I-I didn't!"

"Then will you please explain to me the meaning of *this?*" He slapped a newspaper onto the table.

Elizabeth bent over it, but the words swam on the page. Patrick was looking so very angry! But he couldn't be angry—he loved her! Didn't he?

"I don't understand," she faltered.

"Do not play the innocent with me, Elizabeth," he snapped. "It doesn't become you." He pointed to a line of text.

Elizabeth took hold of the newspaper and forced herself to read.

> Sir Walter Elliot, late of Kellynch Hall, is pleased to announce the betrothal of his daughter, Elizabeth, to Mr. James Rushworth of Sotherton.

What horror was this? "Someone is jesting," she managed to say. "They must be." She attempted a smile.

"You will notice that I am not laughing." His finger jabbed at the newspaper. "According to this you are engaged to be married."

"But I am not! He never proposed! He spoke to my father, but never to me!"

"Never?" There was a knowing look in Patrick Gill's eyes.

She felt her face grow warm. "We had an understanding, but—"

"An understanding?" he cut in. "What kind of understanding?"

Her breath now came in gasps. How angry he was! How could she make him see that it was all a mistake?

"Elizabeth," he said, speaking low, "how could you? How could you offer yourself to him?"

Elizabeth could not bear to answer. The expression in his eyes made her wince.

"I have to wonder," he continued, "what he could have offered you that is worth such a sacrifice." His lip curled. "Was it the money?"

"No!" she flared. "It was not the—" What could she say? For of course he was right! She hung her head. "It was not only the money," she said. "He offered independence."

"Indeed." There was contempt in his voice. How she felt it!

Elizabeth was trembling now. "You can have no notion of how it was," she said thickly. "My situation was impossible. What could I do but find a husband?"

She heard him mutter an oath, and his chair scraped the floor. Elizabeth closed her eyes. No longer would she face him across the table. Any moment now she would feel his arms around her—holding her, comforting her—

and the world would be right again. There—she could hear him moving toward her. She readied herself for his embrace—but it never came.

Elizabeth opened her eyes. Patrick Gill was gone.

A sob rose in her throat; she had not the power to hold it back. She covered her face with her hands. How long she sat this way she could not say.

A movement startled her, for someone had taken hold of the back of her chair. She raised hesitant eyes. Patrick Gill's unsmiling face looked into hers.

"Come," he said, and he held out his hand. "They have prepared a private room. You may have your cry there."

"I am not crying," she whispered brokenly. "And they do not have a private room."

"They do now." A sardonic smile pulled at his lips. "Have you never noticed, my dear, how resourceful men become when money is involved?"

"Beg pardon, sir. This table all right?"

Captain Wentworth gave a start and tore his gaze from the curtained doorway. The serving girl repeated her question.

"No," he said shortly, and pointed to a table that gave a clearer view of the room. 'That one."

She shrugged. "Very good, sir. Will you be having the special, then?"

Wentworth muttered an affirmative, and she went off. He tossed the newspaper on the table, his eyes focused on

the curtain. Unless he was mistaken, Elizabeth was behind it—with a gentleman. No, Wentworth corrected
himself. Hardly that.

The trouble was, he'd only just come in. It was a long
shot that he'd found this place at all, for the chairman's
directions were garbled. Still, he'd seen enough of the
woman to recognize Elizabeth's auburn hair and erect carriage. He'd had the fleeting impression of green—but was
she wearing green today? He frowned in an effort to recall.

He knew he ought to follow the pair and accost them
straightway—and if he were mistaken, what would be the
harm? Then again, if Elizabeth were within, would a
forced marriage be such a bad thing?

Wentworth slid into the chair at the new table, but
carefully. He did not trust it to hold his weight. This was
a fool's errand and no mistake—a waste of a perfectly
good afternoon. What did he care about Elizabeth's actions? But Anne would care. It was for Anne's sake that
he had traced Elizabeth to this place.

He glanced around the tearoom with distaste. Bath offered a variety of spots for lovers' trysts, but this? It was
hardly up to his fastidious sister-in-law's standards. And
women were everywhere—fusty, prying old birds, by the
look of them. If Elizabeth wished to broadcast her indiscretion to all of Bath, this breeding spot for gossip was
the perfect choice.

Sooner or later the pair would have to come out, and
then he would know. He gave a tug to his cravat and,
after another glance at the curtain, opened the newspaper.

The clatter of flatware against porcelain and the nattering of the women made concentration difficult.

"Here you are, sir." The girl's shrill voice caused him to look up. "A nice fresh pot," she said and plunked it down. "And our best selection of fancies."

He managed a tight smile as she filled his cup with the steaming brew—cheap tea, unless he missed his guess. He glanced again at the curtain and, with a sigh, returned to the newspaper. It would likely be a long afternoon.

McGillvary handed Elizabeth into her chair, but did not seat himself. How he wished she would own the truth and be done with it! As it was, her evasive answers were remarkably like the excuses offered by his junior officers— and Admiral McGillvary had no tolerance for excuses.

He allowed his hand to rest on the back of his chair, a reminder to himself that he was not dealing with one of his men. "Tell me again," he said with careful patience. "If you are not engaged to Rushworth, how came your father to place that announcement?"

"I have no idea. Truly."

"That I find hard to believe," he countered. She looked up then; the hurt expression in her eyes caused him to soften his tone. "He said nothing to you about it?"

McGillvary was no stranger to the changes guilt brought to a man's features. He saw Elizabeth's jaw tighten. "H-he mentioned an agreement," she stammered.

"An agreement. The 'understanding' you and Rushworth had made?"

"No."

"Did you inform him of what had transpired between you?"

She bit her lips and said something he could not hear. McGillvary pulled himself to his full height. "Answer the question, please," he said sharply.

"I did not tell my father. I believe he learned of it from Mr. Rushworth himself."

"And was your father pleased with such an alliance? Rushworth has neither the looks nor the title you say your father requires in a son-in-law."

Her eyes flew to his face. Yes, he remembered what she had said. She would be even more alarmed by the time he was finished. The thought crossed his mind that she was not one of his officers and that he ought to temper his responses. This time he ignored it.

"What concerns me most," he went on, "is that you entered into this so-called 'understanding' willingly, did you not?" Memories of the kiss he had witnessed made his tone bitter.

Elizabeth's gaze was now downcast. He saw her swallow. Would she lie or own the truth? The answer, he knew, would be in the eyes. "You will look at me while I speak to you, sirrah," he ordered.

Elizabeth's eyes came up; their gaze held his. This was a good sign. "Elizabeth," he amended, correcting his slip.

"I was willing," she said slowly. "Or I thought I was. But—"

"Was it the lure of his person? As you say, you were not interested in his money."

"I told you. He offered me independence."

McGillvary snorted. "I do not think being saddled with a dullard for a husband is independence, my dear."

Elizabeth lifted her chin. "If you must know, Mr. Rushworth is easy to lead—as is my father! I am accustomed to dealing with fools. Besides," she spoke recklessly now, "Mr. Rushworth needs a woman who can manage him. I am not precisely a green girl."

"That is exactly what you are!" McGillvary drew out his chair and sat. "A mansion, a staff of workers—these look vastly romantic until one takes possession. Then a woman seeks refuge in vapours and spasms."

"I have never had the vapours in my life! And believe you me, I have been tempted. No one knows better than I how difficult it is to manage a large house. As I told you, for thirteen years I have stood in my mother's place."

"I have not forgotten."

Elizabeth's blush became more intense. "And you needn't tell me that I was robbing the cradle by pursuing him," she said thickly. "I know that." A tear rolled down her cheek.

He dug out a clean handkerchief and passed it to her. "The man's wife left him, Elizabeth," he grumbled. "Does that tell you nothing? Her replacement will have it even worse."

She dried her eyes. "I daresay Mr. Rushworth has learned to be more careful about how he treats a wife."

McGillvary gave a snort of derision. "No," he said, "you're out there. Oh, he's learned to appreciate a wife, but not for the reasons you think." He paused, wondering how much he should say. "Have you never wondered why Rushworth is so eager to marry again?"

"He would like to put the past behind him, I suppose."

"Or he has become more particular in his appetites! And misses having them gratified!"

At that her head came up. "Mr. Gill!" she protested. "That remark is not in the best of taste."

"You were the one who wished to take him on as husband. I assumed you'd considered all the angles."

"But I don't wish him to be my husband," she insisted. "Not any longer!"

"Then I suggest you tell him so."

"I shall."

"Indeed?" McGillvary's lips twisted. "Then do so—now."

"How can I? He is in London."

He pushed back his chair. "That needn't deter you," he said, reaching for his hat. "I can take you to London myself. Where is he staying?" He rose to his feet.

Elizabeth's eyes were wide with shock. "I have no idea," she faltered. "His mother lives here, but—"

McGillvary made his way to her side of the table. "Rushworth's mother," he said. "Ah yes. Pug-faced old thing, isn't she? Wears turbans with her hair tucked up underneath—looks like a toadstool, I've always thought." He paused to consider this. "Or is that her sister?"

Elizabeth sat staring up at him.

"At any rate," McGillvary went on, "she's read the afternoon paper and no mistake. We'll see her instead. Come."

"*We?*" Elizabeth looked truly frightened now. "What do you mean, we?"

"We'll go together; I'll take you myself." He held out a hand. "Nothing could be easier. You'll tell her of the mistake, and she will then inform her son."

"But I cannot break an engagement. It isn't done! I know you think it is nothing, but I will be ruined!"

"Perhaps," he said. "But the way I see it, it's the lesser of two evils."

Elizabeth came out of the storeroom with Patrick Gill close behind. The tearoom was filled with patrons—and most of them were looking at her! Their frank curiosity made her squirm. She knew her world; she could guess what they were thinking. Even so, Patrick Gill's hand was at her elbow, propelling her forward. She heard him speak to someone—the proprietor, she supposed.

As before, Mr. Gill reached in front to open the door. He was not wearing gloves today—and across the back of his hand was a pale, jagged scar. Elizabeth winced to see it. Why had she never noticed this before? Here was the man she loved—and she'd never noticed!

The shop's bell tinkled merrily as the door came open. And then they were standing in the sunlight together, surrounded by the clatter of street traffic. Elizabeth stumbled against him, but only for a moment. Immediately she pulled herself erect.

If only he would not be so angry! If only he would forgive! But Elizabeth knew this would never happen. Her father never forgot his anger, and there was no reason for

Patrick Gill to do so, either. Why should he forgive when the entire situation had been her fault?

Instead of heading for the hacking stand, Patrick Gill just stood there. Then he gave shout and plunged into the street. A carriage immediately pulled up, causing havoc for the other drivers. It was jet black and gleaming, and was drawn by two matched horses. A liveried footman jumped down to open the door. Mr. Gill turned and came sprinting back.

Elizabeth was astonished. "You'd better have the money to pay for this, Patrick Gill," she told him. "For I certainly have not!"

Once inside, Mr. Gill was talkative—which would have been enjoyable under other circumstances. "There is no time like the present to put things to right. Mistakes happen. Your father ought to bring a suit against that publisher for libel."

But Elizabeth knew that this was the last thing her father would do, for he had supplied the information! And here was another problem. Even if she could come up with a story to satisfy Mrs. Rushworth, what could be done about her father? He expected her to marry James Rushworth!

She glanced at the door. The latch looked unhappily secure, and Patrick Gill sat right beside it. There would be no escaping for her.

And so Elizabeth held herself prim and erect, portraying a confidence she did not feel. "Perhaps Mrs. Rushworth will not be at home," she heard her voice bleat. "Or she might refuse to see me."

"After reading that notice? I think not."

"Especially after reading that notice," she shot back. "James has told her nothing. It will be a complete surprise."

Mr. Gill stiffened. Instantly Elizabeth regretted using Mr. Rushworth's Christian name.

"I think you mistake your suitor, my dear. There is very little he does not tell his mama."

Elizabeth's heart jumped to hear the words *my dear*, but his tone gave little cause for hope. A glance out of the window showed that they were not far from the Rushworth residence.

With trembling fingers, Elizabeth hunted in her reticule for her card case. She attempted to open it, but her hands were awkward. It fell. Mr. Gill knelt to retrieve it. It was then that she realized that he held a card case of his own, a gold one. He opened it and extracted a stiff white card.

Elizabeth became instantly suspicious. "What are you doing?"

He snapped the case shut and returned it to his pocket. "Give me your card," he said. "I'll present both to the butler."

"Both? Have you lost your mind? You are not coming with me!"

He took possession of her card case. "Oh, but I think I am, my dear." He removed one of her cards. "Don't fret. After all, I am the most experienced duelist." A smile appeared. "Watch and learn, Miss Elliot," he said.

At last the carriage arrived at their destination. McGillvary fingered both calling cards, his and hers, with a smile hovering about his lips. Gad, it was perfect. He could picture the scene that was about to unfold in Mrs. Rushworth's drawing room. Elizabeth would stammer out her version of the tale, and then he would step forward to inform Mrs. Rushworth of the truth—that Elizabeth had never been nor would ever be engaged to her son.

After that, what could Mrs. Rushworth do? Nothing! McGillvary knew very well that the woman would not dare to argue with him. Nor would Elizabeth—at least, not in front of Mrs. Rushworth. Later he would settle up with her.

The only hitch was that Elizabeth might hear the name *McGillvary* before he delivered his set-down. Well, he would simply have to keep her occupied in the entrance hall while he was being announced.

He lifted a hand to hide his smile. He could think of a most excellent way of detaining Elizabeth, though she would probably not appreciate it!

There would be time for that after the interview—a lifetime's worth. Soon Elizabeth would learn the advantages of the McGillvary name. He glanced at her. To be sure, she was adrift at the moment. But she would appreciate the genius of his plan once she saw the look of chagrin on Mrs. Rushworth's face.

"Mr. Gill," said Elizabeth, "you cannot come with me!" The desperation in her voice tore at his heart.

"My dear," he said gently, "I refuse to send you to face that old gorgon alone."

Elizabeth squared her shoulders. "You will wait here, or you will drive away and leave me. But you will not accompany me inside."

"And I," he countered with equal vehemence, "will not allow you to go in alone."

"If you come with me, you will prove beyond doubt that you are a heartless monster!"

"Then so be it." He grinned at her. "My dear, it will take more than one crusty old lady to frighten me."

"Patrick," she cried, "I do not care if Mrs. Rushworth is the devil incarnate! You cannot come into that house with me!"

"I'm no coward." McGillvary took hold of the latch and gave it a sharp twist. The carriage door swung open.

Elizabeth uttered a shriek and pulled it shut. "But I *am!*" she cried.

McGillvary had had enough. He stuffed both calling cards in a pocket and took hold of her shoulders. "Look," he said, giving her a shake, "we stand together, understand? There is strength in numbers."

The despair in her eyes caused him to unbend a little. "Come, dearest," he urged, more gently, "we must not retreat. Now is the time to engage the enemy more closely."

"But my reputation," she protested. "It is bad enough that I must break off my understanding. But if you are with me when I do—!"

So this was the heart of the matter. "You do not wish to be seen with me, is that it? Patrick Gill, the clerk, has no place in Mrs. Rushworth's salon?"

"Patrick Gill, the *man!* What will Mrs. Rushworth think when I say what I must, accompanied by a man who is not a member of my family? She will think I am utterly wanton, that's what!"

"That," he said, "is ridiculous."

"One does not bring an unmarried man when breaking off an engagement. Even you know that much."

McGillvary did know, unfortunately, and he gave himself a mental kick.

Elizabeth shook off his hold and opened the door. He allowed her to have her way, though she did not know it. When she had exited the carriage, she turned to face him. "Do you hate me so entirely?"

Elizabeth's hat was askew and her temper was in shreds, but she did not care. Fortunately Patrick Gill remained inside the carriage. She strode to the door and took hold of the brass knocker. "Odious man," she muttered, and rapped sharply.

The butler came to the door. Elizabeth thrust her calling card under his nose. "I would like to see Mrs. Rushworth, if you please." Anger gave her voice an edge.

The man retreated a step. "Permit me to ascertain whether Mrs. Rush—" he began, but Elizabeth interrupted.

"I am Miss Elizabeth Elliot. Mrs. Rushworth will definitely wish to see me." She pushed past him into the entrance hall. "I will wait here," she told him.

A mirror was there, which was just what she needed. Turning her back to the butler, she made a minor adjustment to her hat. The man remained where he was, staring. Elizabeth looked over her shoulder at him. "Kindly inform Mrs. Rushworth that I am here."

The butler took his time in returning, and Elizabeth fell to pacing. Pacing brought on thinking, and thinking was dangerous. She knew that if she thought too much, she would lose what little courage she had left. She would say her piece to Mrs. Rushworth and hope that the woman would be gracious enough to accept her apology.

For Patrick Gill there would be no apologies. Elizabeth's gaze swept the empty entrance hall. True, it would be reassuring to have a companion just now, but certainly not him! And his advice to her—something about engaging the enemy—was ill-timed and in very poor taste! The more she thought about him, the angrier she became.

The butler returned and begged leave to inform her that his mistress would see her right away. And so Elizabeth followed him up the flight of stairs to the drawing room, her thoughts still focused on Patrick Gill. With each step she pictured his laughing face—mocking her, encouraging her to fight. Fight? Elizabeth's courage was

almost nonexistent. It was the force of her anger that pro-
pelled her up those stairs.

The drawing room door was opened, and Mrs. Rushworth's butler stepped back to allow Elizabeth to pass.
He announced her name and that was all. There came a
sniff and a loud whisper.

The room was darker than she expected, for net blinds
covered the windows. Mrs. Rushworth, grim and unsmiling, sat rigid on one of the sofas. Without a doubt she
had seen the announcement.

Elizabeth made herself come fully into the room. It was
then that she noticed that Mrs. Rushworth was not alone.
Mrs. Leighton sat opposite, her teacup suspended in mid-
air. Elizabeth's remaining courage deserted her.

"You may go, Howell," said Mrs. Rushworth. "And
Howell," she added, "close the door."

Elizabeth raised her chin. Why, Mrs. Rushworth was
being deliberately manipulative! She was intending to
frighten her! The knowledge of this changed everything.
No longer did Elizabeth wish to be apologetic and con-
trite. Patrick Gill's words came flooding back: *Engage the
enemy.* Very well, she would.

It was then that Elizabeth realized what she had to do.
She must be honest—plainly, disastrously honest. And in
order to gain the advantage she must be the first to speak.
If only her voice did not falter!

"Good morning, Mrs. Rushworth," she said crisply. "I
wonder if you would be good enough to explain the announcement in today's *Gazette?*"

Mrs. Rushworth gave a perfectly genuine start. Her mouth fell open, revealing a row of unattractive teeth.

"You cannot imagine my surprise when I read what was printed there," Elizabeth went on. "I wonder if you would be kind enough to explain."

Mrs. Rushworth set her cup and saucer on a small table. Her face was now alarmingly red. "I beg your pardon?" she said.

To Mrs. Leighton she added, "Impertinent girl." She turned again to Elizabeth. "I am the one who should be asking that question of you. To learn of a beloved son's engagement in such a way!"

Tell the truth, Elizabeth reminded herself. *Engage the enemy.*

"How do you think I felt," she countered, "to learn about my supposed engagement from a newspaper column? It has caused a world of trouble for me."

Mrs. Rushworth's lips were white with anger. "Supposed engagement? You are not engaged to my son?"

"I am not." Elizabeth drew a long breath. "He never proposed. That is to say, he wished to, but I would not allow him to speak."

"You would not *allow* him?" Mrs. Rushworth repeated.

"At the time your son was married, ma'am. For all I know he might be married still."

Mrs. Rushworth bristled. "He thinks himself to be in love with you, Miss Elliot. I will have you know that my James is an honourable boy!"

Elizabeth had her own opinion, which she wisely decided not to share. "I am fond of your son, Mrs. Rushworth," she said, speaking carefully. "That is, we are friends, but nothing more." She pulled the glove from her left hand. "Do you see? He has given me no ring."

Mrs. Rushworth's voice shook with emotion. "But he has spoken to your father."

"Very possibly," said Elizabeth, "but my father has not spoken to—" Here she suffered a twinge of conscience. She must say something in her father's defense—but what?

"My father has been ill, as you know, and is under a physician's care." Elizabeth was treading warily now. "He is sometimes confused. I do not know what medications he might be taking."

Mrs. Rushworth's glare was openly hostile. "My James planned to propose when he returned from London," she said throbbingly. "I can scarcely see why!"

"He hinted that he might. But in all honesty, I could never accept."

Mrs. Rushworth made a strangled sound, either from rage or joy, which told Elizabeth that she had gone too far. "I have had time to reflect during his absence," she continued more gently, "and I have come to the conclusion that we do not suit."

"You do not wish to marry my son."

"It is better said that I oughtn't to marry your son. For one thing, I am older than he—"

"Past the age of foolishness, I had hoped."

Elizabeth gave Mrs. Rushworth a measured look. "And for another, the state of my father's health makes a wedding quite impossible."

Mrs. Leighton, who had been silent, gave a malicious laugh.

Mrs. Rushworth appeared to get hold of herself. "And so," she said icily, "you have come to break your engagement."

These words were loaded with meaning. "No," Elizabeth said distinctly, "I have not. I have come to say that there never was an engagement, and that I have no idea who placed the announcement."

Mrs. Leighton coughed. "You father, presumably," she said.

"My father is convalescing. He does not go out."

Mrs. Leighton made an impatient gesture. "Such notices are sent by letter, stupid girl! Or through the offices of another family member—a brother or a cousin."

"A cousin!" The word slipped out before Elizabeth could stop them.

Her surprise did not go unnoticed. Mrs. Leighton exchanged glances with Mrs. Rushworth. They turned to Elizabeth with narrowed eyes.

"Good day, Miss Elliot," said Mrs. Rushworth.

There seemed no more to be said. The interview was over.

And so, Elizabeth knew, was her good standing in Bath.

12 WHAT PRICE FREEDOM?

Lady Russell worried her way through the night, wrestling with thoughts that were both fantastic and uncomfortable. She suffered pangs of conscience as well, not only for the things she was planning, but also for what she had left undone. For instance, she ought to have informed the girls of their father's plight. And yet so much depended upon the timing of events! That dreaded second warrant was nothing to be trifled with.

And so Lady Russell gazed at the ceiling, waiting for dawn and listening to the sound of her clock. With each tick came another accusing thought: What will people say? What will the girls think? What will he think?

She pulled the blanket more closely against her chest. It did not matter what he thought—or what anyone thought. Hers was the most reasonable course of action. Did not desperate times call for desperate measures?

At last she slipped out of bed and found her dressing gown. Soon the new day would come, and with it the beginning of her plan. She eased into the chair behind her writing desk and lit the lamp. The flame continued to flicker, so she adjusted the wick. Immediately the flame grew small and bright. Lady Russell considered this. One small adjustment—just so! —and yet so much improvement was accomplished.

So much improvement.

Her gaze dropped to her hands. The lamplight cast unflattering shadows, causing the veins to stand out in bold relief, an unhappy reminder of her age. Quickly she looked away. A letter, written with the help of her solicitor, was propped against the inkstand. It would be sent to London this very morning by express. There, in her own hand was written the direction: *Vicar-General, The Faculty Office of the Archbishop of Canterbury.*

The dining room was deserted that morning, but the sideboard was not. Elizabeth took up a plate and began to fill it. She had just begun her breakfast when Yee came in with a letter. "An answer is required," he said. "The man waits."

Elizabeth laid down her fork, wishing that he did not speak so loudly. This morning she had a wretched headache. This urgent letter he brought was, no doubt, from her father, demanding an explanation. Or else Mrs. Rushworth had communicated with her son, and James was now making an anguished appeal. Or perhaps Lady Russell had heard the news—but no, Lady Russell would come herself, wouldn't she? Reluctantly Elizabeth broke the seal and spread the sheet.

My Dearest Elizabeth—

A promising beginning. Then she noticed the Elliot crest embossed at the top of the page. Sure enough, there were her cousin's initials. He requested a private interview at her earliest convenience. Obviously he had heard the news and wished to offer—what? Congratulations? Hardly.

She pushed back the chair. If William Elliot required an answer, she would give it. She went directly to the drawing room and sat down at the writing desk there.

Mr. Elliot,

> Mary and I will be meeting friends in the Pump Room this morning at eleven. Since your business is urgent, I shall not object to seeing you there.

Elizabeth signed her initials with a flourish. Meeting him in a public spot would accomplish several things. For one, she would be seen conversing with at least one person besides Mary, which on this particular day would be helpful. Then too, William Elliot would be reluctant to deliver a rebuke before so many watching eyes. Elizabeth sealed up the note and went downstairs to find Yee.

A delivery boy was sitting on a chair in the entrance hall while the main door stood open. "Sir Walter Elliot does not reside here, sir," she heard Yee say, but the person was insistent.

Elizabeth went over to see what was going forward. The man standing there was somberly dressed. His figure was not quite as robust as James Rushworth's and he was considerably older. For some reason he looked familiar.

Elizabeth stepped forward. "I am Sir Walter Elliot's daughter," she said. "Perhaps I may be of assistance. What is it that you require?"

The man removed his hat, revealing a balding head. "Harold Lonk of Madderly Kinclaven, ma'am," he said. "A signature is what I require, if you please. Would you see to it that your father receives this immediately? It is rather urgent." He held out a letter.

Elizabeth could feel Yee's disapproval as she took the letter and signed her name in Mr. Lonk's receipt book.

Upstairs in her bedchamber she tossed the letter onto her bed. What a waste of everyone's time! As before, her father would throw it in the fire, and then where would she be? But Mr. Lonk, whom she now remembered from the counting house, said it was important. If so, shouldn't it be read?

Pressing a hand to her throbbing temple, Elizabeth sat down on the bed. Her father used to say that women were ill-equipped for the world of business, but this was a false-hood. Her mother had been an admirable manager of their finances. Hadn't Elizabeth demonstrated similar skill when she called on Mr. Lonk and negotiated that thirty-day extension? Could it be that the thirty days had already passed?

All at once she snatched up the letter and broke the seals. Sure enough it was a demand for payment, signed by Mr. Lonk. There would be no further Term of Extension offered. He went on to express the hope that the matter would be resolved in a timely manner without involving the services of the bailiff.

The bailiff?

Elizabeth's gaze darted to the bottom of the page. Here were written various sums, including the total amount of the loan. Aghast, she stared at the numbers. The total was staggering—over nine thousand pounds! She willed herself to stop trembling and counted out the digits.

This was impossible. It had to be!

In the end, Lady Russell's honour won out. She would not ignore her goddaughters; she would tell them the news about their father. Therefore, later that morning she presented herself at St. Peter Square and was taken up to the drawing room. The butler brought in tea and biscuits, but no one joined her. Were none of the girls ready to receive callers?

With rising impatience, Lady Russell checked the clock. She could not waste half the morning on one visit. There were things to be done! She dug in her reticule for a paper and pencil.

Anne's drawing room displayed a number of Captain Wentworth's foreign curios. There was something about them that put Lady Russell in mind of a thing she needed, but what? She rose to her feet and wandered about the room, considering each piece in turn. The Chinese chest of drawers by the window? The Turkish carpet? The Venetian mirror?

Venice—now here was an idea. Because Napoleon had recently abdicated, it was possible to travel to Venice.

And then Lady Russell remembered: *passports.* She wrote the word and underlined it twice. Did he have a passport? If so, where was it kept? Passports brought to mind foreign money. *Lira, Marks, Schillings* were added to her list.

Eventually Mary came in. She was looking very much better, and Lady Russell told her so.

"Better than what?" Mary wanted to know. She took a seat on the sofa opposite.

This peevish mood of Mary's could ruin everything, Lady Russell realized. Breaking the news about Sir Walter would be even more difficult. "I've been to see your father," she began carefully.

"How fortunate for him. Imagine, having callers when one is ill. No one comes to see me when I am ill."

"I am come to see you, Mary."

"Yes, but this morning I have something to do, so it is not at all convenient. Elizabeth and I are going to the Pump Room. Can you imagine? After weeks of living like a recluse, she now wishes to walk about in company— which is very odd, considering."

Lady Russell had no idea what this meant. She said, "I trust I will not detain you," and took another look at the clock. What was keeping Anne and Elizabeth?

"So," said Mary, "how is Father these days? Is he crabby? Elizabeth says that he is. But then, anyone would be crabby around Elizabeth."

"He is out of sorts, yes. Your father has many worries, Mary. Many difficulties. Particularly now."

"If Father is cross, I believe I won't visit him after all. Which is too bad, because I wanted to find out about Elizabeth's betrothal."

Lady Russell quickly concealed her surprise. She had forgotten all about Mr. Rushworth. "Betrothal?" she said.

Mary shrugged. "There was a notice in the *Bath Gazette* yesterday. Didn't you see it? I thought that's why you came so early."

Lady Russell's heart was hammering now. If her plan were to succeed, Mr. Rushworth's financial 'gift' must not be encouraged! What she needed most was information, and Mary was the perfect source.

"Please tell me more," she said. "It appears that I am sadly behind-hand."

Mary needed no encouragement. "Well," she said, with unbecoming eagerness, "Anne was tremendously upset when she saw the announcement. You should have heard the things she said to Elizabeth. But that's only because she was thinking of Mr. Rushworth and his awkward manners. She hasn't yet considered the advantages of the match. I think they should be married right away—so romantic! And then, once they return from their wedding trip, we can visit. London is lovely in June, I've heard."

"What I think," said Lady Russell, "is that it is unwise to contemplate marriage—any marriage—without careful consideration. Has Elizabeth chosen a date for the wedding?"

Mary sighed heavily. "Elizabeth says it is all a lie. She told Anne that she hates the very sight of Mr. Rushworth and that she won't marry him. And let me tell you," Mary added, "Captain Wentworth was not happy to hear that. He said Mr. Rushworth is the perfect husband for Elizabeth. He has pots and pots of money, so how can she go wrong? Then he said something about cats in the dark looking alike, which I thought very odd. After all, Mr. Rushworth looks nothing like a cat. He looks more like a hedgepig."

Lady Russell poured out a cup of tea and passed it to Mary. "Captain Wentworth," she said sharply, "ought to keep his opinions to himself, instead of airing them before the family. How wretched for Elizabeth to hear such things!"

"Oh, he did not say that before everyone. Only Anne."

Lady Russell blinked. "Then how did you learn of it?"

"Why I ..." A flush crept into Mary's cheeks.

Lady Russell put down her cup. "Mary, really. A gentlewoman does not listen at doors."

Mary's voice rose to a whine. "Can I help it if his voice carries so distinctly? Well anyway, Captain Wentworth is perfectly right. Everyone we know will read that announcement. Elizabeth has no choice. She must marry Mr. Rushworth."

"Not necessarily," said Lady Russell.

"At her age, who else will have her? A bird in the hand, I say. Now then, if I can contrive to have a new wardrobe made up in time, I shall be perfectly happy."

"In time for what? The wedding?"

"No, in time for our trip to London, of course. Think of it—a house on Grosvenor Square."

Lady Russell was certainly thinking!

Mary continued to talk. "It will be like spending April in Paris," she said, sighing. "I have always heard about that. Except I have never been to Paris. That brute Napoleon *would* have a war—for years and years. It is most unfair."

Lady Russell gave Mary a look. "He did not do so to inconvenience you, my dear."

"But I *long* to travel," Mary cried. "And no one takes me anywhere!"

"Foreign travel," said Lady Russell, "is uncomfortable and inconvenient. And expensive."

"Don't I know it? Oh, to have more money."

Oh, said Lady Russell silently, *to have more time!*

Nine thousand pounds. The very look of the number made Elizabeth shiver. How could even half that amount be raised? The Crofts, she knew, paid a generous sum to live at Kellynch Hall, perhaps as much as five hundred per year. How Elizabeth wished it were more! She did a little mental figuring. If her father utilized every penny of that amount toward the debt, why—

No, that could not be right. Elizabeth went hunting for a pencil. She must work the sum on paper, for the answer she'd come up with was too ghastly to be true. Eighteen. It would be eighteen long years before her father was free of this debt!

And this did not account for interest—wicked usury she'd heard the rector call it. Interest, Patrick Gill had once explained, was how a counting house earned a profit. One paid for the privilege of using someone else's money. He likened it to tenants farming on land belonging to an estate. This concept made little sense to Elizabeth then. Now it was all too clear.

And then Elizabeth remembered something else. Anne had once proposed a plan—a ridiculous, severe plan—that would have freed her father in seven years. Would that he had listened to Anne's advice! But it was useless to plan, for the Crofts were quitting Kellynch Hall. What if another tenant could not be found? What would become of her father? What would become of her?

White-faced and trembling, Elizabeth once again read through the letter. Several others had signed it in addition to Mr. Lonk. One of the signatures looked familiar. A prominent *M*. An even larger *G* and a series of looped letters ending with a *Y*.

McGillvary.

Must he be witness to this, her newest disgrace? When her father could not pay, would Admiral McGillvary keep silent? Of course not. It would be all over Bath that Sir Walter Elliot was bankrupt, hauled off by the bailiff and cast into prison. And his daughter?

Elizabeth rose to her feet and began to pace about the room. The entire amount was clearly impossible, but the quarterly payment was not out of reach. To whom could she turn for help? Not Captain Wentworth; he had made his position abundantly clear. Mr. Rushworth? Thanks to Patrick Gill's interference, there would be no help from him. The only person remaining was William Elliot—and Elizabeth would rather die than go to him! Even now she could see his sneer of refusal. But what choice did she have?

She came to a halt before the window. Here was what she needed, air! The latch was stubborn, but she persevered. At last she got the window open, drew up a chair and sat, leaning her elbows on the sill. No ideas came. There was only Mr. Elliot's mocking face and Captain Wentworth's scorn. Even if she could raise the two hundred pounds, she would have to do so again and again— every quarter—for years. By the end of it, her father would likely be dead and she would be—

Elizabeth took a shuddering breath. She would be almost fifty; the spinster sister, old and faded, supported by the pity of her family. She was being supported out of pity now!

Directly below the window was a flagged terrace. Here was an idea. Elizabeth had heard about women who ended it all by leaping from a window or a bridge. To do so was extremely stupid, for what did suicide solve? Pain, she now realized, provided motivation. Pain and panic and mortification and misery.

Idly, she considered the distance. It was certainly enough to cripple, but would it kill? There was no sense in doing a thing unless it could be done properly.

The size of the opening was another problem. If one sat on the sill—just so! —it could be managed. At best it would be difficult. But did that matter?

Sometime later Elizabeth found herself standing on the seat of the chair, gazing at the pavement below. This, then, was the end. She would fall tragically, yet gracefully, to her death.

She put one foot through the opening. Balance became difficult. With a cry, Elizabeth lost her footing and swayed. Desperately she clung to the sash. This was madness!

And then her shoe fell off.

Elizabeth watched it drop to the pavement below. "Botheration!" she cried.

Somehow, seeing the shoe on the pavement below made a world of difference. Other uncomfortable thoughts followed. How, exactly would she land? Would her skirts fly up and cover her head?

It was one thing to die elegantly, like that painting of a Grecian maiden she'd seen in a London gallery. But to die ungracefully on the pavement of a second-rate house was mortifying. As was being stuck on a window sill with her leg hanging out!

Red-faced and shaking, Elizabeth drew in her leg and climbed off the chair. The floor was smooth and strong and safe. She sank to her knees, trembling.

Within minutes the door opened. Elizabeth looked up to see Yee. In his hand was her shoe.

Silently he held it out to her. His dark eyes never left her face.

Red-faced, Elizabeth got to her feet. Either Yee had seen her absurd attempt, or he thought she'd thrown her shoe out the window in fit of pique!

And yet the man would not go. "Life," he said, "is a precious gift from God, 'who redeemeth thy life from destruction, who crowneth thee with lovingkindness and tender mercies.' We must not lose faith and hope." Yee held out a letter. This has come for you. No answer is required."

"Thank you," she said quietly. Doubtless this was Mr. Elliot's answer. She hadn't the heart to read it.

She watched Yee walk to the window, close it, and force the latch to lock. "Lady Russell and your sisters wait in the drawing room," he added.

Elizabeth hadn't the strength to conceal her dismay. Must she face Lady Russell as well? "Thank you, Mr. Yee," she whispered. "Please send Elise to me. I require assistance with my apparel."

Yee bowed and left the room. Elizabeth put Mr. Lonk's letter and Mr. Elliot's unopened note in her reticule. She would deal with those later, after the ordeal of the Pump Room—and the lecture she knew Lady Russell had come to deliver.

Mary began talking a soon as Elizabeth entered the drawing room. Without so much as a good morning, she announced, "I still say Father will make you marry him."

"And as I told you," said Elizabeth, firing up, "my marriage to Mr. Rushworth is out of the question. Indeed, it is the least of my troubles."

"Now, now," said Lady Russell. "Of course you will not marry him if you do not wish it."

Elizabeth could not believe her ears. Her godmother was never compassionate! It must be the prelude to a scolding—which was a fine bit of hypocrisy, for Lady Russell had no children. What did she know about fathers and daughters?

Lady Russell turned to Mary. "Your father is a just man. He will not force Elizabeth to marry someone who is abhorrent to her." She looked again to Elizabeth. "Good morning, my dear. You look lovely today."

Again Elizabeth was taken aback; Lady Russell did not give compliments freely. She knew she should offer one in return, but she could find nothing to say. Lady Russell was looking unusually haggard. Indeed, old age must be setting in, for the cup and saucer trembled in her hand.

Lady Russell put the teacup down and gazed at each of them in turn. "Since emotions are high over the news of this engagement—this supposed engagement"—she amended, looking to Elizabeth, "I think it is best that none of you visit your father today."

"Not visit Father?" said Anne. "Oh, but I do not agree!"

"Your father will be distressed over the fuss and gossip," she said, "and this might cause him to fall into a decline." She held up a hand as if to silence Anne's protests. "In a day or two, after things have settled a bit, you may call. Is this agreed?"

"But what if he has seen the notice in the paper?" said Anne. "Shouldn't we explain?"

"I will instruct the staff to keep the newspapers out of his reach."

Anne was not satisfied. "What if he hears of it from another source?"

"We will allow no visitors," said Lady Russell.

"Yes, Mr. Savoy will know what to do," agreed Mary. "He is a dab hand at that sort of thing."

Lady Russell turned to Mary. "I believe that we are capable of handling matters without involving Mr. Savoy. And you will kindly refrain from using cant speech, Mary. It is most unbecoming."

Naturally, Mary began to object. "If," Lady Russell went on, "you would care to write your father a note, I will gladly deliver it."

Anne rose and went immediately to the writing desk. Elizabeth remained where she was, tapping her foot and thinking. Should she send Mr. Lonk's letter in care of Lady Russell? It would serve her father right, for Lady Russell would not allow him to destroy it. On the other hand, it was wretched to allow him to be further debased in Lady Russell's eyes.

No, Elizabeth decided, as before she would see to this business herself. Even if it meant—Elizabeth stiffened—consulting Mr. Elliot.

After dropping Mary and Elizabeth at the Pump Room, Lady Russell was driven to the bailiff's house. At this point her courage nearly deserted her. How simple it would be to order the carriage to return to Rivers Street!

Not alone, she told herself firmly. She would not leave this place without Sir Walter. Still, she couldn't help smiling a little. What must Longwell have thought when she told him to lay an extra place for dinner and make ready the spare bedchamber—for a gentleman?

Sir Walter was in fine form this morning. The clothing she had sent yesterday had made an impression on the other inmates. Sir Walter's title and manners, along with the dinner he had provided, caused them to venerate him in a way Lady Russell considered unseemly.

"Really, Sir Walter," she said, after the others had withdrawn from the parlor, "you should not allow these men to call you Your Honour or Your Grace or Your Worship."

"But they mean no harm," he protested. "And it does no good to correct them; I have tried. They think me a capital fellow, and naturally they must show it by their speech. You might like to know that no one has addressed me as Your Serene Highness ... yet." Sir Walter's chin quivered; he began to giggle.

"I should hope not!" cried Lady Russell. She looked at him narrowly. Had he been drinking? Having descended into the Lower Orders, was he now consoling himself with cheap gin?

Presently Sir Walter got hold of himself. "Ah me, the enduring quality of *noblesse*," he said. "Is it not a natural phenomenon, like cream rising?"

Lady Russell did not know how to answer this. She brought out her packet of papers and opened it.

Still smiling, Sir Walter reached out to touch her sleeve. "I wonder, dear Lady Russell, if Longwell could procure another meal for this evening? *Beef en daub* or perhaps *blanquette de veau?*"

"Sir Walter, really. We have serious matters to discuss."

"But this is serious," he insisted. "I must eat. As soon as possible, in fact. I am famished."

Lady Russell selected a page from her pile. "Surely you've just had your breakfast."

He heaved a great sigh. "Breakfast was served—at the ungodly hour of eight—but alas, it was inedible."

"Was it indeed."

Sir Walter made a face. "It was porridge, Amanda. As you know, I do not eat porridge."

Lady Russell turned over a page. "Porridge is a nourishing, healthful food," she said, "enjoyed by thousands throughout the Empire every day. I am surprised at you."

"I do not eat porridge any more than I eat cabbage." Sir Walter gave a perfectly genuine shudder. "It is simply not the thing."

Lady Russell brought out a box and removed a pen and a bottle of ink. "Once we finish here, we shall see about procuring a meal."

"Excellent! If you would kindly deliver the box with today's clothing, I shall be most grateful."

"I have not brought your clothing."

"But Longwell said—"

"I know what Longwell said. After we are finished here, you may choose for yourself what to wear." Lady Russell leaned forward to deliver her point. "We shall now discuss how you are to leave this place."

He smiled. "Why, in your carriage, of course."

"Yes," she said. "But first we must satisfy the legal obligations."

Sir Walter's fingertips danced on the tabletop. "You've brought the two hundred fifty pounds?"

The eager note in his voice was matched by the brightness of his eyes. This was rather startling. "Yes," Lady Russell said slowly. "I have the money with me."

"May I, er, have it, please?"

"In a moment. First we must review the events which have brought you to this unfortunate juncture."

"Mr. Savoy's charges," he said promptly, "and various tradesmen's bills. Yes, yes, we know all that."

Lady Russell drew a long breath. "You have other outstanding obligations, have you not? In addition to the two hundred fifty pounds? May I have the sum of them, please?"

Sir Walter's gaze shifted to the floor. He scratched his head and then studied the ceiling and sighed some more—all without producing a total.

Lady Russell got down to business. "The bailiff tells me that there is a second warrant for your arrest that will be issued shortly. It would be helpful to know what that amount is now, so that we may make arrangements to pay it. Otherwise, if you are going to be arrested again, I have a better use for my money."

"I ... er ... why ... I ..."

It was painful to see him flounder, but this was the best way to drive home her point. At last she said, more gently, "You do not know the amount of your indebtedness, do you?"

Sir Walter's gaze remained focused on the tabletop.

Lady Russell steepled her fingertips. "What you want, Sir Walter, is a manager."

He looked up.

"Not a solicitor like John Shepherd," she said. "That will never do. You have proven that it is too difficult for a gentleman of your rank to submit to a lesser man. No, you need a real manager—like the arrangement you had with dear Elizabeth."

Sir Walter wrinkled his nose. "I don't see what Elizabeth has to do with anything," he objected. "She is set to marry Rushworth, and—" He sucked in his breath. "The express, Lady Russell! Did you send the request to Rushworth?"

"I did not. And it is a very good thing, for Elizabeth refuses to marry him."

Sir Walter's face paled. "What?" he whispered.

"But we digress. I was speaking of Elizabeth your wife, not Elizabeth your daughter. You lived very nicely under dear Lady Elliot's management. You did not overspend your income then."

"But it was not nearly so amus—"

"No," she interrupted. "I imagine not. And yet you lived as a gentleman." Lady Russell put up her chin. "Walter Elliot," she announced, "what you need is a wife."

"A ... wife?" When at last he spoke, his voice squeaked. "What odd notions you have, my dear. I cannot think of anyone whom I ..."

He laughed a little. "I mean, what woman—of proper birth and independence—would wish to undertake such a thing? No, Lady Russell, you put it out of your head. I appreciate your concern, but no."

"I am one such person," she told him. "And I am willing to pay your debts, provided you agree to certain conditions."

Sir Walter's eyes grew even rounder. "Eh, well now, Lady Russell," he said, tugging at his collar. "While yours is a most unusual idea, we needn't be hasty. A wise man takes time to consider his options. Plenty of time. The more time, the better."

Lady Russell was rather hurt by this response. Her fingers ruffled the banknotes. "Forgive me, Sir Walter," she said, "but *time* is the very thing we do not have. When that second warrant is issued, you will need to come up with the money to pay it."

Sir Walter's breathing became laboured. He pulled out a handkerchief and blotted his brow.

"The choice is yours to make. You may leave this place now, with me, and tomorrow travel to London to be married. Or you may remain here and wait for the second warrant."

"Surely it is not as bad as all that," he squeaked. "You say Elizabeth does not wish to marry Rushworth? But Wentworth! Have you consulted Wentworth? Perhaps he can assist me!"

"Captain Wentworth knows nothing about this, nor do your daughters. No one knows about this but me. By the bye," she added, "would you happen to know where your passport is kept?"

Sir Walter was thunderstruck. "My passport?"

Lady Russell ran the tips of her fingers along the bank-notes. "I was thinking that we could have a lovely wedding trip abroad. I believe Venice is especially nice at this time of year." Her eyes met his. "We shall leave England as soon as we are married. And later, once things have calmed down, we shall enquire about settling your debts."

"But—my things! I have only the clothes on my back! I am in no condition to travel."

"I expect we can do a little shopping once we reach London."

Sir Walter blinked. "Shopping?"

Lady Russell preserved an innocent face. "After all, our ship might not depart for several days. Perhaps we shall attend the theatre as well."

Color returned to Sir Walter's cheeks. "The theatre?"

Heartened, Lady Russell enlarged upon this theme. "We might, with luck, be invited to various dinners and parties. You do realize that I am not unconnected with the London social set."

She uncorked the bottle of ink. "My solicitor drew up documents relating to the settlement of my fortune and such. I daresay you won't mind signing them."

Smiling, Lady Russell held out the pen.

13 At One Fell Swoop

Elizabeth gazed at the entrance to the Pump Room with a sinking heart. The Ionic columns on either side of the door seemed enormous. She knew all too well how she would be received and what people would say.

Mary, on the other hand, tripped across the wide marble step eagerly. Once inside she let out a sigh of admiration. "The Pump Room cannot compare with Kellynch Hall, can it," she said, too loudly for Elizabeth's taste. "Those chandeliers, for instance, are notably inferior."

Elizabeth looked the other way. Mary would make outlandish statements today, when her reputation hung by a thread! She nodded politely to the prim and smiling Master of Ceremonies and walked past Mary into the main room.

"Elizabeth," Mary called, "do these windows not put you in mind of the Great House at Uppercross?"

It was all Elizabeth could do not to roll her eyes. The Great House was a rambling country house, built without regard to architectural plan. It had none of the graceful, classical elements that characterized this building.

But today Elizabeth was determined to be pleasant. "Shall we take the water?" she said. She loathed even the smell of it, but her sister needed occupation. Although Mary was noisy and had poor taste, she was better than no one. Several ladies had already turned away; there was much whispering behind gloved hands.

Then Mary gave a little cry. Elizabeth turned to see a young woman coming toward them with hands outstretched. Behind her was a tall man who looked vaguely familiar. "Mrs. Wallis," cried Mary. "How lovely to see you."

Elizabeth's heart gave a bump. Colonel and Mrs. Wallis were particular friends of William Elliot's; it was no accident that they were here. Sure enough, Colonel Wallis stepped aside to allow another to join their conversation.

"Hello, Cousin," William Elliot murmured. "You are late. Thirty minutes late, to be precise."

"I apologize," Elizabeth said stiffly. "I was detained." Her cheeks were hot. This was a bad beginning.

"You have your reasons, I am sure," he said smoothly.

She decided to explain. "Lady Russell read us a lecture on the state of Father's health. She thinks he is heading for a decline."

"Lecturing is Lady Russell's specialty. Your guilt is absolved. And what is your opinion?"

"Of Father's condition? I wish I knew. Lady Russell has told us not to call. She claims a visit would upset him."

A knowing look came into William Elliot's eyes. "Ah," he said. "No doubt referring to the notice in the paper and all the gossip. Is what I hear true? Have you indeed broken the engagement?"

"There was no engagement," Elizabeth cried. "As well you know!"

"Elizabeth, hush." He lowered his voice. "Our every move is being watched. You should not give more fodder than you—"

"—than I already have? I thank you, Cousin, for your support! I was never engaged to James Rushworth. I told you that myself; weren't you listening?"

"But his mother seems to think you were. She is spreading stories all over Bath."

"His mother may go to the devil for all I care!"

A flicker of surprise shot through Mr. Elliot's eyes. "My sentiments exactly," he said. "But alas, I fear they" —he rolled his eyes toward the row of matrons sitting together near one of the windows— "do not agree. Nor does your father."

Elizabeth's chin came up. "I do not care what my father thinks."

"That is patently obvious." Mr. Elliot's expression changed somewhat. "He was very eager to have you marry Rushworth."

"I shall marry whom I choose!" flared Elizabeth. "It is not for him to dictate what I do."

"I quite agree." Mr. Elliot offered his arm. "Shall we stroll for a bit?"

No sooner had she placed her hand on Mr. Elliot's arm than Mary came rushing up. "Elizabeth," she cried. "The most delightful thing! Mrs. Wallis has invited me to join her for shopping and lunch. She will see me home, so you needn't worry about arranging anything for me."

Mrs. Wallis came up from behind. "You are most welcome to join us, Miss Elliot," she said politely.

But this Elizabeth firmly refused. Colonel and Mrs. Wallis departed immediately with Mary, which to Elizabeth's mind was a bit too convenient. Her cousin had invited her here for a reason. Well, she had accepted for a reason of her own. From beneath lowered lashes she studied him. How did one ask a man for over nine thousand pounds?

"Elizabeth," he said, smiling faintly, "you must know that your father only wishes to see you comfortable and happy."

His words were like the flick of a whip. "Comfortable and happy?" she cried. "I am anything but! Father is ill, our home is let to others, and according to you, my reputation is ruined."

And I owe an impossible amount of money!

"But you have not considered. There is another way." His smile reappeared—the cat-like smile that Elizabeth distrusted—and he covered her gloved hand with one of his. "The fondest wish of your father, in point of fact."

His voice was smooth—too smooth! What was he up to?

She turned to face him fully. "Of what are you speaking, Mr. Elliot?"

"Why, of marriage, my dear." He gave her hand an affectionate squeeze.

Her eyes narrowed. "Whose marriage?"

William Elliot's smile grew coy. "Why, ours," he murmured.

But—he was playing right into her hands! This was too easy! What was he about?

Elizabeth pulled her hand from his arm. "As always, Cousin," she said, "you will have your little joke."

"I am perfectly serious."

"I rather doubt that." Elizabeth left him and walked over to the fountain. She dug a coin from her reticule and accepted the glass. She could feel Mr. Elliot's gaze as she took a sip of the warm water. What calculating eyes he had!

"It is quite revolting, isn't it?" he said, coming up to her. "But I thought you knew that."

Elizabeth frowned at the contents of the glass. "Men drink gin without complaint." Casting a scornful glance, she tipped back the glass and drained it.

"Now what," he said, "would you know about gin?"

"I do read! I am not stupid, Mr. Elliot."

"What you are," he said drily, "is stubborn! An alliance between us would be a very good thing."

Elizabeth put down the glass. "I fail to comprehend why we are speaking of this in a public place."

He spread his hands. "But what else am I to do? I am unwelcome in your sister's home, and propriety forbids us from meeting elsewhere. How else am I to see you alone?"

Elizabeth looked at him sideways. Here was an answer to her painful situation, but how thoroughly disagreeable it was! "I have no desire to be married out of pity," she said frankly. "Or, utility!"

Again she saw his eyes widen. His pleasant smile twisted. "Maidenly reluctance," he said sharply, "does not become you, my dear! I have gallantly offered to rescue you from public scorn and ridicule and this is the thanks I receive? I am the man who holds the key to your happiness!"

Elizabeth's throat constricted. There was only one man who held happiness—and he was not William Elliot! But for all his disarming charm and wit, dear Patrick could not help her now.

Again she eyed William Elliot. Would this man, who had married his first wife solely for her money, agree to advance such a large sum? She doubted it.

Apparently her distress was evident, for he cried, "Forgive me," and recaptured her hand. "How can I make you understand? With us, dear Elizabeth, it's destiny!"

"Destiny," she repeated woodenly. His words were impulsive and even romantic, but his eyes were so cold! Elizabeth looked the other way.

"Well?" he said. "What is to be your answer?"

But Elizabeth was no longer attending, for she had seen a face in the crowd. As if aware of her gaze, the woman turned. "Elizabeth?" she called out. "Elizabeth Elliot?" To Elizabeth's surprise, she was smiling.

"Miss Bingley!" said Elizabeth. "Hello!"

Since leaving the bailiff's, a transformation had taken place. The lines that worry and illness had etched on Sir Walter's handsome face were smoothed away. He gazed out of the window of Lady Elliot's carriage with obvious delight. They were very near their destination.

"I had quite forgotten about your little house, Amanda," he said. "Rivers Street is a charming situation—a most charming situation."

The carriage came to a stop, but Lady Russell did not appear to notice. "I cannot understand it," she said, frowning. "The bailiff was so insistent about knowing your address. I cannot like that."

Sir Walter smiled slyly. "Was I not clever to give him Anne's?"

"But you were seen to be leaving with *me*. When that second warrant is issued, the bailiff will come here." Outside, Lady Russell's coachman let down the steps and attempted to open the door, but she held it closed. Then she pulled down the window blind.

"Sir Walter," she said urgently. "You will not be well-hidden here."

"But you said—"

"I know what I said, but my friend, you are not *safe!* I fear we must leave Somerset earlier than planned. In fact, we ought to leave tonight."

"Tonight?" he squeaked. "That will never do." He looked about anxiously. "Surely your coachman must have time to prepare. After all, one must travel properly. I was hoping," he added, "to have my crest painted over Sir Henry Russell's before our departure."

Lady Russell's fingers dug into his arm. "Don't you understand?" she cried. "We daren't use this vehicle! We must travel to London *secretly!*"

Sir Walter considered this. "Do you mean ... in disguise?"

She waved aside his boyish grin. "We must travel on the Mail. Longwell will know how to manage it."

Sir Walter clapped his hands. "I say, that's famous! I've always fancied to travel in disguise!" His smile became cunning. "I'll go dressed as a highwayman."

"A tradesman would be best," corrected Lady Russell. "Or a common labourer."

Both eyebrows went up. "Common?" Sir Walter scoffed. "Me? Impossible!"

Miss Bingley came rushing forward with decided friendliness. Elizabeth went weak with relief, for here was an end to the tête à tête.

William Elliot was looking narrowly at her. "Well?" he said.

Elizabeth feigned surprise. "But—were you expecting an answer today, Mr. Elliot?"

"Eliza," cried Caroline, bursting in. "My dear!"

Elizabeth was forced to present her cousin, who would not go. She could not resist adding, "Mr. Elliot is my father's heir."

"Is that so?" Caroline gave him a wide smile and launched directly into the story of her journey to Bath. Elizabeth listened with rapt attention, aware of Mr. Elliot's growing impatience. After some minutes of this, he politely excused himself—giving Elizabeth a whispered order to meet him here tomorrow. She did not reply.

At once Caroline caught hold of her arm. "Your cousin is very fine, Eliza. I wonder that we have not met before! And he is to inherit your family's estate?"

She paused, thinking. "Dear me, what is the name of it? You've mentioned it often enough."

"Kellynch Hall."

"Ah, yes. Kellynch. A quaint old place, I am sure. Your cousin must be very proud of it."

Now it was Elizabeth's turn to hesitate. She did not wish to reveal the details of the retrenchment to Caroline Bingley! "I believe," she said carefully, "that Mr. Elliot resides in London."

Caroline gave a little laugh. "A country estate is just the thing for a gentleman. How odd that your cousin does not agree. Or perhaps it is his wife who does not agree?"

"His wife is deceased. He has just come out of mourning."

A glint came into Caroline's eye.

"Kellynch is an isolated spot," Elizabeth hurried to say. "A man of the world, such as my cousin, would have little desire to bury himself there."

"A man of the world," Caroline echoed. She beckoned to a woman, who immediately came to join them.

"I have met such a pleasant gentleman, Louisa," Caroline confided, speaking very low. "He is Miss Elliot's cousin, the future Sir William." Elizabeth saw her dig an elbow in her sister's side. "Can you imagine? He is a widower."

Mrs. Hurst's painted brows went up. "Unmarried? How intriguing."

"Mr. Elliot is no paragon," Elizabeth put in. "He is rather too fond of his own opinions."

Mrs. Hurst turned to Elizabeth with smiling eyes. "How refreshing to meet a gentleman who is not a fortune hunter! We have had our fill of those lately.

"My cousin is many things," replied Elizabeth, "but he is *no longer* a fortune hunter."

But this bit of irony was lost on Mrs. Hurst and Miss Bingley. They pressed Elizabeth to join them, and when she refused they insisted on learning her address so that they could call.

Elizabeth wrote the address on one of her calling cards, using a pencil supplied by Miss Bingley. "My father is convalescing, so we have given up our house for the time being," she explained as she wrote. "He is planning to return to the country at summer's end."

"To Kellynch Hall?" said Caroline. "Or might he be persuaded to take another residence if Mr. Elliot should decide to live there?" She exchanged a teasing smile with her sister.

Elizabeth took in the exchange. What new horror was this? Was Caroline Bingley setting her cap at William Elliot? Even in jest it was a dreadful thought!

Lady Russell peered into the stairway below. "Sir Walter," she called, "please! Your trunks are here. We haven't time to dawdle." He did not answer, and she gave an exasperated huff. The man was impossible. "Sir Walter," she called again.

"Coming, my dear" he sang out, and he began to mount the stairs. "Truly, my dear, your house is a marvel. So well preserved. Such taste in its design."

He came level with her, still talking. "So often these little houses are scruffy and worn down." He wrinkled his nose. "The result of scores of lodgers, no doubt."

"I'll have you know that there have been no lodgers here. Sir Henry's aunt was the only occupant."

Sir Walter nodded. "That would explain the scheme of decoration. Charming, but outdated." He shook his head. "A small house has no scope for the imagination."

Lady Russell had her own ideas about scope and imagination, but she kept them to herself. She pointed. "Your trunks are in the spare bedchamber. Choose what you need, and remember," she called after him, "only your oldest, plainest clothes. We do not wish to attract attention."

She came into her own room and sank into a chair. What a business this was! Did the man understand nothing about the need for haste? She heard a soft knocking. "Come," she called.

It was Sir Walter. "I beg your pardon," he said, "but the bell cord in my chamber is not functioning. I wish to summon your manservant."

Lady Russell swallowed her irritation. "I do not keep a manservant," she explained, "except for Longwell, and he is seeing to our tickets for the Mail."

Sir Walter looked so pained that Lady Russell unbent a little. "I am very sorry," she said more gently. "You will need to handle your own packing."

"But what about my bath? You promised me a bath."

It had been many years since Lady Russell had lived with a man. She had forgotten how trying they could be. "When Longwell returns," she said, "he will see to your bath—but only if there is time. In the meantime, kindly attend to your packing."

He went ambling away. Lady Russell gave a sharp sigh. "For heaven's sake," she muttered after him, "do something useful."

Immediately there was a scratching at her door. "Come," she said wearily.

Sir Walter put his head in. "I beg your pardon, my dear," he said. "I did not catch that last."

Lady Russell strode to the bell cord. "Would you like a glass of Madeira, Sir Walter? I'll have Ellen bring it directly."

"Why, a little sherry would be lovely, thank you. I have had a most exhausting morning." With these words he withdrew.

Presently Ellen came, and before she went down for Sir Walter's sherry, she helped Lady Russell into her travelling dress. Amanda Russell surveyed her reflection unhappily. Disguise or no, Sir Walter was a stickler where women were concerned. It would never do for his affianced wife to appear haggish.

Sometime later Ellen came back to say that Longwell had returned. The next sound Lady Russell heard was not her butler's steady tread but another tentative knock. She turned to face the door, hands on hips. "Come," she said sharply.

"I do not wish to trouble you," Sir Walter said, "however—"

"Botheration!" cried Lady Russell. "What *now?*"

Elizabeth's spirits rejoiced. She had been in the Pump Room for close to an hour, and yet she had never been alone. As she left the building and stepped into the street, she met Lord Atherton, an old friend of her father's. The man greeted her with marked affability before he passed on. She could only hope that many observed the exchange.

Watching eyes were everywhere. Elizabeth was mindful to keep her posture erect and her pace serene as she strolled through the Abbey Courtyard. All that remained was to occupy the time until her appointment with Patrick Gill at two o'clock. Normally she would have spent time in the shops, examining goods she could no longer afford to purchase, but she had been on her feet all morning. She searched the Abbey Courtyard for a vacant bench.

"Miss Elliot?"

She turned, shading her eyes against the sun's glare. Here was an unexpected surprise. "Mr.—Shepherd?" she enquired. "How do you do?"

He bowed. "I do not like to intrude upon your reverie, but this matter is of some urgency. Have you seen William Elliot?"

"He was in the Pump Room earlier. I do not know where he is now."

Mr. Shepherd's lips compressed. "He was traced to the Pump Room this morning. I was not quick enough!"

"Is there a problem?"

Mr. Shepherd consulted his timepiece. "A matter of business compels me to find him immediately. Does he call upon you at St. Peter Square?"

Elizabeth was reluctant to answer. "He does not," she said. "We—my sisters and I—have had a falling out with him." She studied his face. "Have you seen Father recently? I have only Lady Russell's reports about him, which seem dramatic and mawkish. What is your opinion of his condition?"

"I cannot say. I am no longer in your father's employ, Miss Elliot."

Elizabeth could only stare. "I know he has been grouchy, but I had no idea he was as bad as that. I shall speak to him on your behalf. He needs you."

"Indeed he does," said Mr. Shepherd "but you do not apprehend the matter correctly. It is I who do not need him."

He stalked off, leaving Elizabeth alone with her thoughts. Certainly Mr. Shepherd knew about the amount of money her father owed. Why was he so eager to find Mr. Elliot?

She could sit no longer; she must walk. Presently she found herself pulling open the thick oaken door at the entrance to the Abbey. From within rolled a darkened, comforting hush.

And then Elizabeth heard her name. A man came toward her across the bright courtyard. He was fashionably dressed, and she could see the gleam of his smile.

"How delightful," he called. "I was hoping to speak to you today. A rather important day for you, is it not?"

Elizabeth let go of the Abbey door; it swung closed with a whoosh. "Sir Henry," she said. "How do you do?"

Lady Russell's unusual request troubled Anne all morning. What possible harm could there be in calling on her father? Frederick was not at home to advise her—and she knew what he would say. In the end Anne decided to go anyway, if only to test the No Visitors Allowed stricture.

She came through the gate at The Citadel, pausing to secure the latch behind her. The walled garden was peaceful; the trees cast dappled shadows on the small lawn. The tranquility was at variance with the agitation in her heart.

What would she find when she spoke with her father? Surely he must know about Elizabeth. Gossip was the sort of thing he delighted in. Of course he would know.

The vestibule was deserted. This did not trouble her; she had often found it so. She knew the way to her father's rooms—and perhaps it would be better to arrive without an attendant. She trod the long expanse of hallway. One look at her father's face would be enough.

Oddly enough, his door was open. Anne could hear voices within—men's voices. This could not be right. Her father did not entertain guests with the door open! Next she heard whistling, and then there was a bang—as if something had been dropped—and a burst of laughter.

Yes, this was the correct hallway; these were her father's rooms. She glanced at the nameplate beside the door—but what was this? The card bearing Sir Walter's name was no longer there.

Anne hurried inside. His sitting room was bare—his things were gone! Workmen in spattered smocks were painting the walls and the woodwork. They gazed at her with open curiosity.

"My father," she cried. "What have you done with my father?"

At last Mr. Crooks and Mr. Pinner took their leave. The library door closed with a comfortable click. Patrick McGillvary leaned forward in his seat behind a wide mahogany desk. His fingers found and rubbed at a sore spot on his left shoulder. Old Crooks and Pinner were good men, but devoid of imagination. They had served his late father well; their loyalty to his family was unquestioned.

McGillvary lifted tired eyes to survey the interior of the library. It had been his father's, as had the house and everything else. While some aspects of a land-bound life were wearing, being master of Belsom was not one of them.

He had not slept well the night before, and it had been a long morning. McGillvary closed his eyes, until he heard the door open. Mr. Starkweather came in with something in his hand. He hesitated, his hand on the doorknob.

"Come in," said McGillvary. "It's been a busy day, I take it."

"It has, Admiral. This came just now. I did not wish to disturb, as you were occupied with the books." Starkweather held out a packet—a letter.

McGillvary took it. "Not from Whitehall," he said, breaking the seals, "but sent, I see, by express. A matter of some urgency." He looked up. "Ten to one it's Ronan asking for money. By express."

Starkweather said nothing as McGillvary spread the single sheet. "Yes," he went on bitterly. "Ronan. What the devil ails the fellow, that he should write in this affected scrawl?" He read only the salutation and part of the first sentence. "No, my dear Ronan," he said, tearing the letter in half, "you must make do with your quarterly allowance."

"I take it there will be no reply, sir?"

"There will be no reply. Let him come to beg on bended knee."

Starkweather withdrew, and McGillvary was left to his thoughts. His half-brother was a scoundrel and worse. What was most galling was that Belsom Park itself would one day pass to Ronan. McGillvary made a mental note to wear his sword while at home the coming week. It would never do to miss an opportunity!

His eyes travelled to the clock, for he had an appointment at two. The thought of Elizabeth smoothed the sharp expression from his face. He reached for the newspaper Starkweather had brought and turned to the society pages. There was the retraction, printed exactly as he had dictated, word-for-word. "That's that," he said, folding the paper.

Anne let herself out of the front gate of The Citadel, allowing it to clang shut behind her. Hateful place! No one knew where her father was—and no one seemed to care! Her father's physician was nowhere to be found. The man in the office informed her that Sir Walter Elliot was no longer a resident. He had no information about where he had gone.

And so Anne was left to fret and worry while she waited for the chairmen to return. She pictured her father ill, helpless, and alone. The longer she waited, the less she was convinced that this was true. Her father was seldom at a loss. He might act the part of the victim, but only when it suited his purposes.

"But perhaps," she whispered, "not this time?"

Where could he be? He had hinted about coming to live with them on St. Peter Square—quite broadly—and yet in his time of need he had not come. Anne could think of only one other person to whom he would turn: Lady Russell. So it was to Lady Russell that Anne intended to go—if only the sedan chair would come!

"You ought to get away from here," Sir Henry said softly. "You have suffered long enough. It will only grow worse if you remain." He raised a gloved hand, as if to ward off her surprise. "I mean no criticism of your performance in the Pump Room just now. You made a brave show of it. I commend you! But it will not answer."

Elizabeth did not know what to make of this remark. She was tired and hungry and she wished Sir Henry would go away.

But he did not appear to be in any hurry to leave her. He indicated the Abbey door. "As for going to church to pray—a bit too obvious, Miss Elliot. The maudlin does not become you. You are better off attending a gay event—a ball, for instance." He smiled. "I understand you attend Mrs. Buxford-Heighton's gala."

"Yes," said Elizabeth. "With my godmother."

"Excellent, my dear. Nevertheless, I cannot hide from you the fact that your sufferings in Bath have only just begun. Shall we walk a little?"

Sir Henry offered his arm, and Elizabeth took it reluctantly.

"I must say," he went on, "you have made quite an enemy in Mrs. Rushworth."

"You mean Mrs. Leight—" Elizabeth caught herself. She had spoken without thinking. She shot a look at Sir Henry.

His eyes glittered in a way that made her squirm. "Ah," he said softly. "Perceptive girl!"

"I beg your pardon, Sir Henry," she said quickly. "Mrs. Leighton is a friend of yours. I had no right to—"

He cut her apology short. "She is a most formidable opponent."

Elizabeth did not like his smile, and she did not like his eyes. He too was a dangerous opponent.

"Yours is a complex situation, is it not?" he went on. "Such a pity, your father's predicament." Sir Henry shook his head. "Run off his legs, by all reports. I, for one, shall miss him."

Elizabeth did not trust herself to speak.

Sir Henry did not appear to notice her discomfort. "You are well rid of Rushworth, by the bye. It was a sporting attempt, my dear, but no." His face screwed into a grimace. "If a beautiful woman must offer herself, she should at least choose a man who is passably attractive."

He caught her eye and winked broadly. "Which the young Rushworth certainly is not, eh?"

"Sir Henry!"

"Now my dear Miss Elliot, there is no need to get in a huff because I speak plainly. It is one of my finer qualities, in fact." He came nearer. "I only wish to offer a little friendly advice. You've no objection to that, surely."

Elizabeth longed to withdraw her hand from his sleeve. What did she want with his advice? And yet she could hardly tell him so!

"As I was saying, what you need is a change of scene, my sweet." His voice dropped to a whisper. "Have you such a refuge?"

Sir Henry did not give Elizabeth a chance to respond. "Your sister, let me see. The short, brown one, married to the up-and-coming squire? Perhaps she has a place for you until winter is past."

"Winter?" said Elizabeth. "I would never stay away as long as that. If I went away at all ..."

Sir Henry gave her a look of mild reproof. "To return sooner would be fatal."

Elizabeth could feel a flush rise to her cheeks. She would never go to Mary's home. Uppercross Cottage was so small; there was barely room for a guest. And besides, Mary was in Bath. Elizabeth stole a look at Sir Henry. She suspected that he knew this.

"Ah well," he said. "The husband is not yet squire; perhaps it would be awkward. You have another sister, if I am not mistaken, with whom you now are living? But since she resides in Bath, she can be of no use to you. There is your worthy godmother, who also lives in Bath." Sir Henry shrugged. "A pity, that."

Elizabeth found her voice. "You are too kind, sir, to concern yourself on my account. I have no relations outside Somerset upon whom I might impose. I shall weather the storm as best I can. I daresay the gossips will find someone new to discuss."

Sir Henry looked alarmed. "But my dear Miss Elizabeth, you have not considered your situation! It is precarious in the extreme!"

Elizabeth's eyes followed a crack in the pavement. "You are too kind," she murmured.

"Nonsense," he replied.

She ventured to glance at him then; a small smile was hovering on his lips. "Truth to tell, Miss Elliot," he confessed, "It so happens that I have a place of refuge to offer." The yellow flecks in his hazel eyes were now especially bright. "Have you ever seen the Mediterranean, my sweet?"

14 THIS BE WAR!

Church Street was narrow and the buildings on either side of it were tall, and yet there were so many passersby. Sir Henry Farley was well-known; Elizabeth dared not cause a scene by tearing herself from his grasp. But how could she escape?

Meanwhile his voice—so quiet and yet so penetrating! —droned on. He must now describe to her in detail her own beauties: the luscious curve of her neck; the shine of her luxuriant hair (which he knew was waiting to be released from its bonds); the hidden deliciousness of her figure. To hear such things made Elizabeth's flesh crawl.

Surely she was imagining this! Sir Henry Farley was her father's friend. How dare he say such things to her!

"What I like most in you," he was now saying, "is your independence, my sweet. You are your own woman. You are not bound by social conventions or by the opinions of others."

"That is not true," she said.

He merely laughed. "My sweet, your modesty is charming! But dissembling is unnecessary with me! For I have seen you with him myself."

Elizabeth's head came up. What had Sir Henry seen?

The man's eyes were bright and mocking. "The fellow in the brown coat," he said, smiling. "One of your many conquests, no doubt."

"I have no idea of whom you are speaking," she said, with a confidence she did not feel. "Bath is filled with men in brown coats."

"But this was a most unusual fellow. You needn't fret; I don't object to a woman having adventures prior to entering my protection. Experience gives a certain spice to life, does it not?"

He lowered his voice. "I do not know him, of course, but I do remember this: his coat had patches on the elbows."

Elizabeth gasped—she could not help it. He had seen her with Patrick Gill.

Sir Henry chuckled at her blushes. He laid his gloved hand over hers and gave it a squeeze. "Charming," he said. "Absolutely charming. His was the admiration due a truly desirable woman. I salute you."

Elizabeth fought to maintain composure. If he had seen her with Mr. Gill, what else had he seen? How much did he know? And when she refused his offer, as surely she must, what would he do?

"You were made for Paris, the eternal city of lovers," he murmured. "In my younger days, that is just where I would have taken you, to my *pied-à-terre* in Paris." He pressed more closely against her. "As you know, these arrangements are understood in Paris."

Bile rose in Elizabeth's throat. She willed it down and kept walking. She lifted her gaze to the Abby. Angels were carved into the walls, angels ascending a ladder to heaven. Elizabeth longed to climb with them—away from Sir Henry's abhorrent whispers!

To reach the Abbey door was now her object. Surely he would not accost her in church!

"My sweet," he lamented, "you have not been attending." He smiled widely, revealing a set of even, stained teeth that once must have been quite fine. "You have not yet given your answer."

"You are too kind, Sir Henry," she managed to bleat. Even now, she knew she should not offend him!

"Ah, but I long to be kinder still."

Hating herself, Elizabeth said, "Must I give an answer right away?"

He gave a sharp sigh. "Do not keep me in suspense, my sweet. For having aroused my interest, I shall not be kept waiting." He lowered his voice further. "The sap must come out of the tree, you know."

This cryptic answer caused Elizabeth's stomach to convulse. "I-I shall think about it," she whispered. She removed her hand from his sleeve and reached for the Abbey door.

"Off to pray, are you?" His mockery was unmistakable. "Perhaps, my sweet, I shall be the answer to your prayers, eh?"

Summoning the last bit of courage, Elizabeth managed to arch an eyebrow. "Perhaps," she said, and pulled open the heavy door.

Her feet stumbled as she made her way into the narthex. She pressed a hand over her mouth—she must not cry out! A sob was stifled in her throat, but it would not be suppressed for long.

She searched for a pew in a dark corner, but there were none. White light came pouring in through the tall clerestory windows; it seemed to fill the Abbey. Where could she hide? Everywhere were watching eyes, pressing at her, accusing her.

She crossed to the side aisle. The pews ended at the wall; she chose one, followed it, and sank onto the bench. Against her shoulder the massive granite was solid, substantial. She bit back a sob and cradled her head in her hands.

"Oh God," her dry lips whispered. "Oh God."

McGillvary came into the Abbey courtyard whistling; he rounded the corner and caught sight of the hanging sign outside Bailey's. It was a glorious day—the sky was bright, the sun was shining, and he was in England. Best of all, he was set to meet his Elizabeth.

"My Elizabeth." He repeated her name aloud, simply for the joy of it.

McGillvary slapped his thigh with the newspaper and grinned. Nothing could be better! For today he would rid himself of the hateful masquerade. He would show Eliza-

beth the retraction, they would exult together in her ex-
oneration, and she would ask how he had done it. For the
retraction was complete, just as he intended it should be.

And then he would modestly confess all. Not, perhaps,
how much the retraction had cost him, but enough so that
she would understand. Naturally, she would fly into a rage
when she learned his true identity. But after the storm
she would forgive.

McGillvary smiled again—a singularly foolish smile
that he was powerless to stop. The forgiveness of his Elizabeth would be delightful.

He checked his timepiece. He was early, as he'd intended to be. The place was crowded, usual for this time
of day, but a glance at the proprietor told him that he
had received McGillvary's instructions. The man nodded
his head at the curtained door. All was in readiness.

Elizabeth was early. She sat at a table by the window,
alone and very erect. Her bare hands were clasped before
her on the white tablecloth; under the brim of her hat,
her face was still. McGillvary stepped aside to have a
word with the serving girl, and he watched as she delivered the message. Elizabeth rose obediently, went to the
curtained door, and passed through.

Within moments, he joined her. "My dear," he said,
smiling broadly, "we've done it!" He slapped the morning
paper onto the tabletop. "We've led the old weevil-box on
a merry chase, and we've clipped her wings!"

Elizabeth stared at him.

He'd been too rash, to throw it at her like that. McGillvary began again. "We've hit her square, my dear! Mrs.

Rushworth, I mean." He gave the *Bath Gazette* to her. "Read this."

She gazed at the page. "What does it mean?" she whispered.

"Victory, my dear! It's as good as in our hands. Mrs. Rushworth has been routed." He took a teacup and saucer from the trolley and placed them. "This calls for drinks all round. On the house."

Elizabeth said nothing. McGillvary took hold of the teapot and gallantly filled both cups. He slid into his chair and watched her take hold of the saucer. The smile left his face. "Your fingers," he said. "They're bruised."

She gave him a quick look—a frightened look? —and hid them from sight. "They are fine."

"You've hurt your hands. Let me see them."

Being occupied with closing an over-stuffed travelling bag, Lady Russell was in no mood for talk. "Longwell, I am surprised at you," she said. "I am not at home to visitors. I do not care if it is the Emperor of China come to call, I am not here!"

"Very good, milady." Longwell took the buckle from her, gave the sides of the leather bag a mighty shove with his knee, and fastened it.

"Thank you." Lady Russell turned her attention to her hat. "The hired chaise is out front, is it not?"

"It will be momentarily, milady."

"Sir Walter—is he ready?" She began to draw on her gloves.

Longwell grunted assent. "I believe I have, at last, arranged the baronet's cravat to his satisfaction, ma'am. At present he is occupied in packing another bag."

"Another? Is he mad? If we are to board the Mail, we must depart at once!"

"Yes, milady." Longwell took up the traveling bag and two bandboxes. "I shall inform Mrs. Wentworth that you are not at home. Or you may do so as you pass the parlour door."

Lady Russell wheeled. "Do you mean to tell me that Anne is in this house?"

"In the front parlour, ma'am. She insists on waiting." He pulled open the door, but awkwardly because of the bandboxes.

"Longwell, stop!" she ordered. "I must think." She struck her hands together. "Blast it all, the chaise will be in full view."

"I take it your ladyship does not wish to be seen by Mrs. Wentworth. Shall I close the draperies?"

"No ... yes! I ... do not know!" Lady Russell frowned at the carpet. "We ought to leave by the service door," she said at last.

"Might I suggest the back stairs," Longwell offered, "in order to escape detection."

"Very well. You'd best put the luggage into the chaise first. We shall await your signal."

"What shall I tell Mrs. Wentworth?"

"Serve her tea. And Longwell, seat her near the fire, away from the windows."

"I shall do my best, ma'am."

Lady Russell began to warm to the plan. "Tell her I shall be down directly—which is quite true, Longwell, you needn't make that face! After we are gone you may tell her that you were mistaken, that I have gone out without your knowledge."

Longwell adjusted his grip on the bandboxes; his gaze never wavered. "What if Mrs. Wentworth desires to wait?"

"Then she may do so, by all means." Lady Russell gave her bedchamber a final look-over. "You will remember to deliver those letters, Longwell? But not before tomorrow."

She did not wait for his reply but went directly to Sir Walter's room. He was dressed for travel in a white ruffled shirt (rakishly open at the neck) and a full-length cloak. Around his waist was knotted a black sash. Imploringly, he held out a waistcoat.

"Might you have room for this, my dear?" he pleaded. "I haven't worn it above twice, and by autumn it will be out of fashion." His smile became sly. "You see? I am able to be thrifty. It would be very bad economy to leave this behind. It is such a becoming shade."

Lady Russell took it from his resistless grasp. He was right; that particular green suited him very well. "Very well," she relented, "but if you cannot find room you must wear it. We must be on our way this instant."

Sir Walter needed no further urging. He snatched up his hat and gloves. "And those bags, if you please."

She took hold of a bulky carryall and lugged it toward the door. "We haven't time to wait for the servants; we must carry these ourselves."

Sir Walter gave a chortle and clapped his hat on his head. "With pleasure," he said. "For I'm gone with the raggle-taggle gypsies, O."

Lady Russell gave him a look. "Mind how you go. We shall be using the servants' stairs."

Humming, he took up the remaining bags and followed, with a thump and a bump. And then Sir Walter began to sing.

> "Then she pulled off her silk-finished gown
> and put on hose of leather,
> The ragged, ragged, rags about our door;
> She's gone with the raggle-taggle gypsies, O!"

Meanwhile, Anne was in a state of agitation: she sat; she stood; she wandered about Lady Russell's front parlour. At last she tired of reading the titles embossed on the spines of books. Why did her godmother not come?

The door opened to admit Longwell. Ellen followed close behind with the tea trolley. This was encouraging.

Longwell made a slight bow. "Her ladyship has been detained, ma'am," he announced and then waited as Ellen positioned the tea things on a low table. Longwell then arranged his features into something resembling a smile and gestured to a chair. "Here is your usual seat by the fire, ma'am."

Anne did not know what to make of this. Longwell was never friendly! She moved to the chair and sat down. Longwell poured the tea and handed the cup and saucer.

"I trust nothing is amiss," Anne said. What was she thinking? One never conversed with Longwell!

"No more than one could expect under the circumstances," he replied. He gave a sidelong glance at the front windows and held out a plate of shortbread for her inspection. "Biscuit?" he enquired, smiling again.

What was wrong with him? Anne took a piece of the shortbread; her gaze never left his face. It seemed to her that Longwell was looking rather harassed.

A loud bump sounded above stairs. Longwell gave a start and so did Anne. "What on earth?" she cried.

Longwell replaced the plate on the trolley. "Her ladyship has lately taken a fancy to moving furniture about," he said, backing toward the door. "If you will permit, I shall ascertain the extent of the, er, damage."

Anne put up her chin. "You will tell my godmother that I must see her at once."

But if Longwell heard this command, he gave no sign. He went out, leaving Anne to stare at the closed door. More scuffling noises followed. Finally Anne had had enough. She rose to her feet and went out to the entrance hall. It was deserted.

Perplexed, Anne returned to the parlour. She took another turn about the room, but this time she looked about with wide-awake eyes. On Lady Russell's writing desk lay a pile of letters. Anne gave a start, for one had Elizabeth's name! She quickly pushed this letter aside. Beneath it was a letter to *Mrs. Charles Musgrove*—Mary! There were several to Lady Russell's friends in Bath and one to a man Anne recognized as Lady Russell's solicitor.

What did this mean? What did this mean? Anne continued her search. The letter on the very bottom was addressed to *Mrs. Captain Frederick Wentworth.*

Anne snatched it up. She gave an anxious look to the door—it would never do for Lady Russell to come in just now! —and went hunting in the drawer for a paper knife. If she could slide it under the seal, she might be able to unfold the sheet without detection.

Outside a carriage came rumbling up and stopped in front of the house. Someone came running down the stairs; a door was slammed. Shaken, Anne pushed the drawer closed and replaced the letter—just as Longwell came in. He went directly to the windows and began to let down the net blinds.

"The sun in Bath is quite destructive," he remarked. "It is our custom to be at the Lodge during this time of year." He fussed a bit with the arrangement of the folds before turning to face Anne. "Shall I bring a candle, ma'am?"

"I would like you to bring my godmother," Anne cried. "Time is of the essence, Longwell. Every moment we waste is precious!"

An odd expression crossed his face. "So it is," he said. "Permit me to ascertain."

On his way to the door, Longwell walked past the desk. He halted, shot a quick glance at Anne, gathered the stack of letters, and went out. The door closed behind him.

Anne gave a cry of vexation. What was Longwell hiding? For surely he was hiding something! Her gaze strayed to the net blinds—there was something going on here. She pushed aside a blind and looked out. A job carriage waited in the street, and there was Longwell, handing cases to the driver!

She was about to cry out when Longwell climbed inside and shut the door. The carriage went rumbling away.

Anne bolted from the parlour and fought with the locks on the front door. She ran out onto the street; the carriage was nowhere to be seen. Grim-faced, Anne returned to the parlour. She gave the bell cord a series of violent tugs. Ellen came in answer to the summons—with a piece of pie on a plate.

"I do not wish for pie," Anne interrupted. "I wish to see my godmother. You will take me to her—now!"

Ellen's face paled. "Oh no, ma'am," she said.

Anne set her teeth. "Very well, I shall find Lady Russell myself."

"Oh no, ma'am!" Ellen went running after Anne, out of the parlour and up the stairs.

"I daresay you won't understand." Elizabeth's voice shook with emotion. "No one could. It is too dreadful."

Where was her courage? Where was her fighting spirit?

"I won't if you do not tell me," McGillvary said reasonably. "Now then, what has happened?"

Elizabeth took a shuddering breath. "My father is ruined, Mr. Gill. And so am I." A tear slid down her cheek.

McGillvary dropped to one knee beside her chair. "The paper has printed a retraction—an apology. Here it is. Do you see?"

She would not be comforted. "I am ruined," she said again. "There is nowhere I can turn for help."

"Surely it is not that bad."

"I can turn to God for help; I know that. But I am to blame for much of what has happened, so perhaps I daren't apply to Him?"

McGillvary did not know what to make of this. "You are not without resources," he said. "What about your sister?"

"Captain Wentworth has made it quite clear that he will not help Father. He says that there is no point because he will only get into debt again."

McGillvary swallowed his amusement at this very apt observation.

"And I know he is right," Elizabeth went on. "But without my father, I am prey to—" She stopped.

"You are prey to—?" he promoted. "Prey to what?"

"I am prey to fears on every hand."

His eyes searched her face. "But that is not what you meant to say, is it?" he said softly.

Her eyes flew to his, confirming his suspicion. He took hold of her hands and turned them palm-up. "What of these bruises?"

"I-I tried to open the window. It was stuck fast. I wished to open it, you see, because I ..."

"Has your sister no servant?"

Elizabeth's head came up. "Surely I am capable of opening a window! I did not wish to wait because I ..." She swallowed several times. "It was so close in that room! You have no idea!"

She gave a queer little laugh. "And then I lost a shoe. Our butler brought it back. I can imagine what he thought of me!" Elizabeth covered her face with her hands. "But in the end," she cried, "I couldn't do it."

McGillvary looked sharply at her, struck by an odd note in her voice. "What couldn't you do?"

She twisted in her chair, away from him, and groped for her reticule. Her fingers plucked at the knot. "I went in for headache powder," she said. "Truly, that is what I meant to buy! But when the man asked what I had come for I told him this, instead."

She was working to remove something from her reticule, but he could not see what it was.

"After calling at the Pump Room, I was waiting," she explained, "but it was not yet two o'clock. And then he came and spoke to me. He said—oh, horrible things!"

Her breathing became laboured. "I escaped into the Abbey. And then I went out and I bought this." She raised her eyes to his. "I had to come to say good-bye first. And I *cannot*."

Elizabeth pushed a slender box into his hand. "Here," she said. Take it away. Please!"

McGillvary turned the box over. Inscribed on the lid were the words *RAT BANE*.

Arsenic?

He gripped her shoulders. "You've not taken this!" he fairly shouted, shaking her. "Tell me you've not taken this."

She would not look at him. "I am too much a coward," she whispered.

"Thank God!" McGillvary moved to take her into his arms, but she pulled away.

"My father," she continued, "received a letter this morning. Or rather, I did. That is to say, it was addressed to him, but it came to me. Mr. Lonk brought it to my sister's."

"The devil he did!"

"And I saw—" She paused to pull the letter from her reticule. "For the first time I saw the extent of his debts. He owes a frightening amount of money." She ventured to look at him. "But I imagine you know that."

McGillvary could think of no suitable reply. "I do," he said.

"When I saw that ghastly amount," she said, "I knew that we were ruined."

McGillvary held out his hand for the letter. Lonk would regret the day he allowed this to come to her hand! "Your father's debts are considerable," he said, "but his situation is not hopeless."

"But it is," she said with equal earnestness. "And the worst of it is, that it is my fault!"

McGillvary was taken aback. "*Your* fault?"

"If you only knew how I encouraged him. I led him to make purchases that I knew were too extravagant. He said we could afford them, and I believed him. But in my heart I knew it wasn't so." She paused. "Until I opened that letter I had no idea he owed so much. It is far beyond his ability to repay. He will go to prison, and I shall be left destitute."

McGillvary fingered the letter, feeling every bit like Judas. "The intent of this letter," he said, "was to bring your father to exercise every means in his power to repay what he owes."

She seemed calmer now, so he decided to explain. "There is, I believe, land adjacent to your estate. He must exert himself to sell this land."

"That is something he will never do. He has his pride."

"Then his pride will choke him."

Elizabeth gave a brittle laugh and reached for the letter. "Poor Father. He used to burn these when they came."

"That was extremely foolhardy."

"Yes, and do you remember? I came to speak to someone at the counting house. That was the day I met you." A smile trembled on her lips. "You spilled ink on your coat, as I recall."

"Yes," he said. "And I went on to make the worst mistake of my life."

He waited quietly, looking into her eyes. Now she would enquire about the mistake, and he would confess his identity.

"I wonder," said Elizabeth, "if I might do that again?"

McGillvary was caught off guard. "Spill ink?"

"No. Speak to someone about paying what we owe."

This was wholly unexpected. "Elizabeth," he said, "I consider myself to be a patient man, but I do not like to repeat myself. Hear this: There is no *we*. You are not responsible, legally or morally, for your father's debts."

She brushed this aside. "I have a few jewels left. My father replaced many of our stones with *paste*, but not everything."

"My dear, I will not take your jewellery as payment."

"You might as well. The pieces that are left I never wear. My grandmother's diamonds, for instance, are in very ugly settings—quite hideous. I also have Mother's pearls." Her voice became wistful. "I don't wear those either."

"Elizabeth—" he said warningly.

She faced him with something like her old spirit. "Should I see Mr. Lonk then? Is he the highest authority in the counting house?"

McGillvary gave a hollow laugh. "The highest authority? Surely not. That would be McGillvary."

There, he had said it. He waited for her reaction.

The hunted look returned to her eyes. "McGillvary. Yes, how stupid of me. He signed this."

She pushed the letter toward him and pointed. "That is his signature, is it not? You of all people would know."

McGillvary felt the skin on his neck prickle. He had countersigned this cursed letter! And he hadn't even known it.

"Is there anyone else I can see?"

McGillvary's mouth was suddenly dry. Here was the answer to everything.

"No," he heard himself say. "You will need to speak to McGillvary yourself. Tomorrow."

15 THE PASSAGE TO REMORSE

Elizabeth descended from the job carriage, shielding her eyes against the glare of the sun. A boy had let down the steps for her, but she did not see his outstretched hand. She did not see him shrug and hold the door, either. The door was slammed shut, and the vehicle drove off.

She watched it disappear around the corner. Patrick Gill had paid the fare when he put her into it, which was a very good thing for her purse. He had also instructed the driver to drop her at the corner. It was like him to attend to such details. This meant nothing, of course. Patrick Gill was thoughtful, that was all.

She made her way to St. Peter Square, mindful to keep her chin up and her eyes fixed ahead. She must remain strong! Patrick had advised her not to allow fears to prey upon her mind, and she had every intention of following his advice.

Did he understand the nature of her fears? She was certainly troubled about the debt and Sir Henry. But now that she was parted from Patrick, Elizabeth was painfully aware that more than anything she feared losing his friendship.

And it was friendship—only that.

Kisses are not promises, nor are gifts guarantees.

Patrick had given both a gift and a kiss, but there was nothing binding in them. Nothing.

She must be realistic. There was no room in her heart for fantasies—not now or ever! The simple truth was this: Despite his many kindnesses, Patrick Gill did not care for her in any extraordinary way. Though he paid the fare today, he had not come with her in the carriage. Nor had he expressed interest in meeting her family or in speaking to her father. None of his actions had been lover-like.

Elizabeth felt her throat tighten. Not for anything would she give in to grief—not here. She was done with tears, at least for today.

In future, she would be more careful. She would guard her heart against Patrick Gill. No longer would she look into his eyes while he spoke or allow herself to be captivated by his smile. Bit by bit she would learn to live without him. This was not impossible; for how many years had she survived on her own?

"For too many years, unfortunately," she whispered. Nothing good ever lasted. Patrick Gill, so precious to her now, would lose interest and fade away, just like all the others. In the end, all that would be left was William Elliot.

Elizabeth was quiet as she entered the house. This time she deliberately kept her back to the mirror hanging in the entrance hall.

The drawing room door opened, and Mary came out to the landing. "Why, hello," she called down. "Are you coming up? I have had the most staggering good luck. Wait until you see!"

Elizabeth bit back a groan. Happy chatter was the last thing she wished to hear! "May I see your purchases another time? I am worn to the bone, truly, and I ..."

Her words of refusal died when she saw their effect on her sister. Mary looked quite crestfallen. "Oh very well," Elizabeth relented. "But only for a moment."

Mary beamed, and as Elizabeth gained the landing Mary took hold of her arm and pulled her into the drawing room. "You just sit there," she said, "and I'll ring for tea."

"Anything but tea, if you please," Elizabeth said faintly.

Mary led her to one of the sofas, talking all the way. "Well. Annette Wallis is a wonder! She took me to the most delightful shops. Not your precious Pultney Street boutiques, but others." Mary spread her hands. "I don't know how she came to be so clever. I suppose an army officer's wife must learn frugality. At any rate, dear Annette knows how to make the most of a pound, bless her."

Elizabeth kept her opinion of 'dear Annette' to herself.

"Look at this," Mary gushed, and held up a lawn under dress. "Compare the workmanship with anything made by your top-lofty London seamstresses. Isn't it wonderful?"

To please Mary, Elizabeth fingered the hem. Her brows rose. Mary was right; the hemstitching was very fine. Caps, handkerchiefs, and silk stockings—one by one each of Mary's purchases was poured into Elizabeth's lap. Mary's eyes shone with pleasure at Elizabeth's admiration.

"I've saved the best for last," Mary announced, pulling at the ribbon on the largest bandbox. "It's a dress, and at such a price! I simply could not pass it by."

It was obvious that Mary had passed nothing by, but Elizabeth did not voice this thought.

"The colour suits me down to the ground, or so Annette says."

Elizabeth knew all about Mary's taste in clothing, so she prepared herself for the worst. Still, she was mindful to keep a pleasant look on her face as the cover came off. Mary parted the layers of tissue and drew out a gown of rose pink. The overskirt was chiffon, embroidered with tiny shimmering flowers of muted green.

Astonished, Elizabeth reached to feel the fabric. "This must have been very dear."

"Not at all." Mary held the gown aloft; the skirt floated into soft folds. "It was made for last season, because the price was greatly reduced." Elizabeth noticed that the dress had long sleeves. Mary correctly guessed her thought and added, "I daresay the sleeves can be changed."

Elizabeth shook her head. "I wouldn't attempt it," she said. "These are beautifully done. It is too easy to bungle the set of a sleeve, and then where will you be? I must say, the colour is perfect for you. Much better than the lavender you wore yesterday."

Mary's cheeks grew as rosy as the gown, but whether this was from pleasure or annoyance Elizabeth could not tell. "It wants a brooch," Elizabeth added, "just there to draw the eye."

Mary looked suddenly suspicious. "Why would I wish to do that?"

"You are a bit pigeon-breasted, dear. A brooch will look very well."

"I am *not* pigeon-breasted," Mary cried, firing up. "You would say something cutting! You always do."

Elizabeth let out a long breath. How like her sister to take everything the wrong way! "It was not meant as a criticism," she said. "One should face one's deficiencies honestly. For in that way a lady is able to compensate for what is lacking, ahead of time, before anyone notices what is amiss. No woman has a perfect figure," she added.

"Except, of course, yourself."

Elizabeth hesitated. There was some justice in this observation. She shrugged. "You can see all the good it has done me."

Mary's expression grew mulish, and Elizabeth rose to her feet. "I believe I'll go upstairs now. I have had a beastly morning, and my head aches dreadfully. What I need is a nap. Be an angel and tell Anne that I'll be taking dinner in my room tonight."

"Tell her yourself!" Mary cradled the dress in her arms. "Pigeon-breasted indeed."

Elizabeth sighed again. Why must Mary make things so difficult? As she moved to open the door, she caught sight of her sister's unhappy face. Perhaps it would be best to make amends?

"I am sorry that I offended you, Mary," she said, more stiffly than she meant. "Never mind what I said about the brooch. The dress is beautiful, and it suits you perfectly." She paused before adding, "I hope your husband won't be angry about the money you spent."

"I do not care what Charles thinks," Mary cried. "We're not paupers, you know."

Paupers. The word was like a slap.

"Yes," Elizabeth said quietly, "I know." She used to say the very same thing and now, because of her excesses, it was quite true.

"For your information," Mary went on, "I haven't got a brooch to match this gown. I am to wear it to Captain Wentworth's dinner. Doubtless the entire company will be overcome by my deficiencies."

The spite in Mary's words stung. "Oh surely not," Elizabeth flung back. "I've asked Anne to use that hideous silver epergne. No one will be able to see you."

"Oh!" Mary shrieked. She dropped the gown; her fingers curled into fists. "How dare you! Not see me, indeed!"

"It is not meant to hide you, silly," Elizabeth amended. "We'll be having the ugliest dinner guests in all of Bath. From what I've seen, the men of the navy are disgusting, both in looks and manners! Furthermore, Anne tells me that we shall be the only ladies at table, which means they will stare at us like schoolboys! I doubt they will notice deficiencies in any of us!"

"You mean me," Mary cried. "My deficiencies!"

"All I ever said was that the dress looks very well on you. Never mind about the brooch. I ought to have kept my mouth shut."

"A truer word," said a masculine voice, "was never spoken."

Elizabeth whirled to see Captain Wentworth standing in the doorway. His eyes held an unpleasant glint.

"Oh blast," muttered Elizabeth. "What are you doing here?"

His lip curled. "Displaying my ugliness and ill-manners to the entire household, apparently," he said. "Where, if you please, is Anne?"

Elizabeth felt her cheeks begin to burn. "I have no idea," she said. "She was here when I left. Charles had the gig out; perhaps he took her to call on someone."

"No," he countered, looking even angrier. "Charles did not take Anne anywhere. He has been with me. According to Yee, she left in a sedan chair." His gaze swept to Mary. "When did you last see Anne?"

Mary began to stammer. "B-bless me, I-I don't know. I've been unwell, very unwell. You cannot expect me to remember who goes here or there."

But Captain Wentworth did expect Mary to remember, and he told her to kindly exert herself. "Anne was h-here this morning," Mary said, "when Lady Russell took us to the P-Pump Room, but that was the last I saw of her."

He folded his arms across his chest. "I have no time to drive all the way to Rivers Street," he growled. "As a matter of fact, I did not have time to come here, but I wanted Anne's opinion on something. Tell her I'll be back in time for dinner."

"Anne's opinion," said Mary, as soon as he was gone. "I like that. Why did he not ask for mine?"

By nightfall, Lady Russell had had enough. The Mail had been bowling along at a rate that shattered her nerves. To make matters worse, it was stuffed with passengers— six in a space not large enough for four! To her left sat a man in a scarlet frock coat, none too clean, whose grizzled face wore a permanent scowl. Lady Russell sat as far away from him as possible. To her right was her man Longwell.

As always, Longwell was neat and composed, unruffled by the exigencies of travel. This was more than Lady Russell could say for herself or Sir Walter, who sat in the opposite corner. At present he was asleep. She did not see how this could be possible, for whenever the coach gave a jerk, his head bumped against the window frame. To Lady Russell, who had not slept a wink, this seemed grossly unfair.

The coach ran onto cobbled pavement, and Lady Russell set her teeth to keep them from rattling. Because of the stifling air, the windows were cracked open and dust was everywhere. Her travelling gown was filthy, and as for her hair—!

The shout of the coachman, warning the roof-passengers to keep their heads down, brought Lady Russell out of her stupor. Sure enough, the coach swept under the arch of an inn. The blowing of the horn came next. Outside were shouts—the hostlers coming to change the horses, no doubt.

"Longwell," she murmured, "this is intolerable."

"Yes, milady."

She peered out of the window. "Might we disembark and proceed to Mayfair on our own? I cannot appear in all this dirt at any civilized place."

"I shall ascertain after we alight, milady," Longwell replied. "However, I fear it might not be possible to remove your trunks until we reach our destination."

He drew a paper from his pocket and consulted it. "We are due to reach London late tomorrow morning. Perhaps it would be best to persevere?"

Lady Russell closed her eyes. What had possessed her to travel in this wretched manner? Her gaze travelled to the sleeping Sir Walter. The test of true friendship was heavy indeed.

The coach came to a halt, and the passengers stirred. Twenty minutes was all they were allowed. The man in the scarlet coat was first on his feet. He yanked the door open and pushed his way out. The young farmwoman's fretful child began to cry.

Lady Russell sighed heavily. "Perhaps you are right, Longwell," she said wearily. "You know best, as always."

Anne bore her part at dinner with weary patience. Frederick and Charles had arrived just in time to change, flush with victory over the purchase of a pair of horses. It seemed like they could talk of little else. Mary's shopping expedition had likewise been a success, and she was in very good spirits. Anne, on the other hand, was feeling rather depressed. For once she was sorry that Elizabeth had taken dinner in her room, for at least she had the goodness to be grieved over their father's disappearance. It seemed Frederick cared only about the new carriage and horses. After the others retired for the night, she confronted him.

"Anne," he replied, "you father is responsible for himself. You are his child, not his keeper."

"You do not know my father."

He gave her a look. "What is it, exactly, that you think we ought to do? Check every back alley and mews in Bath?"

"If necessary, yes."

"Do you honestly believe your father is shivering on a street corner? Be reasonable, darling."

Anne almost stamped her foot. "I am being reasonable. Father has disappeared and so has Lady Russell. And you care nothing about it."

A light came into his eyes. "Oho! Perhaps they have followed our example and made for the border?"

"Frederick! Be serious. Father would never consider such a thing."

Captain Wentworth spread his hands. "Perhaps he was overmastered by passion?" he suggested. "Or, more likely, by the size of her bank balance?"

"This is no joke!" Anne cried. "If you had not spent *all day* at that wretched horse auction, I would not have had to deal with this alone! Lady Russell left behind a stack of letters, one for each of us. If Longwell hadn't come in when he did, I might have learned something."

"So you think her disappearance has something to do with your father's?"

"What else am I to think? I cannot shake the notion that Father is in trouble, and that I ought to help him."

"And since when have you—or anyone else—been able to help him? He has never shown a particle of interest in your advice."

"I know," she said, twisting her fingers. "And yet, I ..."

Captain Wentworth took Anne's hands in his. "My sweet, your father is a resourceful fellow. The explanation is probably quite simple. Ten to one he has come to his senses, realized that the rates at The Citadel are both exorbitant and unnecessary, and has taken new lodgings."

"Without telling anyone?"

Captain Wentworth raised an eyebrow. "Isn't that what he did the last time?"

Anne was not happy with this answer. "I think he is fleeing from the scandal Elizabeth has created."

"Well now, I don't know. It seems to me that he was caught in his own trap there."

Anne's eyes narrowed. "How do you mean?"

"What's the expression? Too clever by half? Anne, the man announced Elizabeth's engagement to a fellow she loathes. Smacks of trying to force her hand, that does."

"Father would never resort to such—such *farcical* tactics," she cried.

"It is rather like something out of a melodrama," he agreed. "What interests me is today's retraction. I wonder how he managed to pull that off. It probably saved your sister's sorry stern."

"Elizabeth," cried Anne, "is not missing. She does not need our help. Father does. If only I'd been able to read that letter!"

"Then let us hope it is posted soon. Unless you wish to keep watch on the front step of Lady Russell's house, we shall have to wait."

Anne's head came up. *"Could we?"*

"Anne!"

Yee came in response to Elizabeth's summons and later, when he cleared her dinner tray, he brought with him the grey velvet bag containing her jewels. With trembling fingers she unfastened its silken cords and poured the contents onto her lap. She gave a cry of triumph for here, wrapped in felt, were her mother's pearls and the Stevenson diamonds. The pearl earrings were also here, along with her mother's amethyst set and the turquoises.

As Elizabeth sorted, her spirits rose, for there were quite a few pieces, including the *paste* emeralds. She had taken the bag with her to Chalfort House, which was a very good thing. If it had been left behind at Camden Place, she would never have seen these jewels again.

But how much were they worth? Some were obviously in need of cleaning, but Elizabeth did not wish to involve Elise. She filled a basin with water and used her toothbrush, a generous amount of tooth powder, and a little soap. The amethysts cleaned up especially well; their rich purple sparkled in the candlelight. She had always disliked this set, and yet tomorrow it would be gone. Sentimentality, she reminded herself, was both foolish and unwise. There was no use crying over what could not be helped.

Elizabeth set the amethysts aside and began to work on her mother's pins. These were more difficult—and painful! —to clean. There were several she remembered very well, in particular a gold-edged ivory cameo which her mother had worn often in the months before her death. Elizabeth remembered this vividly; her mother's skin had been as pale as the cameo. Her poor mother! What she had suffered! And now, all these years later, what would she think of her daughter selling her precious pin to pay her husband's debt?

"My debt," Elizabeth reminded herself. This time she would not shirk responsibility.

Once the dust was cleared away, the cameo's face shone. Elizabeth buffed the gold setting with a towel. She had never realized how fine the setting was or how beautiful the Grecian woman's face. How had her mother come by this piece?

Then she remembered what Mary said about needing a brooch. Objections rose at once: Elizabeth ought to keep this for herself; Mary had been too young to remember; it would have no value in her eyes.

And yet the idea would not go. At last Elizabeth gave up the struggle. She hunted in a drawer for writing materials and cleared a dry area on the dressing table.

Dear Mary,

Perhaps you will not remember this brooch of Mother's, but it is just the thing for your new rose gown. I know she would be pleased for you to have it as your very own.

Elizabeth signed her name and pushed back the chair. In the morning she would slip into Mary's room and place the pin on her dressing table. Her sister might not appreciate its value, but neither would Admiral McGillvary. Now it would never be his.

Admiral McGillvary. The memory of his laughing face, half concealed by shadows on that terrace at Chalfort House, took on a ghoulish aspect. How she would face him tomorrow she did not know.

The following morning found London shrouded with fog, which suited Lady Russell perfectly. "I declare, I could sleep for an age," she said aloud, and she pressed a warm, damp cloth to her face. Of course she would not be able to sleep, but it was a lovely thought.

For one thing, the room was in motion, evidence of how the Mail had preyed upon her mind and body. Although the walls seemed to sway, the chair, at least, was still. Lady Russell leaned her elbows on the dressing table. She and Sir Walter were solidly, if not comfortably, established in a small hotel on Piccadilly. The morning was now well-advanced, and a stream of vehicles clattered over the street outside. Lady Russell was past caring. What a blessed relief to be out of the coach!

The maid brought a pot of tea and Lady Russell helped herself, watching the steam curl invitingly from the cup. A spot of tea would set her to rights. She was mindful to keep her eyes turned away from the looking glass, for the strain of travel had surely taken a toll. Fortunately, Sir Walter was having his bath and would then take a nap.

How she wished she had brought her own maid! Her hair was filthy, although she had tried to repair the damage. She'd washed her face and arms too, but what to do about her stained and creased clothing she did not know. Soon she and Sir Walter would be on a ship bound for Venice, and everyone knew that clothing was never properly maintained at sea.

Despite the hardships, she had to admit that her plan was successful. If Longwell was able to book passage on a ship, all would be well. It would be best not to linger in London, for Sir Walter could not be trusted there. However, Lady Russell knew she could rely on Longwell. Always, he cared for her impeccably. Had he not arranged everything thus far?

Soon a soft knock sounded at the door, and in answer to her call Longwell entered. His face looked pale and drawn—a result of the journey, no doubt. Lady Russell felt a stab of pity. The poor man had been given no time to prepare! At the last moment she had bundled him into the Mail coach.

"The arrangements for your passage are complete, milady," he said woodenly. "You depart tomorrow on the vessel *Sarabande* bound for Venice by way of Gibraltar, Corsica, and Malta. You are required to be on board by four o'clock in the evening, as the ship leaves at the turn of the tide." Longwell shot a look from beneath bushy brows. "Passage for two," he added gruffly, "double occupancy."

"Thank you, Longwell." She gave his arm an affectionate pat. "Most satisfactory. I can always depend upon you." She lifted the teacup and took a tentative sip. "Venice, Longwell. Think of it! I own, I am surprised at that destination—so romantic! However we shan't dwell on it as there is work to be done. Now then," she continued, "there are several articles of business to which we must attend." She began to search through her belongings on the dressing table. "Dear me, where did I put that list?"

Longwell slid a hand into his coat pocket and produced it.

Lady Russell beamed at him. "Why, thank you, Longwell. Where would I be without you? Now let me see. Ah, yes. Banking and the acquisition of the license. If it is not too much trouble, would you be so good as to enquire at the nearest parish church whether we might be—"

Longwell interrupted. "No, milady."

Lady Russell blinked. "I beg your pardon?"

"That I will not do, ma'am." He squared his shoulders. "If I may, I would like to return to my room."

"Why, certainly," she said. "No doubt you are tired and would like to rest. We can attend to business in the afternoon."

Longwell's rigid stance became straighter still. "I misspoke, milady," he said gruffly. "What I meant to say is that I would like to return to my room—in Bath."

"But we need you here!"

"I do not scruple to leave you in your bridegroom's care, milady," he said roughly. "He will see to your needs admirably, I am sure."

"He shall do no such thing, as well you know! Indeed, I do not know what I shall do without you."

Longwell cleared his throat; his Adam's apple bobbed up and down. "Milady," he said, "I've stood by you in good times and in bad, and never have I shirked my duty—even in this madcap adventure, which I must say is next door to breaking the law! But to take you to church to be wed to That Man?" He gave a rumbling cough. "That I will not do."

"Why, Longwell!" Lady Russell was rendered speechless She had never heard her butler speak so many words at once. From all appearances, he was not finished!

Indeed, the torrent of words served to give Longwell courage. "You must do as you see fit, milady, and I'll not criticize your judgment. But I won't be a part of it—never!" He raised his chin. "Your late husband, God rest his soul, wasn't worthy of you, and neither is this man! I won't stand by and watch him lead you into ruin!"

With difficulty, Lady Russell found her voice. "He is my friend, Longwell," she said quietly, "and my longtime neighbour, as well as the father of my goddaughters. The situation is desperate. Sir Walter needs me."

"What about you?" demanded Longwell. "What do you need from him? Not money; he can't give it. Not a title; you already have one."

She thought for a moment, and then looked up at her butler's stolid face. "Companionship, perhaps?" she offered.

"Harrumph! He won't be needing your companionship. Not if he's got his looking glass! He's all the company he needs!"

Lady Russell gasped aloud—and almost laughed. What had come over Longwell? "Well then," she said, "I suppose I must journey to Venice without you ... alone." From beneath her lashes she stole another look at him.

He did not soften. "I had planned to serve you all my days, milady," he said grimly, "but no more. We have reached an impasse."

Lady Russell became very still, feeling more than a little fearful at the direction this conversation was taking. "Longwell, my dear, what are you saying?"

"I'm giving notice, milady. I shall return to Bath with the next Mail to collect my belongings."

"What? Brave the Mail again so soon?" she teased. "But come, I'll not accept your resignation." Her voice softened. "I need you, Longwell. Now more than ever. Please don't leave me."

The imploring note in her voice was not without effect. Longwell's rigid reserve shattered. "Were you expecting me to come on your honeymoon trip?" he shouted. "Serve you breakfast in bed each morning? Wait hand and foot upon your useless fop of a husband, who is no better than a dandified looby? Stand by while he paws at and takes liberties with your person? No, I thank you!"

"Longwell, please!" Lady Russell laid a desperate hand on his sleeve. "You are upset and fatigued. Believe me, I understand. Can we not discuss this later? I never expected you to come to Venice with us, but while we are in London, I—"

He jerked his arms away and folded them defiantly across his chest. "There is nothing to discuss, milady. I won't retrieve your marriage license, and I won't escort you to church. Were you wishful for me to give you away at the altar? Have you no regard for my sincerest feelings?"

With that, Longwell turned on his heel and went out, slamming the door behind.

Lady Russell discovered that tears were streaming down her cheeks. Her butler, she realized, had been weeping as well.

"Oh, Longwell," she whispered.

Soon after he departed another knock sounded. Lady Russell's heart nearly flew from her chest. Hastily she dried her tears. "Come in, dear Longwell," she cried.

It was not her butler but Sir Walter who came sauntering in. He wore a magnificent dressing gown of purple and gold. On his feet were purple velvet slippers. His legs, she noticed, were bare. Quickly she brought her hands to cover her mouth—she must conceal what she was thinking!

"Good day, my dear Amanda," he purred. "My, what an attractive dressing gown."

"Do you mean mine?" she enquired. "Or yours?" For the one she was wearing was very old indeed. She moved away from the lamp, all too aware of the ugly shadows it cast.

It did not appear that Sir Walter heard her remark, for he was smiling at her in a singular way. "Then again," he said, continuing his sentence, "by this time tomorrow I shall be acquainted with all of your dressing gowns, shall I not?"

He put a hand on his hip and made a leg.

"Sir Walter," cried Lady Russell. "You forget yourself, sir!"

"Only until tomorrow," he said with a wink.

Lady Russell was struck speechless. Apparently these were the man's bedroom manners. She much preferred his drawing room manners!

He took a suggestive step forward. "I have been consoling myself, my dear, with the recollection that there are benefits to the married state," he said. "Very nice benefits." His cheek dimpled. "Surely you remember."

He strolled more fully into the room and took a seat on the bed, crossing one bare leg over the other. "My one regret is that we must spend our wedding night aboard ship." He gave a great sigh. "Such a setting, while romantic, is so very cramped and uncomfortable."

"Not to mention un-private!" cried Lady Russell.

"Ah, but never you fear," he said, twinkling. "We shall manage."

Lady Russell pulled her dressing gown more firmly about her person and tightened the knot. "Perhaps," she said faintly, "such intimacies ought to be postponed."

"But why?" he said. "By the bye, I've brought you a gift." Sir Walter slid a hand into a pocket and brought out a bottle. "In anticipation of our wedding night, I would like to present you with this." It was a bottle of Gowland's lotion.

"It is not a proper wedding present, but it is a useful one." Sir Walter's smile disappeared. "Apply this to the face twice daily," he instructed, "and three times while we are at sea. The salt air is treacherous to the complexion! By the time we reach Italy's sylvan shores, your crow's feet will have faded away to nothing."

"Crow's feet?"

"How do you ladies call them? Expression lines? Smile creases? They're facial wrinkles, at any rate, and they are most unsightly."

Lady Russell's fingers closed around the bottle. She did not trust herself to speak.

Sir Walter continued to talk. "The face is the first to show the effects of age—it grows lank and wrinkled. The neck succumbs next and then the breast and arms. You might not realize this, but I have read extensively on this

subject," he explained. "It is known as the Deficiency of
the Fluids. It appears first in the highest parts. But the
lowest parts," he said more brightly, "that is to say, those
below the waist, continue as plump and fresh as ever. Indeed, in those areas it is quite impossible to tell a young
woman from an old one!"

Lady Russell tightened her grip on the bottle. It was a
very good thing that Sir Walter was out of reach!

At any cost she must change the subject. "Sir Walter,"
she said, "I have distressing news. Longwell has given notice."

Sir Walter's brows went up. "Has he indeed? How very
fortunate. It saves us the trouble of dismissing him."[1]

---

[1] Sir Walter is indebted to Benjamin Franklin for his theory regarding
the Deficiency of the Fluids (*Advice on the Choice of a Mistress, 1745*).

16 THE VERY RICHES OF THYSELF

Patrick McGillvary stood before the tall Palladian windows in the yellow drawing room, watching a kestrel glide over the lawn. Beyond the trees, the buildings of Bath shone golden in the morning sun.

It was a pleasant vista, but McGillvary did not linger. His real interest was with the windows themselves—were they perfectly clean? The ormolu-mounted clock on the mantelpiece struck nine. He had two hours to prepare for her arrival. Every detail had been meticulously planned, but even the best-laid plans could go awry.

His mother's round table, clothed in crisp, snowy linen, stood ready for their meal. Everything was of the very best; Lewis had assured him of that. Nothing second-rate would do, for Elizabeth would know if he were shirking! The silver, placed in flawless alignment, had been polished to perfection; the blue and white luncheon plates shone, as did the crystal glasses. It pleased McGillvary to use this china today. His late wife had favored a pink flowered set, which he thought insipid.

The door opened and Mrs. Lewis came in with a floral arrangement and a crystal bowl of berries. "White and purple iris, sir, and pink rosebuds," she said, placing the arrangement at the centre of the table. "And a lovely bowl of strawberries to complement the whole." Her fingers lingered fondly on the bowl. "Your mother's, these were," she added. "Reminds me of the old days."

"Indeed it does," he agreed. His father's second wife, an indolent Italian, had not been fond of hosting luncheons. Constanza McGillvary now lived in London with Ronan. McGillvary never gave them a thought if he could help it.

"By the bye," he said, returning his attention to Lewis, "have you seen Starkweather?"

"That I have not, sir."

McGillvary thanked her and left the room, intent on finding his secretary. There was a foul-up with the warrant—he would have Lonk's hide for that! —and Sir Walter Elliot had given him the slip. But the baronet's departure did not matter. One way or another the man would be found. Together they would hammer out a cordial understanding regarding the debt.

Naturally, he was prepared to abrogate Sir Walter's original contract in favor of another, more favorable agreement. This went against the grain, for his firm would forfeit the interest, but it could not be helped. One could hardly fleece one's future father-in-law! Still, it was irksome that the man was missing. He had planned to show Elizabeth the new agreement today, already signed by her father.

He stopped a passing footman and enquired about Starkweather's whereabouts. The man paled—and almost saluted—before stammering an evasive reply. McGillvary regarded him steadily, then thanked him and moved on.

His staff was on edge today, and he was the cause of it. He had not minced words when he'd issued orders about the house. *Perfect* meant perfect by navy standards; his servants had not lived a year with him as master for nothing. He meant business—and they knew it.

At last he came into his library. This was where Elizabeth would be brought. It was a comfortable room, at variance with the pomp of the entrance hall just outside. McGillvary had always liked this room. He spent some time fussing over the position of the chairs. Elizabeth would sit there. And he, when he gave her the news, would stand just there. Or should he take up a position behind the desk?

Experience had taught him that small details like these were important. On his desk lay Sir Walter Elliot's papers, ready for perusal. He would discuss the situation in a businesslike way, and once that was taken care of, they would move on to personal matters.

He smiled, picturing her relief. They would then lunch together and later take a tour of the house—she would like that. The gallery, which occupied the entire west end, was reputed to be one of the finest in that part of the country. He would show her the portraits, and thus she would be introduced to the McGillvary family line.

It was a good plan. It had to be. There was no time to think of another.

Charles stifled a yawn and turned another page. It was thoughtful of Wentworth to leave the morning newspaper for him. He was trying to appreciate this favor, but it was heavy going. He had already read through the political pages—such stuff, it made his head ache! As for the rest, he could not have cared less. The political cartoons made no sense, and he didn't give a hang about the goings-on in London.

Charles turned another page. The society news was here, but he had no reason to read any of it. Mary would, and later he would hear all about it—endlessly.

Presently the door opened and Yee came in with the silver coffee pot. The last thing Charles wished for was more coffee, but he made no objection as Yee filled his cup.

"Has Captain Wentworth come back?" Charles said, watching the dark, steaming coffee fill his cup.

"I believe not, sir. Would you care for another muffin?"

Charles tried to ignore the quizzing gleam in the old butler's eyes. "I would," he admitted, "but my waistcoat wouldn't." Since coming to Bath it was becoming more difficult to fasten the buttons!

Yee withdrew, and Charles lifted the coffee cup to his lips. What he wouldn't give for an afternoon with his cousins, trading stories in the horse barn at Uppercross or in his aunt's cramped parlour at Wynthrop. Charles knew their stories by heart, but any company would be better than none.

At length he threw down the paper and heaved out of the chair. What a thing, to be cooped up in the house on such a fine morning! There was no game and he had no gun, but a brisk walk around that lake would do him good.

Some minutes later Charles was striding down the grassy hill. But he saw neither the bright water nor the blue sky overhead—for on the far side of the lake someone was sitting on the bench. She was feeding the birds, and she was alone.

Charles moved swiftly to a group of willows and took cover. Why he did this he could not say. He only knew that his initial surge of delight was now replaced by shyness. This was both puzzling and annoying, for he was never shy.

He could feel the skin on his neck prickle, and he rubbed at it with his bandaged hand. What he needed was time—time to work out what to say to her. It was not often that he was at a loss for words.

Ducks and a swan paraded before the bench, greedy for the crusts she threw. The scene reminded him of a story from Little Charles's book of nursery tales, the one about the beautiful princess and her swan brothers. She would probably laugh if she knew what he was thinking, for she was not a beautiful woman.

Charles thought about this. He knew Mary considered her plain, but Mary's opinion did not mean very much.

She rarely saw beyond the obvious. For her, a woman's attire counted for everything. This woman's gown was certainly not new, but the only thing Charles saw was how well she looked in that particular shade of grey-green.

Then he realized something else: he never noticed what she wore or how it became her, not ever. Her beauty was in the brightness of her eyes and the warmth of her smile.

He looked down at his bandaged hand, her handiwork. It was none too clean now, but he was not afraid of what she would say. Perhaps she would scold him a little and say that she needed to bandage it again? Charles would not mind that.

And yet he knew that he ought to mind. He should not stand here gazing at her like this, either. But what harm was there? He simply wished to sit on the bench and talk. He did the same with his sisters, didn't he?

Would she like to speak with him? Would he be a bother to her? Charles's blush intensified. He already knew the answers to these questions. He knew something else as well—she was lonely. She was talking to the birds as she fed them.

Charles gave a long sigh. Very well did he understand this. Lonely people often talked to animals; had he not done the same with the horses and dogs at Uppercross?

He ran his fingers through his hair and straightened his neck cloth. He'd forgotten a hat, but that did not matter. Winnie Owen did not stand upon ceremony the way Mary did. Charles felt a smile forming as he stepped out from behind the willows.

"Good day, Miss Owen," he called cheerfully. "Beautiful morning, isn't it?"

As the longcase clock in the vestibule struck a quarter past ten, Elizabeth was quietly making her way down the servants' staircase. She was dressed in the same navy gown she'd worn for her escape to Chalfort House. Hidden in her reticule were Mr. Lonk's letter and the velvet bag of jewellery.

She spent several anxious moments when crossing the servants' hall and kitchen to reach the service door, but no one was there to see her. She let herself out of the house and made for the front walk.

Her plan was to pay a call on Miss Owen. She had developed this practice during her stays in London—that is, to precede a difficult call with an easy one. The prescribed fifteen-minute visit would steady her nerves.

A maid answered the door and took Elizabeth's card, but before she could announce Elizabeth's presence, Miss Owen herself came out. With a cry of delight, she brought Elizabeth up to the front parlor to meet the company assembled there. A dark-haired smiling woman sat by Mr. Minthorne's side. She was in a wheeled chair.

Mr. Minthorne rose to greet her and introduced Mrs. Berryman as his affianced bride. He turned to her, smiling. "My dear, Miss Elliot is our neighbour."

Mrs. Berryman's eyes were alive with pleasure. "Isn't that fine! Please, Miss Elliot," she said, gesturing to a chair, "won't you sit down? As you are a neighbour, perhaps you are acquainted with that delightful man, Charles."

She glanced smilingly at Miss Owen. "That is his Christian name, is it not? I did not catch the surname."

"Do you mean Charles Musgrove?" said Elizabeth. "He is my brother."

Mrs. Berryman's smile grew wider still. "Such a delightful fellow! So helpful and kind! He assisted with my chair, as there is no manservant in the house."

"No manservant yet," put in Mr. Minthorne. "We shall soon rectify that."

The pair began to speak of improvements they planned to make, obviously a topic of great delight. Elizabeth listened politely. Under cover of the conversation, Miss Owen drew her chair nearer to Elizabeth's.

"We did not expect Mrs. Berryman's visit until tomorrow. My cousin could not manage her chair by himself, not with all those stairs. Mr. Yee was busy—and I don't like to ask him for help. Mr. Musgrove insisted on helping. I am ever so grateful."

Before Elizabeth could reply, Mrs. Berryman addressed her directly. "Won't you tell me about yourself, Miss Elliot? I understand from Michael that Mrs. Wentworth—your sister? —is musical. Do you have similar talents? Miss Owen tells me you are very clever, and I can see that it is so."

Elizabeth glanced at the clock. There was little hope of escaping this vivacious women in less than fifteen minutes. She would be fortunate to escape at all!

Just around the corner from St. Peter Square, McGillvary waited in a hackney carriage. He checked his timepiece again—three minutes past eleven. Elizabeth was prompt in keeping appointments. She had promised to come.

Recalling the proverbial watched pot, he leaned against the hard seatback and ran a finger along the bubbled varnish on the sill. From time to time he flexed his shoulders, but there was no getting comfortable in this seat.

Today he wore Mr. Gill's ratty tweed coat, more for old time's sake than anything. Pym had altered it to fit his frame exactly, but either he had gained weight or Pym had been overzealous in laundering it, because it felt too small. McGillvary extended his arms. The sleeves were all right, but the shoulders and waist were too tight.

Some minutes later he saw Elizabeth hurrying along the pavement. He jumped to his feet, knocking his head against hack's low ceiling, and opened the door.

She looked up at him with some anxiety. Her eyes told their own story.

"My dear," he murmured, and drew her inside. "You came."

"I am so sorry! My neighbours would talk; I had to practically force my way from their house!" She glanced over her shoulder. "If I am seen here with you, I'll catch it for sure. That Mrs. Berryman does not miss much."

She settled herself on the seat, keeping well away from the window. "I ought to have worn a veil," she added.

McGillvary shut the door and the hack jolted into motion. "Oh I don't know about that," he said. "A lovely young woman all in black, heavily veiled, at this time of day? A bit early for a funeral."

"I am not wearing black. For your information, this is navy blue. I—thought it appropriate, considering."

McGillvary could not hide his grin. "One of your tricks to soften an old sea dog's heart? Very good."

She gave an impatient sigh. "It is not a trick. The only trick I employed this morning did not work. I am done with tricks."

Naturally he could not let this pass. He made her explain her strategy of calling on less-intimidating neighbours and chuckled at her ingenuity.

"I fear you are right about my dreary gown—although you are not much better. What possessed you to wear that old coat?"

He did not bother to conceal his pleasure. "Yours was the inspiration, my dear. You asked if I had patches on the elbows on one of my coats, and I remembered that I had."

"I am heartily sorry that I chose this dress," she said, "for it is prickly and uncomfortable. I wore it when I ran off to that house party, which ended in disaster. And now I must meet Admiral McGillvary in it." She paused. "It smacks of trickery, as you say."

"Are you worried about McGillvary? Don't be. His bark is far worse than his bite, I assure you."

"I am well aware of the man's opinion of me, thank you. You needn't rub it in. He put me in a dreadful situation at that masked ball."

"Did he?"

"He encouraged me to make a fool of myself, and then he laughed at me. I was never more humiliated."

McGillvary's brows rose. "If you must kiss Rushworth in the garden, that is your affair. Don't go blaming McGillvary."

"Oh!" she cried. "So he told you about that? Insufferable man!"

"Only after your engagement was announced," he countered.

"He is rude and unfeeling. And he despises me."

"I rather doubt that," McGillvary said drily. "My dear girl, can you not understand? His actions that night were motivated by chivalry."

"Chivalry?" Elizabeth was incredulous. "He laughed at me! He mocked me—openly."

This was too much for McGillvary. "But he got rid of Rushworth sure enough," he pointed out. "And that without causing a scene. Rushworth was the fool that night, not you."

"Oh, I was the fool, Mr. Gill, and no mistake," she said. "I shall play the fool's part today as well."

"Kindly do not call me that," he said quietly. "It was not my intention to start an argument."

Elizabeth's face fell. "Please," she said, "the fault is mine. These days I find myself arguing with everyone. I do not mean to. It just ... happens."

He laid his hand on hers. "My point was to make you realize that sometimes a man sees a situation differently than a woman does."

She drew her hand away. "Yes. Men and women are very different." She turned her head to gaze out the window. Silence fell between them. "Look," she remarked. "Is that the gate?"

McGillvary leaned forward to see. The massive arched entrance loomed ahead. The carriage came to a stop and the gatekeeper came trotting from the gatehouse. McGillvary let down the window.

"Hello, Roberts," he said, passing the man his card.

Roberts' face was incredulous. "*Sir!*" he cried. "I'm sorry, sir, for stopping you, but this here mangy excuse for a—"

McGillvary cut him off. "Very good, Roberts. Carry on." He raised the window and glanced at Elizabeth. There was no evidence that she had heard this exchange. The grind of iron against iron meant that the heavy gates were being opened.

As the hack rolled forward, Elizabeth started up. Her eyes were strangely bright. "Mr. Gill," she said, "I mean, *Patrick*. You know Admiral McGillvary fairly well, do you not?"

She was leading up to something, he could feel it. But what? "I do," McGillvary said carefully.

"And he is a gentleman, is he not? In every sense of the word? Because what you said about men and women being different—that is very true."

His instinct for danger seldom failed him. What was she about? "Go on," he said.

"I—acted against your advice," she confessed. "I brought with me the last of my jewellery."

"That," he said, "was unnecessary."

"But it is," she insisted. "I must have something to offer him. Business is business; I know that much. Admiral McGillvary is not running a charity."

His brother Ronan thought he was, but no matter. "No," said McGillvary slowly, "no, he is not."

"But you see, I must offer *something* of value. Something ... honourable."

Her expression filled McGillvary with foreboding.

"Have you ever noticed," she continued, "that a man behaves very differently when he is with a woman? Alone with a woman, I mean." She hesitated before adding, "I daresay you haven't thought much about it, being situated as you are, but I have." Again she paused, as if weighing her words.

"Patrick," she said slowly, "you won't leave me alone with him, will you? You'll stay with me during the meeting?"

McGillvary frowned over this request. How the devil could he promise not to leave her alone with himself?

"Promise me," she said, this time more earnestly. "I can bear anything if you are with me, but you must not leave me alone with him."

"My dear," he reasoned, "you will be quite safe. He shall not harm you."

She found his arm and clutched it tightly. "Promise me," she whispered. "Please, Patrick."

"Elizabeth, you are being nonsensical. There is nothing to fear."

"Am I?" Desperation was in her voice. "I thought I could trust Sir Henry Farley," she said haltingly. "But then he—" She turned her face away.

What had Farley done? McGillvary took hold of her shoulders. "Elizabeth," he said. "What did Farley do?"

She did not answer; he tightened his grip. "What did he do, Elizabeth?" he demanded. "Tell me at once!"

She raised a frightened face. "He offered me his ... protection. He said he would take care of me ... beautifully ... in his villa abroad."

"The devil he will!"

"Don't you see?" she cried. "What if Admiral McGillvary does the same? You mustn't leave me alone with him!"

She was trembling. McGillvary knelt on the floor. "Elizabeth, my dear." His voice was ragged. The next instant she was in his arms, crushed against his chest. "You must trust me," he said.

The hack slowed in order to navigate the circular drive. She swayed with the turn and clung to him. "You must trust me," he repeated.

At length the hack slowed to a stop, which meant they were now at the house. McGillvary lifted his eyes to heaven. What else could he do but follow the plan he had set in motion?

"We will see this through together," he vowed. "And then, my dear,"—his voice changed somewhat—"I'll crush that devil Farley."

The handle of the door began to turn. Silently cursing his over-zealous footman, McGillvary reached behind and held it closed. With his other arm he kept Elizabeth tightly against his shoulder.

And then she began to pull herself together; he could feel it. The tension remained, but her trembling subsided. Abruptly she drew away, and just as quickly he released her.

"Better?" he whispered. "Shall we go in?"

She nodded, her eyes wide. Fear was there, but not tears. McGillvary let go the door and it swung outward. A footman caught hold of it; another let down the steps. Both men kept their eyes averted, but their curiosity was palpable.

McGillvary descended first and offered a hand to Elizabeth. She emerged with stiff, silent dignity. Since he had paid the driver beforehand, he gave his nod to his butler. The hack was waved on.

Elizabeth's panicked eyes met his. "Shouldn't the driver wait?" she protested. "We shan't be long."

He kicked himself for making such an obvious blunder. The poor girl! And yet, what could be done? The hack was now well away from the house. He shrugged and threw her a lopsided grin. "One never knows with him," he said. "The fellow can be devilishly long-winded. We'll manage."

She looked at him for a long moment. "Well," she muttered, "he can be devilish, anyway."

"Shall we go in?"

"Not just yet, please." Elizabeth turned and gazed at the sweep of the drive. The hack was just visible as it made its descent to the gate. Would she run after it?

Again he became aware of the footmen's curiosity, but he issued no rebuke—he did not dare take his eyes from Elizabeth. She stood erect and still. Abruptly, she drew her shoulders back and her head came up. Resolve was hardening into action. McGillvary had seen this countless times before battle. This was the moment—it was now or never.

"Here we go then," he said and offered his arm.

Willing herself to stop shaking, Elizabeth laid a hand on Patrick Gill's sleeve. Through her gloves she could feel the roughness of the wool. She took a swift look at him. He was cheerful; that was heartening. Of course, being a man, he would not understand the position she was in. Still, his bracing good spirits were no bad thing. After all, what was Admiral McGillvary? An upstart! A man of no particular distinction!

But as Elizabeth came into the entrance hall of Belsom Park, flanked by footmen and attended by the butler, it took effort not to gasp. The room was enormous. *Heroic* was the word that came to mind, for Greek columns and marble statuary adorned the walls. Elizabeth itched to look up at the ornate ceiling overhead, but pride kept her eyes fixed straight ahead. This house was far grander than Kellynch.

She cudgeled her brain, trying to recall something, anything, about the McGillvary family. Why had she not looked into this before now?

Mr. Gill's whisper interrupted. "Feeling better?"

"No," she whispered back. "I'd have to snub him to do that. And under the circumstances that would not be wise."

He gave a crack of laughter, hastily subdued. "Good girl," he said. "That's the stuff."

What understanding eyes he had! But she could hardly stand here gazing at Patrick Gill. "Admiral McGillvary has a large number of servants," she observed.

"Hasn't he just?" Patrick Gill's voice held a note of irony. His gaze swept the room and he coughed. The servants standing about began to move.

This was too much for Elizabeth. "Stop staring," she whispered.

"How's that?"

"You mustn't stare, Patrick," she said, very low. "It makes you look like a poor relation." She tipped back her head. "We won't give him—or his servants—the satisfaction."

"Yes, madam," he said meekly. He presented a card to the butler. "Would you kindly give this to Mr. Starkweather? He is expecting us." The butler departed.

"Mr. Starkweather is the secretary," he explained. "Would you like to remove your hat?"

"Certainly not. This isn't a friendly call." Something about his expression caused her to explain. "Only among particular friends does a lady remove her hat—when she will be staying for a good while. Which I shall not be doing."

"I see." Again she saw his gaze sweep the room. They were quite alone now. "Would you care to sit down?" he offered. "I cannot imagine what is keeping Starkweather.'

Patrick should not have omitted the *Mister*, but Elizabeth refrained from correcting him. His reference to her hat brought an uneasy thought. "Mr. Gill," she whispered, "is my hat straight?"

"You look fine." He smiled. "Do you doubt my word? There are mirrors, as you see."

The thought of a mirror made Elizabeth flinch, and this did not go unnoticed. "Did I say something wrong?" he whispered.

"I've been avoiding mirrors lately," she confided. "They confirm that my worst fears are true."

His eyes gleamed with sudden amusement. "The beautiful Miss Elliot? Never!"

Elizabeth could feel a blush rising. Why had she given this answer? Now he would press her to explain. And she would capitulate! "It's my face," she confessed. "The mirror tells me that I am old—old and drab and haggish."

He grinned. "I find that hard to believe."

"Nevertheless, it is perfectly true. I am, in fact, a spinster. I do not mind that—much. What I mind is looking like one."

Patrick Gill chuckled. "Then we'd best avoid the green drawing room," he said, "for there are five or six mirrors in there."

"You will have your little joke. I could well end my days as an old maid."

"Never." His eyes were smiling into hers. "I have known you only a short while," he continued, "and look at all the fellows who have lost their hearts to you."

By this he meant Mr. Rushworth and Sir Henry. Elizabeth inclined her chin. "That is not amusing."

Patrick Gill laid his hand on hers. "My dear," he said, smiling all the more, "I think you'd be surprised at whose heart you have managed to capture."

His eyes looked into hers with an expression of such intensity that Elizabeth found it difficult to breathe. "Why, Patrick," she stammered, flushing a little, "are you ... are you ... making a proposal?"

Silence hung between them, punctuated only by the fearful hammering of her heart.

The impact of her words showed first in his eyes. Shock and surprise shot through their blue depths, and with this came uncertainty.

Fearfully she studied his pale countenance. She saw him take a ragged breath. And still she waited, longing desperately for the warm, friendly sparkle to return. But his eyes showed no merriment, only grave concern. She saw his lips part, but no words came.

The sound of an opening door caused them both to jump. A dark-haired man came forward. Elizabeth pulled her hand from Patrick Gill's.

"Starkweather." Mr. Gill's voice was strangely rough.

Together they followed the secretary into Admiral McGillvary's library. This was a noble room, but Elizabeth noticed little about it. She walked across the thick carpet as if in a daze. A leather-upholstered chair was pulled forward for her. She stood beside it, staring at the admiral's massive mahogany desk.

Patrick Gill made a stiff bow and said, in a strained voice, "If you will excuse me for a moment, Miss Elliot," he said. To her horror, he turned and strode away.

"But—Mr. Gill!" Elizabeth was startled by the bleat of her own voice. How small and shrill it sounded! "Where are you going? I thought you would remain!"

He turned, his hand on the latch of the door. "Starkweather will wait upon you while I am away," he said.

"But—"

"All in good time, Miss Elliot."

"Would you care to sit, Miss?" The secretary politely indicated the chair. Elizabeth remained where she was, gazing at Mr. Gill.

The forbidding expression in his eyes softened somewhat. "Sit down, my dear," he said gently. "I shall return in a moment, I promise."

Trembling, Elizabeth did as she was told. The door swung shut behind Patrick Gill.

McGillvary came into the passageway cursing beneath his breath. Of all the things to go wrong, surely this was the worst! "Pym!" he shouted, fighting his way out of Patrick

Gill's hateful tweed coat. "Pym!" He glanced down the empty passageway. Where the devil was Pym?

A door opened and Pym came hurrying forward, cradling in his arms a garment of deep blue.

McGillvary caught the glint of gold braid and winced. "Blast it all, Pym!" he exploded. "My plain coat! Not the dress uniform!"

Pym blanched. "But, sir," he stammered, "you said you wanted the best blue coat, and I thought you meant—"

"My best *plain* blue coat. Confound it, Pym, I thought I made that perfectly clear."

The little man began blubbering something incoherent, which McGillvary ignored. Over his shoulder he took a swift look at the clock. There was no time to rectify the error. He had promised Elizabeth that he would be away for only a moment, and this was one promise he meant to keep.

"Don't just stand there, man," he growled. "Help me into it, instead of carrying on like a goose."

Pym sprang into action, fussing over the set of the coat on McGillvary's shoulders and taking swipes at it with his brush. "Your hat, Admiral," he said, offering it.

"Put it away, man. I'm only going as far as the library."

But McGillvary knew he might as well be headed for the guillotine. He took the brush from Pym and used it for his hair, ignoring the man's wail of protest. Soon Mr.

Gill's scraggly locks were smoothed into a more conformable style. Then, much as Elizabeth had done, McGillvary squared his shoulders and made for the library door.

Starkweather emerged. He came forward to report that all was in readiness and added, "She desires no refreshments, sir."

"Of course she does not. This is, after all, a business meeting." McGillvary studied his secretary's expression. "She is comfortable, Starkweather?"

"She is, sir."

"Thank you. That will be all." McGillvary put his hand on the latch. Gad, he was trembling like a schoolboy! It would never do for Starkweather and Pym to see him this way—along with God only knew who else.

He glanced behind. Who knew better than him how to spy on the occupants of this house? And Elizabeth's comment about a proposal—disaster! He'd made a mull of it, and she would surely hate him for it! But how could he have spoken then? Right there in the entrance hall before so many sets of prying eyes? Or ought he to have thrown caution to the wind?

Thus Patrick McGillvary stood before the door to his library, cursing himself for being a weakling. Again he put his hand to the latch, and again his hand trembled. This would never do. He would use the inner door!

Abruptly McGillvary turned and stalked down the hallway. Some battles were better faced privately.

Small and alone, Elizabeth sat in the leather chair. The secretary had departed, which was a relief because now she could get hold of herself. She fought to order her thoughts, but along every line of reasoning lurked danger. Patrick Gill she could not think about. She had made a fool of herself a few minutes ago, and she could only hope that he would forgive her. The man was a sincere friend, and she had ruined everything by mentioning a proposal.

She focused on Admiral McGillvary instead. Any minute now she would see him, if the secretary were to be believed. Her only comfort was that Patrick Gill would be present as well. Admiral McGillvary would sit in that large chair behind the desk, and he would speak. What would she say in return?

Her carefully-rehearsed speech, which she had recited to Mr. Gill, was gone from her mind. After all, what could she tell him? Surely he knew everything about her father's situation! Elizabeth continued to study his chair. The man who would sit there was the man who stood between her father and debtor's prison—or worse!

She then became aware of the ticking of a clock. All at once Elizabeth came out of her seat—she could sit and wait no longer. Her feet began to move of their own accord; she found herself pacing back and forth before the desk. No doubt he would read her a lecture on the evils of debt—as if he knew anything about it! And then what would happen? Nothing dishonourable, according to Patrick. How she prayed this would be true! Patrick had also mentioned a new payment contract, which was probably there on the desk.

Elizabeth glanced swiftly at the closed door and, after a moment's hesitation, she edged closer to the desk. Cautiously she came around the corner of it. There! On one of the documents she spied her father's name written in bold letters. After another look at the door, she reached over and carefully moved that page aside. Her father's familiar signature greeted her.

"Dear God," Elizabeth breathed.

It was the only prayer she could manage.

Again she paused to listen, but she heard no approaching footsteps. Again Elizabeth grew bold. She examined another of the documents and then another. She even found a copy of Mr. Lonk's letter, the duplicate of the one in her reticule.

She bit her lip, thinking. It was all here, every bit of evidence against her father. What if she tore these pages up and threw them in the fire? It would then be her word against Admiral McGillvary's!

Such exhilaration was short-lived. This would be the worst course of action she could take. With trembling fingers she replaced the copy of Mr. Lonk's letter.

So intent was Elizabeth's concentration that she did not hear the click of the latch on the library's private inner door. This door, designed to resemble one of the bookcases behind the desk, took her completely by surprise.

She gave a gasp and backed away. In the shadowy passageway stood Admiral McGillvary.

Her friend, Mr. Gill, was nowhere to be seen.

If the admiral noticed her discomfort, he gave no sign of it. Without hesitation he stepped forward and turned to secure the door. Light from the windows caused the gold on his uniform to glitter.

He turned to face her fully. "Miss Elliot, I presume?" he said.

End of Book 2

Patrick and Elizabeth's story concludes in
The Lady Must Decide

Mercy's Embrace: Elizabeth Elliot's Story
A *Persuasion*-based Regency Romp in three parts

ABOUT LAURA HILE

My Regency novels feature intertwined plots,
cliffhangers, and laugh-out-loud humor.

I write escapist, sweep-away romantic
stories for thinking readers ... like you!

The comedy I come by in my work as a teacher.
There's never a dull moment with teens!

I live in the Pacific Northwest with my husband,
sons, and a collection of antique clocks.

Visit me on-line at Laurahile.com.
Do stop by. I'd love to meet you.

For news of my new releases, follow me
on my Amazon author page.

ALSO BY LAURA HILE

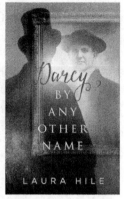

Darcy By Any Other Name
Mr. Darcy, trapped in Mr. Collins body?
What could be worse?
A delightful *Pride and Prejudice* body swap romance

Marrying Well for Fun & Profit
Laughable advice from Jane Austen's Sir Walter Elliot

LAURA HILE

If you enjoyed So *Lively a Chase,* you will probably enjoy this book by Robin Helm

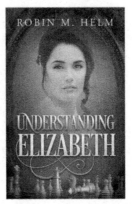

Understanding Elizabeth
A *Pride and Prejudice* romance

Made in the USA
Monee, IL
08 July 2021